In memory of Carol

ACKNOWLEDGMENTS

Writing a mystery series focused on cookie cutters and baking is great fun, in part because of the folks whose paths I cross during the journey. I am grateful to my editor, Michelle Vega, and to the skilled staff at Berkley Prime Crime; their perceptive queries more than once helped me clarify a scene or deepen a character. As always, my longtime writer's group — Ellen Hart, Pete Hautman, Mary Logue, and K. J. Erickson — gave support and friendship, for which I am endlessly grateful. They also offered insightful critique, which I truly appreciated . . . after a few deep breaths and a couple cookies. And I am especially grateful to my husband, who missed celebrating a landmark birthday because the manuscript was due four days later. Instead, he helped enter my edits into the final draft and hardly complained at all. Not to worry, however; I threw him a big party a month later.

CHAPTER ONE

Olivia Greyson made a mental note to develop spontaneous deafness the next time someone asked her to serve on a committee.

Olivia and four other Chatterley Heights citizens sat in a circle near the large front window of her store, The Gingerbread House, ostensibly planning the two-hundred-fiftieth anniversary of the town's founding. For Olivia, the aroma of cinnamon, ginger, and cloves drifting from the store kitchen held more allure than the clash of egos going on around her. Planning a birthday bash for Chatterley Heights had brought out the worst in some of its citizens.

"Mauve," said Karen Evanson, the newly elected mayor of Chatterley Heights. As always, Karen wore a tailored suit, rich burgundy, which showcased her slender figure. The knee-length skirt revealed toned calves. She looked both professional and younger than her forty-six years. "Absolutely, the banner for the band shell must remain mauve. It's a Victorian color, most appropriate." The mayor's authoritative voice left no room for argument. "Anyway, it's far too late to change. The sewing club has nearly finished the banner. You should have spoken up sooner, Quill."

"I did. You ignored me, as usual." Quill Latimer, PhD and town historian, crossed one long, thin leg over the other. Quill's languid voice, tinged with disdain, exuded professorial superiority. He was in his mid-fifties, with a receding hairline, though Olivia suspected him of shaving the top of his head to look more scholarly.

Olivia's mind flashed to her father, who had died of cancer when she was a teenager, half a lifetime ago. He had been a scholar and author of popular books on ornithology. He was vague and forgetful, but never arrogant. Quill Latimer, on the other hand, often behaved as if he had something to prove.

"Since Chatterley Heights's founding date was close to the Revolutionary War," Quill said, "I still maintain that mauve is the wrong color for the banner. Red, white, and blue would be far more —"

Proving Quill's point, Karen ignored him.

"We're running late, and we have several more topics to cover. First, I should remind you all that I expect you will return your keys to the Chatterley Mansion directly to me once this weekend is over. And I assume that no one has lost theirs and everyone has been using them to check in and make sure everything is on schedule?" The committee members nodded in unison, and Olivia half expected them to singsong like schoolchildren, "Yes, Miss Evanson." Karen seemed satisfied. "We'll continue with a report from Mr. Willard." She held a voice-activated recorder toward a gaunt, elderly gentleman and asked, "Are all the permits finally in place?"

Mr. Willard, whose real and cumbersome name was Aloysius Willard Smythe, had been advising the committee on the legal aspects of their proposed weekend celebration. He was also Olivia's attorney. With a gentle smile that stretched his skin across his prominent jaw, Mr. Willard said, "Rest assured, we may now parade the streets of Chatterley Heights without fear of arrest."

Olivia laughed softly, appreciating the lightened mood. The mayor, however, was not amused. With an impatient shake of her honey blond hair, Karen turned to Binnie Sloan, editor of Chatterley Heights's only

11

newspaper, *The Weekly Chatter.* "I don't suppose you've managed to arrange publicity from any of the major DC or Baltimore newspapers, Binnie."

Binnie answered with a derisive snort as she dug into one of the many pockets in her wrinkled cargo pants. Given her plump, squarish build, Binnie usually wore men's clothing. She preferred styles with deep pockets, so she could carry enough equipment to be prepared for any journalistic opportunity, whether real or fabricated.

Olivia's cell phone vibrated in the pocket of her tailored linen slacks. While Karen frowned at Binnie, Olivia sneaked a peek at her caller ID. It was a text from Del, Sheriff Del Jenkins. They hadn't planned to get together later, but since it was a text, Olivia opened it and read, "Call me ASAP." This was not a typical message from Olivia's "special friend," as her mother called him. Del was normally easygoing with a light sense of humor . . . except when his town or Olivia was in danger.

Karen Evanson's commanding voice interrupted Olivia's thoughts. "We all agreed, Olivia. No cell phones during our meetings. Please put it away and pay attention." Another snicker from Binnie drew a glare from Karen. Olivia slipped her cell back into her pocket.

Before the mayor could repeat her demand for a publicity report, Binnie said, "I didn't bother with the DC and Baltimore papers. They won't be interested in our little birthday party. At least, not unless something really juicy happens. I could put something on my blog, maybe hint that one of Chatterley Heights's prominent officials is about to be arrested for fraud or —"

"As usual, I'll have to complete your assigned tasks for you, Binnie. Now about the opening parade on Saturday morning . . ." Karen consulted a typed list. "I have determined the order in which notable Chatterley Heights citizens are to march in the parade. As mayor, I will lead. Following behind . . ."

Through the store's front window, Olivia watched streetlamps flash on, creating a rectangle of light around the Chatterley Heights town square. Inside the park, one old-fashioned streetlamp illuminated the historic band shell. Olivia wished she were sitting in it, watching the surrounding shops go to bed for the night.

A rich, sweet fragrance wafted from the kitchen. Molasses. Olivia's mind drifted, as it often did, toward cookies. A decorated gingerbread cookie might help alleviate her current frustration. Normally she loved being in the store, surrounded by cookie cutters, cookie cookbooks, and the colorful array of icing decorations, but if she had to hear one more heated disagreement about nothing . . .

Not that their task wasn't important. Two hundred and fifty years of survival was something to be proud of, especially for a small town. Olivia was not above feeling a tingle of pride and excitement. Chatterley Heights, her home until she left for college, nestled between Baltimore and Washington, DC. The little town was steeped in history, some of it downright amusing. Certainly the antics of their revered founder, Frederick P. Chatterley, made for some delicious stories. A number of town residents had recently discovered, through intensive research, that they were descended from Frederick P., though not strictly in a respectable way.

"Olivia? I hate to interrupt your reverie, but our task would go more smoothly if you would try to pay attention." Mayor Karen Evanson raised her perfectly shaped eyebrows at Olivia.

"Everyone calls me Livie," Olivia said before she could stop herself. If she'd been paying attention, she would have remembered that Mayor Evanson, as she preferred to be called, disapproved of informality. Nevertheless, perhaps in defiance, everyone in town called her Karen.

"You know my attitude toward nicknames," Karen said with an impatient shake of her head. She made an exception only for Mr. Willard. A strand of shiny hair grazed her chin and fell obediently back into place. "It's your turn to report on your events planning. We only have three days before the celebration begins, so I hope you've made progress."

"The events are in place," Olivia said. "Del and Cody will handle traffic during the parade, and —"

"That's Sheriff Del Jenkins and Deputy Sheriff Cody Furlow," Karen articulated into her recorder. "And?" she asked, turning to Olivia.

Suppressing a sigh, Olivia said, "And local businesses are lined up for the fete on Sunday."

"The tours of Chatterley Mansion? Are they arranged?" Karen's clipped tone conveyed impatience with her less-than-competent assistants.

"All arranged," Olivia said. "As you know, Professor Latimer will lead the tour groups. He has a vast knowledge of Chatterley

Heights history, and he knew Harold and Sally Chatterley for many years before they died." Olivia noticed that when she began to compliment Quill, Karen stopped recording.

"You really need to learn to be more efficient with your reports, Olivia. We don't have time to waste."

Olivia's little rescue Yorkshire terrier, Spunky, was curled on the needlework seat of an antique chair facing the front window. He lifted his head and growled at the mayor's sharp tone.

"Why you keep that dog in a place of business, I'll never understand," Karen said. "I'm not sure it's even legal."

"Oh, it is quite legal," Mr. Willard said. "And Spunky is very popular with customers."

Spunky slapped his fluffy tail on the chair seat and settled back to sleep.

Ignoring Karen's criticism of her pet, Olivia consulted her brief notes on her committee assignment. "As you've probably noticed, Maddie is making fragrant and delicious progress on her gingerbread house replicas of the oldest and most important buildings in town." Olivia's best friend and business partner, Maddie Briggs, was known for her creative, exuberant cookie designs.

"In fact, she is just finishing the last gingerbread house, the Chatterley Mansion. She's also decorating cookies with indoor scenes to put inside the rooms. It's all amazing."

"I doubt they will hold up through the weekend," the mayor said with a tight smile. "In my opinion, gingerbread houses are frivolous and potentially unsanitary."

"Can the attitude, Karen," said Binnie Sloan. "Folks love stuff like gingerbread houses. They're great for publicity photos."

Olivia would have appreciated Binnie's support except it wasn't given in defense of The Gingerbread House or Maddie's baking skills. Binnie was sniping at Karen for insisting *The Weekly Chatter* hew to higher journalistic standards than had been its practice. Binnie's stories favored sensationalism over truth. Olivia, who had been stung more than once by what passed for reporting in *The Weekly Chatter,* had to agree with Karen.

The mayor's flawless makeup couldn't hide her flushed cheeks and tight jaw. She drew in a breath to speak, but before she could put Binnie in her place, Quill Latimer said, "Fascinated as I am by this weighty conversation, I must point out that I am teaching an evening class beginning" — he made a show of taking a pocket watch from his sweater vest pocket and springing open the lid — "beginning less than an hour from now. I have a twenty-minute drive, and I must stop at home to pick up my materials."

"Perhaps you should have been more prepared," Karen snapped.

Quill cocked one bushy eyebrow at Karen and said, "Perhaps you should beg the unpaid services of another PhD historian who happens to be an expert on the history of Chatterley Heights."

Olivia wondered if she should move the heavy mixing bowls and rolling pins out of snatching distance. She relaxed when Mr. Willard cleared his throat, a sign he was about to speak. To her irritation, she felt her cell phone vibrate inside the pocket of her linen pants. She should have left it in the kitchen with Maddie. She decided to ignore it.

"I am eager to hear how your research is progressing, Quill," Mr. Willard said with a sheepish grin. "Especially with respect to the possibility that our own Frederick P. Chatterley might have left a number of, shall we say, unacknowledged descendants?"

As the gathering responded with expressions ranging from amusement to disgust, Olivia's cell vibrated yet again. This time she checked the caller ID. It was Del. His persistence gave Olivia a twinge of concern, but Karen was watching her. She'd call back as soon as the meeting ended.

Mr. Willard chuckled. "I realize it is perhaps unseemly of me to be so interested in our revered founder's less-than-estimable pursuits, but nevertheless . . ." He shrugged his bony shoulders.

"It's downright fascinating," Binnie said. "I plan to do a whole spread on the old reprobate's illegitimate descendants. How many have we got?" She retrieved her ever-present notebook and a ballpoint pen. "Okay, five so far. The latest is that kid who's working with Lucas on the Chatterley Mansion, Matthew something. Don't know the guy myself."

"Matthew Fabrizio?" Olivia asked. "I didn't realize his family lived in Chatterley Heights so far back. I met him when I was taking pictures of the Chatterley Mansion for Maddie's gingerbread house design."

"Yeah, Fabrizio, that's it," Binnie said, jotting the name down in her notebook. "So old Frederick must have knocked up some Italian chick back in seventeen-something-or-other."

"That is incorrect," Quill said. "There was no one of Italian descent living in Chatter-

19

ley Heights until —"

"Yeah, whatever," Binnie said, stuffing her notebook into a pocket. "I think I'll interview the kid."

Olivia barely knew Matthew Fabrizio, but she felt sorry for him.

"It is important to be precise," Quill said in his lecturing voice. "Matthew Fabrizio is descended from Frederick through his mother, who belonged to an old Chatterley Heights family. And while intriguing, as Mr. Willard said, this obsessive search for Frederick's illegitimate offspring has no real significance. Harold and Sally Chatterley, knowing of Frederick's proclivities, wisely foresaw this dilemma. Their will made it clear the family mansion was to pass to the town of Chatterley Heights if there were no more descendants born within wedlock to Chatterley parents."

"That is correct," Mr. Willard said.

"So if I may report my more important historical findings, I —"

An insistent generic ring tone from Karen's cell phone interrupted Quill, who glared at the mayor. Without apology, Karen dug her cell phone out of a stuffed expanding file next to her chair. As Karen frowned at the caller ID, Olivia realized her own cell was vibrating once again. She

20

slipped away from the group and escaped to the relative privacy of the store's cookbook nook. Flipping the phone open, she found two voice mails and a text message, all from Del. The text read, "Call me. Now."

Del answered at once. "Livie, you won't believe this. You are about to have visitors. I tried to stall them by directing them to the mayor's office, but sooner or later they will find out the celebration committee is meeting at your store."

"Del, what are you — ?"

"Hold on to your hat," Del said. "It seems the Chatterley family has not died out, as we all assumed. Harold and Sally's son, Paine Chatterley, is still alive."

"You're kidding!" Olivia lowered her voice. "But he didn't show up for either Harold's or Sally's funeral."

"Nonetheless," Del said, "Paine is alive, and he has returned to Chatterley Heights. He and his wife Hermione are heading your way. They want the key to their mansion back."

"This is outrageous!" Mayor Karen Evanson's face reddened right down to her earlobes.

Paine Chatterley, a slight man with silver hair, eyed Karen with detached amusement.

His plump wife, Hermione, stared at the mayor with frank curiosity.

"We will most certainly not give you our keys to the Chatterley Mansion," Karen said. "You've presented no proof of your identity. You two are nothing more than scam artists. Do you honestly think we didn't confirm Paine Chatterley's death before taking possession of Chatterley Mansion?"

Paine Chatterley, if that's who he was, gave Karen a faint smile, which conveyed a hint of superiority. "We have papers, of course," Paine said. He selected several official-looking documents from his soft leather briefcase and handed them to Karen.

Karen's eyes narrowed with suspicion as she snatched the papers from Paine's hand. She barely glanced at them. "You assured us he was deceased," she said as she thrust the papers toward Mr. Willard. "I assume these are fake."

Mr. Willard's gaunt face turned ashen as he pored over the documents.

Maddie emerged from the kitchen carrying a plate of decorated gingerbread cookies, cheerfully unaware of the unfolding drama. "Lucas called and told me we'd be receiving special visitors. I thought we could all do with some sustenance." Maddie studied the Chatterleys, and they returned the interest with amusement. Olivia could understand why. Maddie had been baking and decorating for close to ten hours straight. Her curly red hair frothed around her head like cotton candy gone viral. Bits of gingerbread dough and colored icing dotted her jeans and T-shirt, and she had flour on her nose.

"So you're Paine Chatterley," Maddie said. "I heard you were dead."

Paine appeared charmed by Maddie's bluntness. But then, Olivia suspected he was able to present himself in any way he wished. His emotional reactions must be under remarkable control, Olivia thought, if Karen's brusque, mistrustful manner hadn't phased him.

"I'm sure I shall shuffle off one day," Paine said as he selected one of Maddie's gingerbread cookies. "But not just yet." His accent was faintly English, as one might expect given his story, relayed by Del, that he'd been living in and around western Europe since he left Chatterley Heights at about age twenty-five. "Meanwhile, it is lovely to be home. Hermione and I wish only for a quiet retirement. We were never blessed with children, so it means a great deal to us to regain a connection with my family."

Olivia's curiosity grew as she noted the physical differences between Paine and his wife. Paine was slender with fine chiseled features and straight silver hair combed back from his forehead. Hermione Chatterley, on the other hand, had broad shoulders and a plump figure with almost no waist. Her hair might once have been red and curly, like Maddie's, but was now thin, white fluff.

"You can call yourself a Chatterley all you want," Karen said, "but we'll need more proof. We will, of course, conduct our own investigation."

"Karen, my dear," Paine said, "I am devastated. How could you not recognize me?"

All eyes turned to the mayor, who gave Paine Chatterley a hard look and said nothing. Binnie Sloan whipped out a small digital camera and began clicking away. Karen snatched the camera from Binnie's hand and shoved it into her expanding file. "We do not need any publicity about this. These two *persons* will be gone by tomorrow."

Ignoring her, Paine turned to Professor Latimer. "And Quill, old friend, it's good to see you again. I hear you've achieved a . . .

well-deserved position."

Paine's hesitation was so slight, Olivia wondered if she'd imagined it. Until she saw Quill Latimer's gaunt cheeks redden. She felt like a spectator at a skillfully directed play. The greetings to Karen Evanson and Quill Latimer felt personal yet lacked intimate detail, as if Paine were conveying a private message to each of them. On the other hand, Olivia understood that a practiced con artist could take little or no information and make it sound as if he knew a secret.

"If I may interject," Mr. Willard said, "these papers appear to be official, but I am not sufficiently conversant with British legal documents to verify their authenticity. I do have a professional acquaintance in DC, a legal scholar of international repute, to whom I suggest faxing these items."

"How could you have allowed this to happen?" Her fists on her hips, Karen scowled at Mr. Willard. "You assured us you had seen the death certificate with your own eyes."

"Yes, I . . . well, to be precise, I was sent an authorized copy of the death certificate, along with supporting documents. I saw no evidence the death certificate had been forged, but I suppose one can never be certain."

"How intriguing," Paine said. "I'm curious . . . when was my alleged death? And how did I die?"

Mr. Willard looked so confused and alarmed that Olivia wondered, for the first time, how old he was and if his considerable intellect was beginning to dim.

"Well, I . . . I would have to check my files, but as I recall you died in a skiing accident while still a young man. I believe you were in your midtwenties. We requested the information some years later, given you had not returned for either your father's or your mother's funeral."

"Ah," said Paine. "You see, I was not terribly close to my parents, and I felt no need to attend their funerals. Furthermore, I detest skiing. You must have been sent another Paine Chatterley's death certificate."

Karen turned her wrath toward Paine. "How many Paine Chatterleys can there possibly be?"

"My dear Karen, you of all people should know there is only one of me. However, given dear old Frederick's predilections, I'll wager there are numerous Chatterleys running around England, spawned before his escape to the colonies. Surely one or two of them had the misfortune to be named Paine. I'm certain this will all be straightened out soon."

"Perhaps," Karen said, "but meanwhile, no key to the mansion. I'm sure you two can find a motel to stay in."

Paine Chamberlain flashed her a smile, revealing stained teeth. "Send off our materials to your expert, by all means. However, my dear Karen, our coming here to talk with you was merely a formality. We stopped by the mansion on our rather circuitous way over here. A kind young man made a copy of his key for us, and we have deposited what belongings we were able to transport with us. I believe he is working on the restoration of our family home. It seems the town had allowed it to fall into a sad state of disrepair."

"*Lucas* handed over his key? Lucas Ashford?" Maddie frowned at the emerald promise-to-think-about-it, almost-engagement ring on her finger, as if it owed her an explanation for her true love's questionable judgment.

"Lucas . . ." Paine Chatterley caressed his chin with long, slender fingers, as if deep in thought. "No, I believe the name was more, shall we say, continental. Italian, perhaps."

"Matthew Fabrizio," Karen Evanson muttered through clamped teeth.

"That's the young man," Paine said. "He seemed quite eager to help."

"I'll bet he was," Karen said.

Paine gave her a curious look. Karen did not elaborate, but Olivia thought she understood. If Matthew Fabrizio was, in fact, a descendant of Frederick P. Chatterley, he had every reason to curry Paine's favor. Illegitimate or not, Matthew might hope to become the son and heir Paine and Hermione never had. If Paine were to acknowledge Matthew as Frederick P.'s descendant, he might also be convinced to write a new will.

"We are rather tired," Paine said. "We'll be toddling along home for a nap before we unpack. I'm sure we'll be seeing a great deal of all of you, once we've had a chance to settle in."

Speaking for the first time, Hermione said to Olivia, "The Gingerbread House is such a lovely store. I can't wait to explore it." She reached out to touch Maddie's arm. "Did you really make these adorable decorated cookies? When I was a child, we had a cook who made such wonderful confec—"

Paine's hand clamped onto Hermione's arm. "Come along, my dear, we have unpacking to do. There will be plenty of time for all that."

Anger flashed in Hermione's eyes, but it was gone so quickly, Olivia wondered if she'd imagined it.

"Oh, by the way," Paine said, "we are in dire need of quiet, so the Chatterley Mansion will be closed to the public during your little celebration. The grounds as well. I'm sure you understand. It is our home, after all, and we prefer privacy." With a brief smile, he herded his wife toward the front door of The Gingerbread House.

The door closed behind the couple, followed by some moments of silence. Olivia was itching to know if Paine Chatterley had been playing mind games with them when he hinted at knowing Karen Evanson and Quill Latimer. Olivia hesitated to ask them directly because, frankly, she was too tired to deal with Karen's sharp tongue.

Binnie Sloan felt no such qualms. She pulled out an old handheld recorder and thrust it toward Karen and Quill. "So, you two, spill it. What connection does the long-lost Paine Chatterley have to our new mayor and our esteemed local historian? And why do you deny knowing him?" She pushed the recorder close to Karen's face. "We'll start with you, Karen. I figure Paine left Chatterley Heights before you were older than . . .

what, ten? Fifteen? Did he hang out at your playground? Maybe he visited DC while you were working for that loser congressman, what's-his-name? Or did you and Paine have a clandestine affair somewhere in Europe?"

Karen's face turned the color of burgundy royal icing. "This meeting is dismissed. And if you, if any of you, repeat a word of what transpired today, I will see to it that you are punished to the full extent of the law."

Spunky jumped to his paws on the soft chair seat and began to yap at Karen. For his own protection, Olivia grabbed him and held him to her chest, shushing him quietly.

Mr. Willard cleared his throat and said, "Actually, Mayor Evanson, I don't believe there is any legal recourse for —"

"I don't care!" Karen stalked to the front door and slammed it shut behind her.

Unfazed, Binnie pointed her recorder at Quill. "Your turn, Professor Latimer. What is your secret link to Paine Chatterley?"

"Forget it, Binnie," Quill said with a brief laugh. "Paine and I are the same age. Of course we knew each other. There's no story, but I'm sure you can make one up." Quill turned his head and gazed out the window, which gave a view of the town square. The Chatterleys were visible as they passed under the band shell lamplight, heading south through the park. This struck Olivia as odd since the Chatterley Mansion was several blocks north of the square.

As he watched the Chatterleys' receding figures, Quill Latimer added, "I will say one thing. That man is no impostor. He is definitely Paine Chatterley, and he hasn't changed a bit."

CHAPTER TWO

Olivia gazed with satisfaction and a rumble of hunger at the five dozen cutout ginger-bread cookies covering half of the worktable in the store kitchen. The other half held Maddie's rectangular cookies, on which she would "paint" scenes to be attached inside gingerbread house windows. Since they'd become partners in The Gingerbread House, Maddie had done most of the cookie decorating, while Olivia handled the business side of things. The arrangement worked well. Olivia had a business degree, and Maddie was a bona fide cookie-decorating genius. But Olivia missed the fun of rolling out the dough, cutting shapes, mixing lovely colors of royal icing . . . and the joy of watching a design take shape on each cookie.

Through the kitchen door, Olivia heard Spunky's delighted bark of greeting, which meant Maddie had arrived. They had agreed to begin work at five a.m., so they'd have plenty of time to finish several batches of gingerbread cookies before the store opened at nine.

"Hey," Maddie said as she slid through the barely open kitchen door. "No, Spunky, you guard the store. You know the rules. We don't want another stern lecture from the health department, do we?" She closed the door firmly behind her and deposited a bag with handles on the counter. "I made us some tuna salad," she said. "I refuse to order pizza at five in the morning. People would talk."

"Which they are doing enough of already."

"Oh yeah?" Maddie began to gather royal icing ingredients from the cupboard. "Did you and Del do something delightfully scandalous last night?"

"Only if you call meat loaf sandwiches at Pete's Diner scandalous," Olivia said.

"Wow. How can you bear the excitement? You know what I think? I think you need another mystery to solve — something to shake up your relationship with Del."

Olivia laughed. "That would shake it up, all right. No, I'm fine with things as they are. When it comes to crime fighting, Del and I agreed to meet each other in the middle. I assured him I wouldn't go looking for dangerous situations to throw myself into, but if it happens, it happens. Del said he'll always worry about my safety, but he won't tell me what I can and can't do."

"So rational," Maddie said, "and so unlikely."

To change the subject, Olivia said, "Del did tell me something last night that will drive Karen Evanson to the brink of madness."

Maddie's green eyes lit with pleasure. "Cool. What?"

"When Paine and Hermione left the store last night, I wondered why they headed south through the park, rather than north to the mansion. Del told me they stopped in at the police station. They, or rather Paine, ordered Del to assign his 'entire staff' to guard Frederick Street day and night from Friday evening until Monday morning."

"No kidding," Maddie said. "Talk about noblesse obnoxious."

"Oh, now you aren't even trying," said Olivia, who spoke decent if rusty French.

"Well, you're always correcting my French, so I might as well mangle it on purpose."

"As long as you're having fun." Olivia opened Maddie's canvas bag to put the tuna salad in the refrigerator. "Hey, what's all this?"

"Oh that," Maddie said as she selected a small red bottle of food coloring. "I finally convinced Aunt Sadie to allow some of her embroidery to leave the house. She's so shy about sharing her work. Between you and me, she's running low on funds, so I suggested we sell some of her aprons in the store."

"Are you sure that's a good idea? What if they don't sell?"

"Not sell? Livie, are you implying that my aunt Sadie, the woman who rescued me from orphanhood and raised me as her own, who is related to me by blood, could possibly lack artistic talent? I suggest you take a look at those aprons before you leap to conclusions."

"I didn't mean *you* aren't an artist of the first order, only —"

"Look at them, okay?"

"Okay." Olivia lifted an armful of folded aprons from the bag and placed the pile on the counter. Choosing the one on top, she shook it open and stared, speechless.

"Well?" Maddie reached for a second apron and spread it out on the counter.

"Amazing." Olivia hung the remaining aprons over chairs and examined them one by one. Each displayed a different decorated cookie theme. Olivia's favorite was an intricate gingerbread house complete with icicles hanging from the roof and lit candles in the windows. Sadie Briggs had used a variety of stitches and shades of color to create impressions of depth and shadow. "These are lovely. I had no idea. I know nothing about embroidery, but . . ."

"But you know what you like?"

"I know this is extraordinary work." Olivia picked up the apron with the Victorian house and examined it more closely. Sadie had chosen fanciful colors for the design; the house exterior was peach, decorated with burgundy trim. Yet somehow it looked familiar to Olivia. "Wait, is this our very own Chatterley Mansion?"

"Took you long enough," Maddie said. "Have we got any more meringue powder?"

Olivia took her eyes off the apron just long enough to locate a fresh bag of meringue powder in the storage cupboard. She handed it to Maddie and returned to the apron. "Look, there's a little face in an upper window. It's a child, I think."

"That's Paine Chatterley," Maddie said.

"You're kidding." Olivia squinted closely at the dark-haired figure in the window. The boy's upper torso was visible above the window frame; his clothing looked vaguely eighteenth century. His embroidered mouth curved slightly down at the edges, giving an impression of sadness. "What made Aunt Sadie use Paine's image?"

"She babysat him for a number of years." Maddie measured two teaspoons of vanilla extract into the mixer.

"Wait a minute," Olivia said. "Not long ago you said that Aunt Sadie is sixtyish. She would have been too young to babysit Paine."

"Hang on a sec." Maddie lowered the beaters into the bowl and whirred up a batch of royal icing. When she'd finished, she said, "Okay, here's the scoop, but don't talk about this, okay? Aunt Sadie is still sensitive. She really wanted to marry and have kids of her own, but it wasn't happening, so at some point — Aunt Sadie is vague about when — she knocked a few years off her age. Well, maybe more like ten years. She looked really young. You left for college at eighteen and only returned recently, which is why you probably didn't figure it out. Most people know, of course, but they don't broadcast the information because Aunt Sadie is such a sweetheart." Maddie shot a warning glance at Olivia.

"My lips are glued shut," Olivia said.

Maddie began dividing her icing into containers for coloring. "Aunt Sadie used to eke out a living babysitting lots of Chatterley Heights kids. She stopped when I moved in and needed a permanent babysitter. Luckily, my folks were frugal and left enough money so she could concentrate on raising me. Now I pay her for room and board, but really, she needs more income. Especially since . . ." Maddie glanced at her emerald ring.

"Are you closer to accepting Lucas's proposal?" Olivia tried to make her question sound casual. For years Maddie had adored Lucas Ashford, owner of Heights Hardware. Yet when he'd proposed marriage, Maddie had found herself terrified.

Maddie shrugged. "At least I don't run screaming from the room at the mere mention of wedding gowns. Anyway, Lucas and I are fine. He doesn't push. So can we sell those aprons for Aunt Sadie?"

"They'll be gone in about twenty minutes," Olivia said. "I'll price them high to slow down the feeding frenzy. I may have to buy the Chatterley Mansion apron myself. Does Aunt Sadie have any more of them?"

"Does she! Only about eighty or ninety, and that's a conservative estimate. They aren't all cookie or cookie-cutter themes, though."

"Everything is a potential cookie-cutter theme." Olivia moved the aprons away from the baking area to protect them from stains. "What was your aunt's impression of Paine Chatterley? What kind of kid was he?"

Maddie picked a small bottle of forest green gel coloring and held it to the light to see how much was left. "You mean, did she see in little Paine the arrogant jerk he grew up to become? No, she did not, and Aunt Sadie is a pretty good judge of character. She thought Paine was a sweet, quiet little boy. He was lonely, she said. Paine was, as they say, an unexpected child. I guess he intruded on his parents' free-wheeling lives, which is why he spent most of his childhood with Aunt Sadie when he wasn't in school. She lost touch with him once he started high school. Maybe that's when he started to change."

Aware that time was passing quickly, Olivia and Maddie worked quietly for a while. Their focus was so intense they both jumped when the kitchen phone rang. Olivia checked the clock over the sink. Five forty-three a.m. Not a good sign. Her heart racing, she picked up the receiver.

"Olivia? It's Mayor Evanson. You sound breathless. You need more exercise to keep in shape."

"Karen, when the phone rings at this hour, it usually means someone died. I hope you're not calling to tell me —"

"Died? Don't be so melodramatic. You're a businesswoman, I'd expect you to be up and working by now. Why, it's already . . ." Karen paused, presumably consulting her watch.

"It's five forty-three." Olivia checked the clock again. "Excuse me, five forty-five. People don't normally call each other this early except in dire emergencies."

"Nonsense. Anyway, no one is dead, although I have a candidate should you be feeling homicidal at the moment."

Olivia resisted temptation and let that one go. "As it happens, we are working against the clock, so if there's something you want . . ."

"I want you to knock some sense into Paine Chatterley, if that's who he is, which is far from certain. Let me know how it goes."

"Whoa, hold on a minute, Karen. I have no idea what you are talking about."

An exasperated sigh traveled across the phone line. "You are part of the two-hundred-fiftieth anniversary celebration planning committee, of which I am chair, and I am assigning you to go talk to Paine Chatterley. Reason with him, threaten him, whatever it takes. Just convince him to open the mansion for visitors during the festivities. We've invested a ton of money in that house, not to mention the donated materials and volunteer skilled labor. We have the right to get something in return. Talk to him as soon as possible. Get him to cooperate."

"Karen, I do have a store to run." Olivia couldn't keep the irritation out of her voice.

"That tiny store can't possibly take all your time. Use your lunch hour to talk to the Chatterleys. Surely Maddie can keep an eye on things while she's working on those little gingerbread houses. And listen, if we must, the town could pay for a motel room for the weekend, although nothing beyond the room, of course. Anyway, you handle the negotiations. Make it happen. You seem to be the only personable member of the celebration committee. Except for me, of course, and I'm too busy."

Olivia didn't mention that Mr. Willard was quite a personable gentleman and could probably do a better job of reasoning with Paine. She saw no reason to subject Mr. Willard to Karen's bullying. "Wait, Karen, I . . . you can't possibly expect me to convince the Chatterleys to leave their home and stay in a motel room for a weekend so strangers can wander among their personal belongings and —"

"That's it exactly. The sooner the better." A definitive click signaled the end of the discussion.

By nine a.m., when The Gingerbread House opened, Olivia had accepted her fate and decided to make the best of it. She would talk to the Chatterleys, but on her terms. She would bring Spunky and cookies. She could understand Paine and Hermione's reluctance to let the town use their mansion during the celebration weekend. They had only just arrived after a long journey, they were tired, and they wanted to settle in without strangers tramping through their home. In their shoes, Olivia suspected she would react with impatience, as Paine had — though without the arrogance, she hoped. A friendly, welcoming visit might soften Paine's resistance. Starting with decorated gingerbread cookies.

Leaving Maddie and their part-time employee, Bertha, in charge, Olivia and Spunky walked toward Chatterley Mansion, located on Frederick Street, north of the town square. The original mansion grounds took up most of the north side of the block. The south side consisted of four cottages, all once owned by the Chatterleys. As the family's financial situation declined, they'd sold off the cottages and some of the land.

Frederick P. Chatterley had never lived in the mansion, which was built nearly a century after his death. The midnineteenth-century Chatterleys were rolling in money from their plantation farther south, so they built a large Victorian summer home in Chatterley Heights. Following the Civil War, the family lost their plantation, much of their fortune, and four out of five sons. They never fully recovered. Eventually, their summer home became their only home. By the time Paine's parents died, in the early 1980s, the mansion had fallen into disrepair. The town tried to keep it presentable, hoping to draw tourists. Few visited. The house was inspected regularly but had been closed to the public for some years before the current renovation began.

Olivia paused across the street from the mansion to admire the restoration efforts by Lucas Ashford and his team. The work was incomplete; scaffolding covered the west side of the mansion from the ground to the top of the roof. The trim around two upper windows was only partially painted. Viewed from the front, though, the house gave Olivia the feeling she'd stepped back into the nineteenth century.

Lucas had chosen a medium-dark periwinkle blue as the dominant color. He'd used a paler version of the same color for the window trim, as well as the spindled railing and pillars of a wraparound porch at the southeast corner. Under each peaked roof, Matthew Fabrizio had re-created the mansion's original three-part decorative design, most of which had broken off over the decades. Two shell pink circles, with sinuous red curlicues flaring out on either side, sat atop two burgundy curves that tapered up to points. Olivia laughed as she realized what the design represented. Two pink nostrils, a mustache, and smiling lips. A fitting symbol for a family named Chatterley. She couldn't help but connect the image to Frederick P. Chatterley's infamous dalliances as well.

Olivia felt a thrill of anticipation as she and Spunky followed the newly repaired stone walk leading to the Chatterley Mansion. She hadn't been inside since elementary school, when her class toured the house.

Olivia rang the doorbell twice, to no avail. She began to wonder if an unannounced visit had been the best choice. She pressed the doorbell again. When she heard the sound of an upper-story window opening, she took a step back and looked up. Paine Chatterley's head appeared through a screenless window in the turret. His gray hair looked matted, as if he'd been rousted from a sound sleep.

"Whoever you are," Paine said, "please leave our property at once. We buy nothing door-to-door."

"Mr. Chatterley? It's me, Olivia Greyson. I brought you and your wife some ginger-bread cookies from our store. You were there yesterday evening, remember?"

Paine stared at her for several moments. Olivia felt like a kid selling unwanted candy to support the school marching band. Another upper-story window opened and Hermione's head popped out. "Oh hello," she said. "You're the young woman with that darling store, aren't you?"

"Once again," Paine said, "please go away. And take that beastly animal with you."

"Don't be silly, Paine. Ignore him, dear. I'll be right down to let you in." Hermione closed her window gently. Her husband slammed his shut.

While she waited, Olivia admired the freshly stained front door, with its leaded glass insert. The insert had been boarded up for years because most of the original glass in the design had shattered. The materials for the entire renovation must have cost the town and Lucas Ashford dearly. Olivia knew Paine's parents had died penniless, so she doubted Lucas would be able to recoup his losses.

Hermione was alone when she opened the front door. "Do come in, both of you. Such a fetching little creature. He's a Yorkshire terrier, isn't he? We have many terriers in England. Such determined dogs. One can count on them to do their jobs. Are these cookies from your store? How lovely." She latched the door behind them. "Please forgive Paine. He hasn't been well lately, and the trip was hard on him. He is normally quite gracious. I'm just brewing tea. Do stay and join me. I'll put out these lovely cookies. Paine doesn't care for tea; I can't think why, it's so soothing when one is ill."

Spared the necessity to talk, Olivia followed Hermione down a short, dimly lit hallway. She was surprised to notice that Hermione's gait was quick and light, despite her bulk. She wore a straight dress, black with gray polka dots and belted at the waist. It reminded Olivia of a black-and-white photo of her own great-grandmother wearing a similar shapeless style. As a child, she'd thought of it as an "old lady dress." Since Paine was in his midfifties, Hermione might easily be younger than Olivia's mother, Ellie, who at sixtyish would never, ever wear such a dowdy outfit.

"Now you stay right here, and I'll be back in a tick with the tea." Hermione hurried off, leaving Olivia alone in the parlor. She knew it was a parlor because it looked like one, with its carved chairs and tea tables. The padded brocade seats on the chairs were freshly recovered. Olivia remembered from her childhood visit how poor the lighting had been throughout the mansion. Now a shiny milk glass chandelier hung from the ceiling, illuminating the entire room. Even the heavy velvet curtains, though Victorian in style, looked new. Chatterley Heights citizens had been busy. Lucky Chatterleys. Olivia had to wonder if they'd known about the renovation and timed their return to coincide with its supposed completion.

Olivia noticed a photo on a dark mahogany bureau against the wall. She crossed the room, carrying Spunky, who had been good so far but couldn't be trusted. With her free hand, Olivia picked up the photo. It was a color shot, faded with age, of a young bride and groom. She recognized the groom as Paine Chatterley, holding the bride's

hand. In his free hand, Paine held a ciga-
rette. His smile had a wistful quality, as if
he didn't quite believe his happiness could
last. The bride was a slender young woman
with curly, light brown hair and a pleasant,
round face. Olivia noticed she had a boyish
figure, with slim hips not much wider than
her waist. Hermione had been, if not quite
a beauty, at least attractive.

Hearing the sound of teacups clinking on
a tray, Olivia hurried to take a seat. Spunky
stiffened, as if to bark, but relaxed when he
recognized Hermione.

"What utterly delightful confections,"
Hermione Chatterley said as she entered
with a tray of tea, milk, sugar, and Olivia's
gingerbread cookies arranged on a plate.
Olivia saw another item on the tray, something small, wrapped in white paper.

"Shall I be Mother?" Hermione poured
the tea, adding milk and sugar without asking what Olivia preferred. "I do wish Paine
would join us. He can be so charming when
he wishes. Unfortunately, this is not one of
his good days." As Hermione leaned forward
to deliver a teacup, Olivia noticed her
unusual copper-colored eyes.

"You must both be exhausted." Olivia
sipped her tea. Not bad.

"Oh, I have the constitution of a horse,"

Hermione said with a laugh that verged on a neigh. "But poor Paine . . ."

Spunky stood up on Olivia's lap, his nose twitching. He jumped down and trotted over to Hermione.

"Hello, little one," Hermione said. "Yes, I've brought you something, too." She opened the folded white paper and placed it on the rug. Olivia got a glimpse of red meat before Spunky devoured it. He'd be impossible to live with now.

"I hope you don't mind," Hermione said. "I went out this morning to buy a nice little steak to cook for Paine's breakfast — he needs to build his strength, you know — but he refused to eat it. He can be so fussy about food, and he does get the strangest ideas sometimes. Why, can you believe he actually accused me of putting strychnine in it?"

Olivia's gaze dropped to the white, blood-stained paper still on the floor, and her mouth went dry. But Spunky settled at her feet, showing no signs of sudden illness, and Olivia told herself that Paine's erratic behavior did show a touch of paranoia. Still . . . there was something about Hermione Chatterley that made Olivia uneasy. She'd keep an eye on Spunky just in case.

"Is your husband very ill?" It was a personal question, but Olivia had the sense that Hermione was eager to discuss Paine's condition.

Hermione placed her teacup on a round marble-top table next to her chair. She tilted her head as if pondering how best to answer. Something about the mannerism bothered Olivia, but she told herself she was still on edge about Hermione's mention of poisoned meat.

"It's difficult to explain, you see," Hermione said. "Paine used to be so vibrant. When we first met — nearly thirty years ago, it was — he was brimming with life. Oh, he was so handsome he fairly took my breath away. But over the years he has become . . . well, melancholy. He doesn't seem to enjoy life anymore."

"Forgive me, I don't mean to intrude, but has he seen a doctor?" Olivia didn't want to use the word "psychiatrist," though it sounded as if Paine might be suffering from depression or worse. She had to wonder why, in this day and age, Hermione was acting as if she couldn't find a name for her husband's condition. In fact, Olivia was beginning to feel as if she were in a play set in a previous era.

"Paine hates doctors," Hermione said with an exasperated flap of her hands. "He absolutely refuses to even discuss consulting one."

"We have some of the finest medical facilities in the world nearby — Johns Hopkins, for a start. I used to live in Baltimore, and I was married to a surgeon. I could call around. . . ." *Focus, Livie. Remember why you are here.* "But perhaps your husband is simply lonely?" she suggested. "He's back home now, and at such an exciting time, too. He might perk up if he got involved in the festivities this weekend. In a way, we are celebrating the Chatterleys. Everyone is thrilled to have the family back here."

"How kind," Hermione murmured, sipping her tea. She reached for a gingerbread cookie. "Isn't this adorable," she said. "It's a gingerbread boy with a little blue crown on his head. The Chatterleys were royalty in England, you know. Although Frederick, poor dear, was the youngest of seven sons, so he decided to make his way in the colonies." Hermione took a delicate bite of the cookie, eliminating the crown.

"That's just the sort of story everyone wants to hear," Olivia said, trying to sound enthusiastic but not gushy. "I know you're both tired and jet-lagged after your long trip, but I was wondering . . . it might cheer up your husband if he could meet some

Chatterley Heights citizens — carefully selected, of course — and tell a few of his stories about the family. Maddie and I could provide decorated gingerbread cookies and make sure the visits are short."

"Oh, I don't know. . . ." Hermione glanced up at the ceiling as if worried her husband might hear. "There are some individuals here who have been rather cruel to Paine. He was quite upset last evening when he saw two of them gathered in your store."

"That was a long time ago." Remembering Paine's exchanges with Karen Evanson and Quill Latimer the evening before, Olivia wondered who had been cruel to whom. "I'm sure they regret any unkindness. Besides, I'll give you a list of potential guests, and you can cross off anyone who might upset your husband."

Hermione nibbled through her gingerbread boy's head and shoulders.

Olivia sensed it was time to back off. She had done her duty. If the Chatterleys insisted on privacy during the celebration weekend, Karen would have to accept it. "Well, I'll let you continue to settle in, Mrs. Chatterley. I should get back to work." Olivia picked up Spunky, who wriggled as if he wanted to stay. "If I may, I'll call again before Saturday and show you a list of people who would love to meet you and Mr. Chatterley. You are free to alter the list or say no to the whole idea."

"How thoughtful," Hermione said as she rose to show Olivia out. "And do call me Hermione." At the front door, she added, "You know, I do think I could arrange a little visit with us. Do bring me a list of visitors and let me work on convincing Paine. I think it would be good for him to meet some people."

Olivia paused on the stoop for several moments after the front door latch clicked shut. She had not expected Hermione to make such an abrupt turnaround. She'd gone from timid to confident in a matter of minutes. Olivia began to wonder which Chatterley really ran the family.

Chapter Three

Olivia sighed with relief as she entered The Gingerbread House, having completed her obligation to "reason" with the Chatterleys. She vowed she would never again allow Mayor Karen Evanson to order her around. Although Olivia had to admit the visit had been intriguing. She'd been left with a number of questions. Such as, which Chatterley was the real force to be reckoned with in the family, Paine or Hermione? And was Paine Chatterley a smooth, manipulative character, as he'd seemed the evening before, or was he depressed and irritable? Or both? Not that these were earth-shattering issues. Interesting, though.

Unlike Olivia, who felt energized, little Spunky was exhausted. He'd allowed Olivia to carry him all the way back to the store. As soon as his little paws hit the floor, he headed for his chair by the window for a nap. "Lazy bum," Olivia said with a fond pat on the head. Spunky curled up tighter. Olivia reminded herself this was how he normally acted after a long walk, only . . . maybe she was being paranoid, but it wouldn't hurt to ask Bertha to help keep an eye on him. If he wasn't perkier soon, she could drive him over to Chatterley Paws and let the town's veterinarians, Gwen and Herbie Tucker, look him over.

Bertha Binkman emerged from the cookbook nook with a customer in tow. "Thank heavens you're back," she whispered to Olivia. "My goodness, it's been busy." Bertha had been the full-time, live-in housekeeper for Olivia's late friend Clarisse Chamberlain. When Clarisse died, she left Bertha enough money to retire, but Bertha, who was in her sixties, was too full of energy to "sit on the porch and knit," as she'd put it. Besides, now that she and the widowed attorney Mr. Willard were an item, Bertha preferred to be in town.

While she asked Bertha to keep an eye on Spunky, Olivia heard the front door open behind her. She put on her customer-friendly smile and turned around. Her petite mother, Ellie Greyson-Meyers, floated across the sales floor wearing a long pink sweater over black harem pants.

"Mom, have you been belly dancing again?"

"So good for one's flexibility," Ellie murmured.

"And you've done something to your hair," Olivia said. "I like the effect; it brings out your eyes. That isn't a ribbon, is it?"

Ellie's wavy gray hair, which hung below her shoulders, had a navy blue streak down the left side. "Thank you, dear. I was inspired by my belly dancing teacher, who has the loveliest pale lavender streak through her black hair."

"Has Allan seen the new you?" Olivia's meat-and-potatoes stepfather, Allan Meyers, was so different from his ever-active wife that the marriage shouldn't work. But somehow it did.

"He was speechless, poor dear," Ellie said. "He, too, asked if it might be a ribbon, but I assured him it is quite permanent, unless I decide to let it grow out. I don't think that's what he wanted to hear."

"How is Allan's new Internet business going?"

"Oh, you know how Allan is when he starts a new venture," Ellie said.

"Barely communicative?"

"Exactly. I leave coffee and plates of food next to his keyboard, and I remove them when empty. It's probably just as well, since I'm so busy with the gingerbread houses. I am worried he'll freeze into that hunched-over position, though. Once our schedules have settled down, I'm taking him to yoga with me."

"Does Allan know this yet?"

"Of course not, Livie. Yoga terrifies him. The very thought would make him start traveling again, and I want him home more."

A customer entered the store, and Bertha hurried to help her. Olivia glanced at her watch. The lunch hour would arrive soon, which meant another influx of cookie-cutter enthusiasts. With Maddie hard at work on gingerbread houses for the weekend celebration, Olivia would be busy.

"I'm heading for the community center," Ellie said, "and I promised to pick up a few items for the gingerbread house project." Ellie extracted a torn scrap of paper from a deep pocket in her harem pants and handed it to Olivia. "But first tell me, how did your visit with the Chatterleys go? Really, Karen had no right to order you to talk to them, but since you did . . ."

"You want to be the first to know?"

"I have my reasons," Ellie said. "I'm concerned about Paine. And about Karen."

"Karen? Really? And Paine?" Olivia's

astonishment caught the attention of Bertha's customer, who turned to stare.

Ellie cupped Olivia's elbow and guided her into the store's cookbook nook, a semiprivate area that was once a dining room. "I knew Paine when he was young, you know. He was . . . complex. In fact, I was never sure I really did know him, despite the many afternoons I spent at Sadie's house, learning to embroider."

"You spent . . . why did I not know this?"

"Possibly because you weren't born yet, Livie." Ellie's gaze wandered to a display of gel food coloring for icing. "You do carry rolled fondant, don't you? I'll need several packages."

"Fondant is easy to make, and it would be much less expensive."

"I know that, Livie, but we are running out of time."

It was unusual for her mother to sound testy, and she seemed disoriented as well. "Are you okay, Mom?" Olivia asked. "It's only Wednesday, and the gingerbread houses don't need to be finished until the celebration begins Saturday morning. Or Friday evening, I suppose, if all of you insist on getting some sleep."

Ellie sighed. "I realize it's not every day a town achieves two hundred and fifty years of existence, at least here in America, which is still so young. In Europe, of course —"

"Weren't you feeling pressed for time, Mom?"

"Not only that," Ellie said, "but I can't tell you how many activities I have missed to help Maddie's crew with those gingerbread houses — like my reading group, yoga, two weekly nature walks, and I haven't had a minute to help with our protest march on Washington. It takes a lot of planning to occupy Congress, you know."

"I'm surprised you aren't *running* for Congress." Olivia was sounding a bit testy herself.

"I've thought about it, dear. Maybe later." Ellie frowned at the scrap of paper in Olivia's hand and sighed again.

Olivia scanned the list. "Five packages of rolled fondant, two boxes of confectioners' sugar, gel coloring . . . dried tagliatelle pasta?"

"Maddie's idea for quick and easy windowpanes," Ellie said. "We're getting desperate."

Olivia finished reading the list in silence. "We have most of this stuff, like the cookie cutters and pastry bags, and I can give you some of our baking supplies from the kitchen. You're on your own for the dried tagliatelle. Although it's an interesting idea."

As they gathered the items, Olivia asked her mother, "Why are you worried about Karen and Paine?"

Ellie gazed off into space as if trying to find words to express her concerns. "Paine Chatterley . . . such an endearing little boy, for the most part. But sad, too, which is hardly surprising. You'd think his parents would have been thrilled when they discovered they were pregnant, after all those years. His mother was over forty, as I remember. However, not all couples are meant to be parents."

Olivia unlocked a small room that had once served as a pantry. Olivia had hired Lucas Ashford to move the door so she could access the room from the sales floor, and now the store's inventory lined the old wooden shelves. Selecting a box, Olivia said, "I think the vegetation cutters are in here." She skimmed a list taped to the front of the box. "Yes, here they are." Olivia lifted a cookie cutter out of the box and handed it to her mother. "This is an elm tree shape I had custom made. If it gets lost, I will be most unhappy."

"I will guard it faithfully," Ellie said. "I used to love the old elm trees. Such lovely shade."

"You know," Olivia said, "from what I saw of Paine yesterday evening and this morning, the word 'endearing' isn't the first that would spring to my lips. 'Cranky,' maybe, or 'haughty.' "

"Sad can look like a lot of things," Ellie said, "including cranky and haughty. However, I do see your point."

"Here's a shady oak tree shape," Olivia said as she handed her mother a shiny copper cutter. "Hermione seems to think Paine is depressed, although she didn't use that word."

"That would not surprise me," Ellie said.

"And Karen?"

"Hmm?"

"Our esteemed mayor, the other person you're worried about. Although if Karen is sad or depressed, I'll eat an entire gingerbread house, dried tagliatelle and all." Olivia found the last cookie cutter on her mother's list, a rosebush. The cutter was no more than a lumpy oval shape, but Maddie would recognize it. Olivia slid the box back on the shelf before correcting the attached list to reflect the change in its contents.

"I wouldn't call Karen sad, exactly," Ellie said, "but she does seem overwrought. It isn't good for her. She's taking this town celebration far too seriously. History is important, of course, and our young people do need more exposure to the idea that time did not begin with their births, but still, one can become too involved in something."

"This from the woman who takes yoga classes seventeen times a week?" Olivia escorted Ellie out into the cookbook nook.

"A gross exaggeration," Ellie said. "Anyway, yoga is only yoga."

"I have no idea what that means."

Ellie tilted her head and smiled up at her daughter, who was taller by a good eight inches. "You'd understand if you would come to yoga class with me. I tried to get Karen to come along, but she insisted she's too busy. She said yoga would only increase her stress, which is absurd. Karen is well into her forties. I told her, now is the time to lay the groundwork for a more flexible and graceful aging."

"And did she take that well?"

"Not at all, dear."

Olivia scanned the display of add-ons for decorated cookies and selected a large jar of white sugar sprinkles for snow on the gingerbread house roofs. "Mom, what's your impression of Quill Latimer?"

"Quill, yes . . ." As Ellie tilted her head, the navy blue streak in her hair shone in the light, reminding Olivia of deep blue luster dust. "I've got it," Ellie said. "Misplaced."

"Um . . . could you use a few more words, Mom?"

A thought furrow formed between Ellie's bright blue eyes. "Poor Quill always seems to me as if he isn't where he ought to be, and he is terribly unhappy about it. Some years ago, I took a class taught by Quill at the community college. It was called the History of Chatterley Heights: Pre-Revolution to the Present. Although, as I recall, the present ended at World War II, which is significant, I think."

"Misplaced, Mom? Quill?"

"That's what I'm talking about, Livie. The class content said it all. Quill is obsessed with the past."

"Aren't most history professors focused on the past?" Olivia handed her mother the last jar of chocolate pearlized jimmies.

"Of course, Livie, just as literature professors are focused on literature, but most of them have other interests as well. One of my friends specializes in the poetry of Gerard Manley Hopkins. She goes into a trance when she discusses his work, but she is equally delirious when she bowls a strike."

"Bowls a strike? Mom, I'm —"

"Confused, I know," Ellie said. "What I'm trying to say is that Quill is happy only when he is lost in the past. He was a different person in the classroom — entertaining, good-natured, approachable. But when I visited his office to correct an error in my registration, he'd turned sullen and grumpy."

"The Quill we all know and —"

"Exactly," Ellie said. "Quill belongs in a previous era. He doesn't fit in the twenty-first century. It makes him very uncomfortable."

"That makes a kind of tortured sense, Mom."

"Thank you, dear. Now, about the rolled fondant?"

As Olivia led the way to the store kitchen, she noticed several customers browsing while Bertha rang up purchases at the sales counter. "Let's get the remaining items from the kitchen," Olivia said. "Then I need to help out on the sales floor."

"Can't Maddie help me? She said she'd be back here in the afternoon."

"Maddie is as frantic as Karen, but she handles it much better. You know she's trying to finish all the gingerbread window scenes before heading over to the community center this evening to help decorate the houses."

Olivia held open the door and followed

her mother into The Gingerbread House kitchen. They found Maddie looking worried all right, but not about her gingerbread window scenes. She wasn't paying any attention to the partially decorated gingerbread cookies that covered the worktable.

Lucas Ashford, Maddie's almost fiancé, sat in a kitchen chair with her arm around his shoulders. Lucas looked as angry as Olivia had ever seen him. In fact, she couldn't recall seeing him even mildly miffed. Now his chiseled features were tinged with red, and she noticed his jaw work as he ground his teeth. Maddie flashed her a concerned frown. Even her wildly curly hair had deflated.

"Maddie dear," Ellie said, dumping her baking items on the kitchen table, "what has happened?"

Olivia noticed the Mr. Coffee was empty and started a new pot. She could tell this was a time for cookies and coffee.

"Lucas just called his team off the mansion renovation," Maddie said. She hesitated a moment, turning to Lucas to tell the story. When he said nothing, she added, "Paine Chatterley demanded that Lucas renovate their kitchen and put in all new appliances, free of charge."

"What?!" Olivia and Ellie said at the same time.

Lucas sprang from his chair and leaned against the kitchen counter, his muscular arms folded tightly across his chest. "Paine said it's the town's fault the mansion was in such bad shape. He said that Harold and Sally's will made us responsible for upkeep, in exchange for the use of the house as a tourist attraction after their deaths."

"That's absurd," Olivia said. "Updating the kitchen has nothing to do with maintaining a historical building. If anything, the kitchen should be left as it was a hundred years ago."

"Tell that to his lordship," Lucas said. "Anyway, it doesn't matter. He isn't letting the town show the mansion this weekend, so I pulled my guys off the job. I wouldn't care except . . . well, I've invested a lot of time and money in that restoration, and so has the town. Now it's all down the drain."

Maddie hitched herself up onto the kitchen counter next to Lucas. "Here's the deal," she said. "Lucas agreed to offer free labor and some of the materials in exchange for the opportunity to do a video of the restored house, inside and out. He wants to expand his business. In this economy, a plain old hardware store can't really survive.

Plus Lucas still has some debt from his parents' medical care."

Lucas's shoulders slumped as his spent anger turned to dejection. "Some of the guys I recruited for the project, they were working for free, even though they needed to be out looking for paying jobs. They were all counting on me to get some new business out of this. They've got skills; I could have put them to work."

Maddie's arm wrapped around his waist as she leaned into him. "It's not your fault, honey. None of this is your fault." She caught Olivia's eye and mouthed the word "cookies."

Olivia nodded her understanding. She and Maddie believed in the power of decorated cookies to smooth social relations and sooth an aching heart, so they always kept a small stash ready for any such contingency. Olivia slid a tin off the top of the refrigerator and opened it. Inside were a dozen cookies, carefully stacked. She could feel the tension in the kitchen ease at once.

While Ellie handed out cups of coffee, Olivia arranged the cookies on a large plate and passed it to Maddie, who selected two heart-shaped cookies with marbled pink and red icing. Lucas attempted a faint smile as Maddie aimed one of the cookies toward his mouth.

The kitchen door opened, and Olivia saw Sam Parnell's hawklike face appear. Not a welcome sight. Sam was a Chatterley Heights postal carrier with a fondness for gossip, and he wasn't particular about accuracy. Hence his nickname, Snoopy.

"I've got this overnight priority package for you," Sam said to Olivia. "I figured it might be important for the celebration, so I brought it right on over. That clerk of yours, Bertha, she's real busy. I noticed she's all alone out there." When no one reacted to his barb, he slid through the kitchen door and shut it behind him. "Anyway, she said you were all back here."

As always, Sam wore his United States Postal Service uniform, complete with hat, but he wasn't carrying his mail bag. Olivia suspected he'd seen The Gingerbread House address on the package and made a beeline for the store, hoping for a free cookie and a chance to check up on her and Maddie. A few weeks earlier, Sam had hand delivered a package and found Olivia chatting with Del in the kitchen. For days afterward, folks dropped by the store only to ask Olivia when she and Del planned to "share their big news." Binnie Sloan had come right out and announced in *The*

Weekly Chatter that Olivia and Del were engaged. Which they absolutely were not.

Sam's glance fell on the plate of cookies, now in Ellie's hands. "Looks like you're having yourselves a little party. Starting the celebration a bit early, are you?"

"Not at all," Olivia said a shade too hastily. She could see the glint in Sam's eyes. "We're taking a break from our preparations for the big weekend. It's a lot of hard work in not much time. Thanks for the delivery; we do need these items for Saturday's opening ceremony." She took the package from Sam's hands and left it on the kitchen counter, unopened.

"I heard you got a visit from Paine Chatterley and that wife of his last evening," Sam said. "He doesn't look so good, does he? Maybe he came home to die."

"I don't think he's —" Maddie's cheeks flushed as she realized she'd fallen for Sam's exploratory gambit. "I mean, are they receiving mail so soon?"

"They got a package already. From London, England. I thought I'd hand deliver it. I always like to meet new folks on my route," Sam said. "I was glad to see they didn't bring along a dog." He shot a glance at Olivia. Getting no reaction, he said, "Mr. Chatterley looked like he just got out of bed

69

when I saw him. Must have tied one on last night. I heard he was quite a teenage drinker back when he lived here, so I figure he kept it up in Europe. They drink all the time over there." Again, Sam's contribution was met with stony silence. "Well, I can't hang around and chat," he said without moving. "I'm on duty."

Ellie bestowed a beneficent smile on Sam and held the plate out to him. "Do take a cookie with you, Sam."

"I don't know, what with my diabetes and all," Sam said as he scooped up two cookies. Without so much as a murmur of admiration, he tore off a paper towel, wrapped the cookies, and shoved them into his uniform jacket pocket.

Olivia unlocked the alley door and held it open for Sam, who exited in silence. She knew he'd be back, angling for gossip, but it didn't bother her much anymore. She was learning how to handle him. Sometimes she could get more information from Sam than he could wheedle out of her. Whether any of it was true was another matter. She wondered . . . was Paine seriously ill or perhaps a heavy drinker, as Sam had implied? Either might explain his inconsistent behavior and desire to be left alone.

As Olivia relocked the alley door, the

kitchen phone rang. Maddie answered and said, "Let me see if she's able to come to the phone." Holding her hand over the receiver, Maddie whispered, "Livie, it's Karen. She sounds frantic. Should I tell her I don't know where you are?"

"Tempting, but no, I'll handle it." Olivia took the phone. "Yes, Karen, what is it?" She heard the brusqueness in her own voice and tried to soften it. "Is anything wrong?"

"Is anything *wrong*? Are you kidding me? *Everything* is wrong. The entire celebration is hanging by a thread. Now I hear that Lucas Ashford has stopped work on the mansion, without so much as a word to me. Even the mansion's exterior won't be finished by Saturday. At least Matthew agreed to keep working, but he only does that Victorian gingerbread trim. If Paine thinks he's going to get away with —"

"Matthew Fabrizio is still working on the mansion?" Too late, Olivia remembered Lucas was in the kitchen. She watched his features harden and tried to shift the direction of the conversation. "Karen, you know Lucas and his team have all been volunteering their labor, and Lucas donated supplies. It's unfair to expect them to keep working when the mansion is now off-limits to the public. After all, Lucas is busy, he has

71

Heights Hardware to operate."

"I'm tired of hearing about stores that have to be run. It's just a store, for goodness sakes, it can survive another day or two. I'll be a laughingstock if we can't even finish a paint job in time for such an important event." Karen's normally alto voice was scaling up into a panicky soprano range.

"Karen, none of this is a personal reflection on you." Olivia couldn't help rolling her eyes at Maddie, who shook her head in disgust. A flush spread up from Lucas's neck, while Ellie smiled benignly at nothing in particular.

"Not personal? Are you completely clueless? This celebration is my baby. It was my idea, I planned it, and if anything goes wrong . . . well, nothing can go wrong, that's all there is to it. You must get the Chatterleys to understand that if they intend to live in this town, they'd better learn to cooperate with us. I have a long memory."

Olivia felt increasingly confused and uneasy about Karen's emotional investment in what was essentially a birthday party for Chatterley Heights. "Karen, I think it might be helpful if you'd step back for a few moments. If we can't bring visitors into the Chatterley Mansion, it won't ruin the celebration. We do have photos of the mansion, and of course we have all the ginger-bread houses, and —"

"You just don't get it!" As Karen shouted into the receiver, Olivia held the phone away from her ear. Everyone in the kitchen heard the outburst. Karen lowered her voice and said, "Okay, we got off on the wrong foot. I should have explained to you that the *press* will be there, at the mansion, this Friday morning. Not just reporters from the little weeklies, either. Binnie got them interested, which was easy, but then she dropped the ball, so I convinced the big DC and Balti-more papers to come. I promised they could get pictures of the mansion, inside and out. Maybe even a quote or two from Paine Chatterley, if he's sober enough. I'll meet them in front of the mansion and give a statement about our celebration and our history and . . . so forth."

"That's great," Olivia said, forcing a show of enthusiasm, "and I'm sure you'll handle it beautifully." She figured it was useless to mention that Paine had asked — more like demanded — that the sheriff keep the block clear of gawkers. "I really think the report-ers will understand when you explain the mansion is again a private residence and that —" Olivia heard a sharp intake of breath and knew she was in for another explosion.

Ellie tapped on her shoulder and whispered in her ear, "Shall I give it a try?" Olivia held her hand over the mouthpiece as Ellie added, "Karen and I often run together. She can easily outpace me, so she feels a certain benevolence toward me."

Olivia mouthed a heartfelt "yes" and handed the phone to her mother.

Using her patient-parent voice, Ellie said, "Hello, Karen dear, it's Ellie. Olivia has been summoned to resolve a store crisis, so I offered to help you with your dilemma."

Olivia sank onto a kitchen chair. Maddie reached for the plate of cookies and brought it to her. "This should be both interesting and instructive," Maddie whispered. "Perhaps even amusing."

"Yes, dear," Ellie said into the phone, "I most certainly do understand how important this is to you. And for your future." She paused for Karen's reply before saying, "Oh, I don't think it would completely destroy your chances, but I can see that if this celebration goes well, it will showcase your considerable leadership skills and administrative talents."

While Ellie listened to the mayor, Olivia nibbled on a shortbread cookie in a butterfly shape with pink and lavender wings. The cookie worked its calming magic on her. She ought to go out to the sales floor and help Bertha, but she felt glued to her seat. So, apparently, did Maddie and Lucas, both of whom hung on Ellie's side of the phone conversation.

"Yes, I see the reasoning in everything you've argued," Ellie said. "I was thinking, though. . . . Perhaps I might throw out another strategy, simply for you to think about? I've always been most impressed by congresspersons who project a calm presence and are skilled negotiators. Of course, anyone of average ability can negotiate successfully with a reasonable opponent, but . . . Yes, I agree completely. An angry, obdurate opponent is more of a challenge. Only a truly gifted leader should even try to negotiate with someone like that."

Olivia was fairly sure she was being insulted. If it got her out of another visit to Chatterley Mansion, though, she'd take it with good grace.

"I think that's an excellent idea," Ellie said, "although I wonder about . . . but of course you were only joking about that. You'd never do such a thing. I wish you every success, Karen dear. Do let me know how it goes." Ellie hung up and beamed at her rapt audience. "Karen intends to speak with Paine herself," she said, "and I need a cookie."

"You deserve one." Olivia passed her mother the last cookie on the plate, a yellow and blue winged butterfly. Ellie took a bite and moaned with pleasure.

"Mom? What was the thing you said Karen would never do?"

"Oh nothing, I'm sure. Karen was feeling feisty, which is a good thing. Within reason, of course. It was a show of bravado, that's all."

"What was a show of bravado?" Olivia asked.

"Oh, you know how it is. Karen was simply expressing her frustration. She said she'd get Paine Chatterley out of her way even if she had to strangle him."

CHAPTER FOUR

Spunky insisted on a walk in the cool of dusk, and Olivia allowed herself to be persuaded. After a steamy summer, it felt good to need an extra layer of clothing. She considered leaving her cell phone at home, fearing she could expect another frantic, demanding call from the mayor. At the last minute, she slipped it into the pocket of her thigh-length sweater.

After locking the store behind her, Olivia asked, "Where to, Spunks?"

The little Yorkie yanked his leash in a northerly direction. Olivia knew better than to object. Spunky was particular about his walking route, preferring to avoid such irritants as heavy traffic or rowdy teenagers. Guarding The Gingerbread House all day was a demanding job. For his evening outing, Spunky required peace and quiet.

As Spunky sniffed every inch of a fire hydrant, Olivia's cell emitted a garbled tune from the recesses of her pocket. She checked caller ID and saw her younger brother's number. "Jason! How's life inside the Beltway?"

"Technically, I'm not inside the Beltway, Liv," Jason said. "In fact, I guess I won't be in DC at all pretty soon. That's why I'm calling. I'm moving back home."

"Oh." Olivia restrained herself from adding her next thought: *Yay!* She hadn't been happy with her brother's decision to follow his girlfriend when she moved from Chatterley Heights back to DC. Charlene had abruptly closed her new business, a health food store, after her abusive ex-husband sneaked into town and got himself murdered. Olivia had worried that Jason's devotion to Charlene had more to do with overprotectiveness than love. She rather hoped they had split for good. Jason deserved better. "So," she asked, "are you okay?"

"Yeah, I'm fine. Things just got . . . well, you know how it is. I couldn't find a job, with this recession and all. I wasn't about to live on Char's money."

"I can understand that," Olivia said. "It's a tough situation."

"Yeah." Jason was silent so long that Olivia thought he'd hung up. He startled her by saying, "I called Mom and Allan, and they said I could stay with them till I can afford a place of my own again. That'll be weird, but . . . hey, the good news is Struts said I could have my old job back."

"That's great!" Olivia wasn't surprised. Struts Marinsky owned Struts & Bolts, Chatterley Heights's garage. She was a gifted mechanic and a great boss. She recognized skill when she saw it. "It'll be good to have you around again."

"Don't get all mushy on me. Bye." Click.

Happily distracted by Jason's news, Olivia strolled another block before she realized Spunky was retracing their morning route to the Chatterley Mansion. And no wonder. During their visit to the mansion that morning, Hermione Chatterley had slipped Spunky a bite of meat. Olivia had not objected, but only because she'd hoped for Hermione's help to convince Paine to open the mansion to strangers. Naturally Spunky would head back in hopes of another tasty treat.

"I'm on to you, kiddo," Olivia said to her determined little dog. "Let me remind you that I am bigger than you, and I'm not about to follow you back to that mansion for every walk from now to infirmity."

Spunky paid no attention. He turned north onto Sycamore Street, which would eventually lead them past the mansion. When Olivia slowed her pace, Spunky strained at his leash until it pulled his front paws off the sidewalk. Olivia picked him up and tucked him under her arm. "You're lucky I bought you a harness leash so you wouldn't strangle yourself," she muttered. Spunky let out a yap in response.

"Shush, boy." Something in her voice made an impression on the Yorkie, who for once obeyed her command. They had come within sight of Chatterley Mansion, where Olivia saw a car parked in front. The car, a red Cadillac, looked familiar. As she crossed Frederick Street and headed north up Sycamore, she saw the driver's door open. A shapely leg emerged, followed by the rest of Mayor Karen Evanson. Karen paused to straighten the jacket of her suit and fluff her hair before striding toward the Chatterleys' front door.

Olivia's first thought was to call her mother and tell her she was a genius. But she wanted to put some distance between herself and the Chatterley Mansion in case Karen glanced down the street while she waited for someone to answer the front door. Knowing Karen, she would corral Olivia into helping her manipulate Paine Chatterley. Going around the block was

Olivia's safest option.

"Sorry, Spunks, no forbidden treats this evening. We're going home." As she bent to put Spunky down, he jerked the leash from her grasp. She grabbed at him, but he was too quick for her. Olivia sprinted after him, consoling herself that at least he was heading north, not toward the mansion's front door. Spunky, though, had another surprise for her. He suddenly veered to the right and disappeared. Olivia realized at once that he'd found the alley behind the Chatterley Mansion. Perhaps it was merely a coincidence, but Olivia suspected he'd planned the whole maneuver.

Olivia followed Spunky into the alley, strolling, in case anyone was watching. At first, she couldn't see the tiny dog ahead of her. Then she spotted him next to a short trash can behind Chatterley Mansion, his tail wagging at warp speed. Spunky was positioning himself for a jump. Before Olivia could capture him, his little hind legs and fluffy tail disappeared inside the can.

"Oh, Spunky . . ." Olivia peered into the can. Garbage filled about half of it, which might explain why it hadn't toppled as Spunky leaped inside. A furry Yorkie face gazed up with delight, though not at the sight of his mistress. Between his teeth, he held a piece of red meat. To be precise, a small steak, cooked rare. "You are a bad, bad boy." Olivia's admonition had no effect, probably because she'd whispered it.

Olivia reached into the can and clutched the meat with her bare hands. As she tried to pull it out of Spunky's mouth, he growled and backed up to the edge of the garbage can. The can shifted, scraping the pavement. Olivia saw no other option; she let go. She was grateful the mansion's only window onto the alley was in the kitchen door, which was several feet away from them.

While she considered her dilemma, it occurred to Olivia to wonder why the Chatterleys had tossed the steak into their garbage. Even if Paine refused to eat it, why wouldn't Hermione have done so? She felt a chill as she remembered Hermione's comment that Paine thought she was poisoning him. But no, Spunky weighed only five pounds; if he'd eaten a piece of poisoned meat in the morning, he'd have shown symptoms before evening.

And why was the garbage can already more than half full? Maybe Paine and Hermione were cleaning out items the workers had left in the house, like old wallpaper? Olivia didn't care enough to examine the can's contents. She wanted to go home.

Olivia lifted Spunky out of the garbage can, steak and all. As she did so, she noticed an empty whiskey bottle lying amidst the trash. She wondered if perhaps a neighbor had used the mansion's garbage can to dispose of telltale evidence. A heavy drinker might want to avoid putting too many empty bottles in his or her recycling bin. On the other hand, Snoopy Sam Parnell might have been right for once. Maybe Paine Chatterley did have a drinking problem.

Olivia grimaced at the bloody object hanging from her otherwise sweet pet's mouth. "That's probably spoiled. You'll get sick, which will serve you right." Olivia felt a guilty twinge. She reminded herself that Spunky had spent months on the loose after his escape from the puppy mill. He'd eaten out of many a garbage can without becoming ill. However, she'd have to find a way to separate dog and meat. Later.

First, Olivia had to get them both away from Chatterley Mansion and back home, as quickly as possible. The most direct route was back the way they'd come. That meant crossing Frederick Street in view of the mansion's front yard. Well, it couldn't be helped.

Once he realized his mistress wasn't trying to steal his delicious prize, Spunky allowed Olivia to carry him off. They left the alley and headed south, toward home. Before leaving the cover of a cottage on the corner lot, Olivia peeked down Frederick Street. It looked deserted. Mayor Karen Evanson's car was still parked in front of Chatterley Mansion, so Hermione, at least, must have been willing to talk to her. If Karen succeeded in gaining Paine's cooperation, it would be a miracle.

With his teeth sunk into a hunk of meat, Spunky couldn't yap, for which Olivia was grateful as she carted him across the street in sight of the mansion. Spunky concentrated his energy on trying to chew the meat without letting go of it. It wasn't going well, but Spunky was a terrier, after all. Giving up was not in his nature.

When The Gingerbread House came into view, he still held that bloody mess clenched between his teeth. By then, Olivia estimated, half of Chatterley Heights had seen them, laughed, and taken pictures on their cell phones. Olivia's only hope was that the evening light had faded enough to make Spunky's plunder unidentifiable.

Exhausted and embarrassed, Olivia entered the foyer of her Queen Anne and plunked her pup onto the doormat. Gritting her teeth, she took hold of the meat with both hands and played tug-of-war with the tough little Yorkie. Spunky threw himself into the game. He growled, Olivia cajoled, and they were getting nowhere. The deciding factor turned out to be Maddie, who heard the ruckus and flung open the door of The Gingerbread House.

Spunky's protective instincts kicked in. He began to yap fiercely, which required him to open his mouth and drop the steak. Olivia, caught off guard, fell back against the foyer wall and slid to the floor, still clutching the meat.

"If you're going to play rough," Maddie said, "don't you think you should go outside? This is a place of business, and you've gotten blood on the rug."

"There are cell phone cameras out there," Olivia said.

"Ah. That's unfortunate. So I guess we'll be seeing this in Binnie Sloan's blog?"

"Afraid so."

Maddie made a face at the mangled steak. "That thing is gross."

"The steak or Spunky?" Olivia struggled to her feet, holding the meat out of Spunky's reach.

Maddie stood aside to let Olivia and

Spunky enter the store. A dejected pooch straggled across the sales floor to his chair. He jumped up to the padded seat and curled in a ball. Maddie led the way to the kitchen, where Olivia disposed of the meat and gave her hands a thorough washing. With a dampened old dish towel, she wiped the stains off her clothes. More or less clean, she sank onto the chair at the little kitchen desk, where the day's receipts lay in an untidy but healthy heap. No matter what Karen Evanson thought, it took time and attention to run a business.

"I won't bother changing my clothes," Olivia said. "Those receipts aren't going to reconcile themselves."

"Good," Maddie said, "because I want company while I finish up these window scenes for the gingerbread houses. A little admiration would not be unwelcome, either."

"Looks like we had a good day," Olivia said as she picked up the receipts.

"An excellent day, which Bertha mostly handled." Maddie pointed to a decorated rectangular gingerbread cookie resting on a rack. "Now, about that admiration?"

Olivia joined Maddie at the worktable to get a closer look at the design on the cookie. "Exquisite, as always," she said. "Hey, is that the little boy in the mansion window, the one your aunt Sadie embroidered on an apron?"

"You got it in one," Maddie said. "This is sad, lonely little Paine Chatterley staring out an upper window of Chatterley Mansion, which is where I'll put this cookie scene — in a window of the gingerbread mansion. I wonder if anyone else will figure out who he is. Aunt Sadie said Paine's hair lightened as he grew up."

"I'm definitely keeping that apron, by the way," Olivia said. "Maybe we should use this cookie in a contest. Whoever guesses the child's identity gets to keep the gingerbread mansion after the weekend."

"Aha! I knew it was only a matter of time before you created a mystery to be solved. You are so addicted. Except we'd have to eliminate Aunt Sadie from the competition, of course, and swear her to silence. Not that she talks much anyway. Your mom could be a problem, too. Ellie is likely to figure out that little boy's identity in a matter of seconds because she's . . ." Maddie's forehead furrowed as she searched for the right word.

"From an alternate dimension?" Olivia suggested.

"I was reaching for 'intuitive,' but your

theory has merit. Anyway, the contest idea sounds fun. I'll talk to Aunt Sadie, and you make sure your mom is on board, okay? Then I'll put together a flyer." Maddie started gathering the dirty baking equipment.

"You can leave those," Olivia said. "I'll load them in the dishwasher as soon as I finish the receipts."

"You are a true friend." While she arranged decorated gingerbread cookies in single layers inside sheet-cake pans, Maddie said, "The icing is almost dry, and I'm getting antsy to see how the scenes look inside our gingerbread houses. As soon as I've got all these cookies packed, I'll head over to the community center. Lucas is bringing corned beef sandwiches from the Chatterley Café. At least we'll get to spend a little time together while I work on the exteriors of the houses."

"How is Lucas? I imagine he's still pretty upset about Paine Chatterley shutting down the renovation project and making those crazy demands?" Olivia decided to load the dishes and leave the receipts until Maddie had left. They'd both been so busy with preparations for the celebration, they'd had little time to catch up with each other.

"Between you and me, right now Lucas is

more worried than angry." Maddie slid a lid on one of her cake pans. "I mean, sure, he's irritated with Paine and upset about the labor and materials he and his team ended up giving away for free."

"Except for Matthew Fabrizio, that is," Olivia said. "I hope Matthew isn't hoping to work at Heights Hardware ever again."

Maddie paused with another pan lid in her hands. "You didn't hear? Paine took advantage of Matthew, too. The poor kid thought if he kept working on the Victorian trim on the mansion, Paine would welcome him into the Chatterley dynasty and help him prove his lineage. He suggested the exchange to Paine, and Paine played along. Matthew worked a while and decided to finish the next day. Before leaving, he went to the Chatterleys and told them more about his great-great-great-whatever's dalliance with dear old Frederick P. These revelations were not well received by Hermione, and Paine did a sudden about-face, claiming he had no idea what Matthew was talking about."

"I can't imagine why Matthew would expect anything different."

"I can," Maddie said. "Matthew is an artist. He can imagine wonderful possibilities."

"So you're saying artists don't have a good

grasp of reality?"

"I'm saying he's broke, and this seemed like a good way to become part of a wealthy family." Maddie lifted her covered pans into a large Gingerbread House bag. "So yeah, Matthew's grasp of reality is limited. Also, he has that dark, tortured-soul thing going for him, so now he's probably drinking away his disappointment. By the way, Heather Irwin seems to have fallen for Matthew. She sure knows how to pick 'em." Maddie double-bagged her precious cargo and carried it to the alley door. "Close up behind me, would you? I can't afford to drop these cookies. Thanks."

As Olivia locked the kitchen door behind Maddie, she thought about Heather Irwin, the town's shy young librarian. Heather had misjudged men in the past, trusting when she should have run for the hills. Olivia had hoped Heather had learned her lesson the previous summer after falling for a thief with a violent temper. On the other hand, Maddie might have overstated Matthew's negative qualities. He was, after all, a fine craftsman. Olivia had heard Lucas say that Matthew would work on a curlicue of Victorian trim until it was flawless, no matter how long it took.

Lady Gaga declared her love for Judas

from the direction of the kitchen desk, where Olivia had left her cell phone. Maddie had been messing with her ring tone, again. Olivia was tempted to let the call go to voice mail until she saw it was from Del Jenkins.

"Don't shoot the messenger, okay, Livie?" were the first words out of Del's mouth.

"I don't like the sound of that," Olivia said. "What's up?"

"Remember I told you that Paine Chatterley more or less ordered me to guard his block over the celebration weekend? Well, Friday morning Karen and members of the press intend to descend upon Chatterley Mansion, cameras and microphones at the ready. And Karen insists that Cody and I accompany her."

"So you're caught between the dog and the tree," Olivia said.

"Exactly."

"Karen is really getting on my nerves." Olivia opened the refrigerator to scour for a spare cookie, her solace in moments of irritation. "Who does she think she is?"

Del heaved a manly sigh. "She thinks she's mayor. She's threatening to get me removed as sheriff if I refuse. And here's the wrinkle: Karen insists she talked at length to Hermione Chatterley, who promised she'd get her husband to consent to letting the public wander through the mansion this weekend. I find that hard to believe."

"Hermione made a similar promise to me when I visited them this morning," Olivia said. "To be honest, I got the impression she has more power in that relationship than we've been assuming."

"Or maybe she was just trying to get rid of you."

"So cynical of you, Del. But you have a point. Did you call the Chatterleys to check on Karen's story?"

"I tried. I called the old number, the one from the mansion's museum days, but it's been disconnected. The phone company said they've had no new request to provide service for the mansion. So I sent Cody over to knock on the door. No one answered. He went around back, too, and looked in some windows, but there was no sign of life. I'm hoping the Chatterleys skipped town to avoid our celebration altogether."

"That's what I'd do," Olivia said. "But I also know how determined Karen can be."

"Either way, I'm stuck," Del said. "I'll have to show up at the mansion Friday morning and see what happens. If Karen is right and the Chatterleys do allow the press to invade their privacy, I'll hang around to keep the peace. If Karen misunderstood, I'll have to cart her off and disperse the reporters."

"Sounds like a fun time," Olivia said, laughing. "Stop by the store afterward. I'll feed you gingerbread cookies and coffee, and you can vent."

"Not so fast, Livie. I am to convey a message to you from our mayor."

"Gee, maybe later. I think I hear Maddie calling for —"

"You are to be at the mansion Friday morning at seven thirty sharp. Karen plans to drill us until eight, at which time she, and she alone, will knock on the mansion door. You've been assigned to help Karen coordinate the interviews. She said something about you being the only more or less levelheaded committee member."

"What she means is I'm the only committee member she thinks she can control," Olivia said. "I'm in a mood to prove her wrong."

"Livie, you know that if you refuse to show up, Karen will blame me. And she is not without political influence."

"I think you're tough enough to handle her. Besides, I do, in fact, have a store to run. I know Karen doesn't take that seriously, but you should."

93

"And I do," Del said. "I will try my very best to get you back to The Gingerbread House by opening time. Karen also instructed me to remind you to arrive in costume. I'm envisioning you as a serving wench."

"Thanks, but Maddie already claimed that role. We wouldn't want too many serving wenches wandering around."

"Livie, there's no such thing as too many serving wenches."

"Good-bye, Del." Olivia flipped her cell shut.

CHAPTER FIVE

After a busy, productive Thursday morning in The Gingerbread House, Olivia felt ready to tackle anything Karen decided to throw at her. During a lull, she used her burst of energy to straighten and restock shelves. Olivia had displayed three of Sadie Briggs's embroidered aprons, all of which had sold in one morning. She hung three more aprons on an antique oak coat stand in the cookbook nook. On each, she pinned a new price tag reading "$125.00."

"Such lovely work," said a familiar voice behind her.

"Mom, you startled me."

"Sorry, Livie. It must be the moccasins. Bertha said you were in here." Ellie's attire was, for her, understated: a long, soft faux-suede skirt, in dark brown, and a light brown T-shirt that read, "Will Protest for Food."

Ellie chose one of the aprons, decorated

with a riot of spring wildflowers, and ran her hand over the embroidery. "Sadie's work is exquisite. These are underpriced," she said, checking the tag. "Not that I could afford it, of course, but I know several well-to-do women who would snap these up at twice the price."

"Is this your way of telling me you aren't leaving me millions?"

"Livie dear, if I ever have millions, you may rest assured that I will spend them." Ellie retrieved a piece of paper from a small pocket at the waistband of her skirt. "I can't stay long, I just need to pick up some emergency supplies for the gingerbread houses. Maddie called and gave me a list. I'm heading over to the community center to help."

"More supplies? But you and Rosemarie were both here yesterday with long lists. Rosemarie said she didn't think you'd need anything more." Rosemarie York ran the Chatterley Heights Community Center, which possessed a kitchen large enough to accommodate Maddie and her team of gingerbread house bakers.

Ellie's normally serene face puckered with concern. "I know, but we seem to be running through our icing ingredients quickly. It worries me, though I hate to think that anyone from Chatterley Heights might be involved."

"Mom, you're leaving out sentence parts again."

"Hm? Oh, sorry. I haven't said anything to anyone else, especially not Rosemarie. She'd feel responsible because she's the community center's administrator, but what can she do? She has to leave the front door unlocked so the decorating team can come and go, which they are doing until well into the night. And, of course, the kitchen door doesn't have its own lock."

"Mom, are you saying someone is walking off with the icing ingredients? The Gingerbread House is donating most of the baking items. Have you mentioned this to Del?"

"Not yet." With a slight shake of her head, as if she couldn't believe her own observations, Ellie said, "I'll be glad to cover the cost from my own pocket, dear."

"That's not the point."

"I know that, Livie. To be honest, I can't be certain that ingredients are actually disappearing. Royal icing can be tricky, as you know. Our less experienced bakers might be trying to hide their failures out of embarrassment. Silly of them, of course, but . . . forget what I've said, Livie. I'll keep my eyes open, and if I think someone is

97

stealing, I'll report it to Del at once."

Olivia nodded, silently vowing to tell Del as soon as she saw him again.

With Maddie at the Chatterley Heights Community Center, frantically working on the finishing touches for the gingerbread houses, Olivia and Bertha were kept busy through lunch and beyond as a steady stream of customers visited the store. Spunky held court from his chair in front of the window. He had merely to lift his head or thump his tail, and most customers succumbed. Now that school was back in session, he was safer from kids who thought it was fun to yank the long hair that flopped over his eyes.

By one p.m., The Gingerbread House had run out of prepared gingerbread mix. An hour later, Olivia noticed an empty shelf that had held a large display of gingerbread boy and girl cookie cutters. It seemed as if everyone within a twenty-mile radius had entered the celebration spirit. If she didn't restock the gingerbread items soon, she figured she'd have to change the name of the store.

Another half hour passed before Olivia finally had a few minutes to begin refilling the shelves. She raided the inventory in her storage closet, filling a large basket with various colors of gel food coloring, gingerbread cookie-cutter sets, and the last three gingerbread house kits. As she locked the storage closet door behind her, she heard Spunky's happy yap. She turned to see Hermione Chatterley gazing around with the rapt attention of a child in a toy store. She wore a maroon dress covered with tiny pink rosebuds. Once again, Olivia thought of her great-grandmother, dressed to go shopping in the city. She also thought of wallpaper.

Spunky jumped down from his chair and trotted over to Hermione.

"Hello, little one," Hermione said as Spunky stood on his hind legs to greet her. "What a sweet boy you are."

Olivia knew he was angling for another piece of meat. "Spunky, down. Mrs. Chatterley, welcome to The Gingerbread House. Is there anything I can help you find?"

"Olivia, I'm so glad to find you here," Hermione said. "I was feeling rather cooped up in the house and wanted a walk, so I thought I'd toddle on over to your charming little store. I'll wander around a bit, if I may. I don't want to be in the way." She stood aside as two women entered the store, chattering to each other.

Since Bertha was busy ringing up purchases, Olivia helped the two women find a set of football-themed cookie cutters from among the displays in the cookbook nook. When she returned to the main sales floor, Hermione had gravitated to the sturdy, glass cabinet that housed, under lock and key, the more valuable vintage cookie cutters.

"Are you interested in antiques?" Olivia asked when she joined Hermione.

"Dear Paine is rather fond of antiques," Hermione said. "I prefer new things myself. So much sturdier. Paine has a birthday coming up in a month, and I'm looking for something he might enjoy. Cookie cutters do seem an odd gift for a man, but if you have one that is especially valuable . . ."

"Cookie cutters tend not to be the most valuable of antiques," Olivia said, "at least not in monetary terms, though some are pricier because they are rare. The truly valuable antique cutters are mostly in museums or private collections. I think many collectors are drawn to the sense of human history attached to cutters — you know, the thought that generations of mothers and grandmothers used them to fashion beautiful cookies for their loved ones." Olivia unlocked the cabinet and selected one of her favorite vintage cutters, an aluminum gingerbread man with a pointy head. "This cutter was sold in the 1950s and isn't terribly unique. But I'm fond of the little guy because I can see how well loved he was. See the handle, where it's nearly broken in the middle? Someone used this cutter over and over until the handle weakened from being pressed into the dough and lifted up. Vintage cookie cutters are often bent or even broken, but for many of us those little imperfections make them even more fascinating. We imagine the story behind every dent."

"How sweet." Hermione had barely glanced at the cutter. "I do think Paine would be more appreciative of something with a bit more value. He had rather an unhappy childhood, you see. I doubt his mother ever made cookies for him. His family had a cook, of course; I believe she might have baked treats for him."

"I hope I'm not being rude," Olivia said, "but I was wondering . . . why was it important to your husband to return to Chatterley Heights? I mean, if his childhood memories are painful, won't he be unhappy here?"

To Olivia's surprise, Hermione giggled. "Oh, you don't know dear Paine the way I do," she said. "I do think he enjoys being

101

miserable. Although" — Hermione's gaze slid across the shelves of vintage cutters as if she were looking for one in particular — "now that you mention it, I've wondered if he wanted to come back here to, shall we say, settle some issues from his past."

Olivia thought of Paine's odd comments to Karen Evanson and Quill Latimer. Was "settle some issues" a euphemism for exacting revenge? Only Quill had admitted to knowing Paine Chatterley before Tuesday evening, but he'd shrugged it off as casual. Karen had ignored Paine's oblique reference to a prior meeting.

"But never mind all that," Hermione said. "Do you perhaps have a truly antique cookie cutter? Something at least a hundred and fifty years old? Perhaps a cookie cutter that one of Paine's ancestors might have used? You see, sad as his memories are, he is frightfully proud of his heritage. Why, he can trace the Chatterleys back at least as far as written records exist, and even further from stories handed down through generations of Chatterleys. His grandfather told him that Sir Cedric Chatterley fought in the Crusades."

Olivia thought of the extensive cutter collection she'd inherited from her friend and mentor, Clarisse Chamberlain. Clarisse had managed to obtain a number of tin cookie cutters that were one hundred or more years old. She'd amassed an enviable collection of cookie molds, precursors to cutters, that had been brought to the colonies by German immigrants. Those molds and cookie cutters were valuable in every sense of the term, but Olivia had no intention of selling them. Someday, when she was ready to let go of them, Olivia planned to donate them to museums.

Gesturing toward the glass display case, Olivia said, "I'm afraid these vintage cutters go back only sixty or, at the most, seventy years. Occasionally we come across an older piece; I could keep an eye out for one, if you'd like."

"That would be nice," Hermione said, but her attention had already wandered toward the view of the town square through the front window.

Olivia was grateful when Bertha called to her from the sales counter that Maddie was on the phone and needed to talk to her. The interchange with Hermione had left Olivia feeling uncomfortable, though she couldn't pinpoint the reason. She felt as if there'd been two conversations going at the same time, and she'd been privy to only one of them.

Answering the call from the kitchen phone, Olivia said, "Hey, Maddie, how come you didn't call my cell? I have it in my pocket on vibrate, as usual."

"My reasons will become clear in a moment," Maddie said, "but it will take a bit of explanation, so don't get impatient with me, okay?"

"When am I impatient with you? Don't answer that. Tell me what's up."

"I'm in Rosemarie's office at the community center," Maddie said. "First, act normal, okay? Is Hermione Chatterley in the store right now?"

"I think so. Let me check." Olivia peeked out the kitchen door. She saw no one in the main sales area.

Bertha was helping two customers at the same time, so Olivia quickly checked the cookbook nook herself and found it empty. Back in the kitchen, she picked up the phone and said, "Looks like she's gone. Why?"

"Okay, here's the scoop," Maddie said. "My friend Lola is helping with the last-minute decorating here at the center, for which she took the afternoon off from her job at Lady Chatterley's." Lady Chatterley's Clothing Boutique for Elegant Ladies drew wealthy customers from well beyond Chatterley Heights. "Lola is a manager," Maddie said, "which is why she had to deal with this."

"Okay, but —"

"Don't interrupt. I warned you this would be complicated. Your mom's right, you need a yoga injection or something. Anyway, Hermione came into Lady Chatterley's this morning and said she was looking for a nice dress. Lola said she tried on six or seven dresses. They were all in the seven- to eight-hundred-dollar range. Hermione picked one she liked and told Lola — told, not asked — to put it on her account. Well, Lola made it clear that Lady Chatterley's did not do business that way. Hermione got all huffy and mentioned that the Chatterleys were nobility in England, so *she* was the real Lady Chatterley, and the store was using her name without permission."

"Wow." It crossed Olivia's mind that Hermione Chatterley was both gutsy and quick-witted. "How did Lola handle that zinger?"

"Lola doesn't rattle easily. She can do the raised-eyebrow thing, so I'm imagining she did that first. Then she explained that 'Madame' was welcome to charge her purchase with any major credit card accepted in the United States. Hermione said she never used such middle-class objects as credit cards. Back home in England, she said, she simply authorized her bank to pay the shopkeepers' bills directly each month."

"So did Hermione walk out of Lady Chatterley's with a dress or not?"

"You're getting impatient again," Maddie said. "The answer is no, but there's more in between. Trust me, you'll want to know this. Lola decided to play along a bit, so she said the store might consider such an arrangement providing the bank in question dealt directly with U.S. banks. She got Hermione to rattle off the supposed name of her supposed bank. Lola said it would take a day or two. After Hermione left, Lola called her husband, who is, as it happens —"

"A vice president at Chatterley Heights National Bank, I know," Olivia said. When Maddie responded with silence, Olivia added, "Sorry, couldn't help myself. I really am hooked. What did Lola's husband say about Hermione's bank?"

"That it doesn't exist."

"I wonder why . . ." Olivia's mind was popping with possible explanations for Hermione's use of a false bank name.

"Lola thinks she might be hiding her real identity," Maddie said.

"Except Paine seems to be the real Paine

Chatterley." Olivia thought back to the Chatterleys' surprise appearance at the celebration committee meeting on Tuesday evening. "At least he seemed to recognize Karen and Quill. From their reactions, I'd say they both recognized him, too."

"Aunt Sadie definitely recognized him," Maddie said, "and she isn't easy to fool. She might use a walker, but her mind is as sharp as ever. Maybe Hermione has some sort of control over Paine?"

"That thought crossed my mind after my first visit to them Wednesday morning." Olivia glanced at the clock over the kitchen sink. Interesting as this information was to her, she needed to get back to work. The Gingerbread House closed in an hour.

"I know you're checking the time," Maddie said, "but there's one more tidbit I want to tell you. Lola called around to a few of the other business owners, and guess what she discovered. Three more upscale stores also experienced the joy of a visit from Hermione, during which she bought nothing. After she left, all three owners noticed some expensive items were missing from their shelves. So we might want to schedule a thorough inventory once we get through the weekend festivities."

"Good idea." After Olivia hung up, she

thought about her impression that Hermione often seemed to be acting a role. Yes, she might be some nefarious and powerful criminal holding Paine Chatterley under her control. But maybe there was a simpler explanation. Maybe she and Paine were flat broke. Maybe they'd decided to use the last of their resources to come home because they had nowhere else to live.

With only Thursday evening and Friday left to prepare for the weekend celebration, Maddie had practically moved into the Chatterley Heights Community Center kitchen. While she and numerous volunteers rushed to finish an ambitious number of gingerbread houses, all representing the town's historic buildings, Olivia was left to close The Gingerbread House on her own. Not that she minded. She loved everything about the store, right down to the dirty dishes cluttering the kitchen.

Once Olivia had finished tidying up and restocking the shelves, she dimmed the lights in the store and sat on the soft chair near the front window. She shifted the chair so she could see both the town square and the store's main sales area. Since Spunky considered the chair and Olivia to be his property, he hopped onto her lap. He watched the action in the park, where volunteers hung banners and strung lights for the celebration, while Olivia soaked up the peacefulness of The Gingerbread House. The faint scent of cinnamon, cloves, and ginger hung in the air. Though it wasn't yet dusk, the store's ever-changing cookie-cutter mobiles twinkled as the low sun peeked into the room.

Spunky jumped off Olivia's lap and pattered to the front door. "Hang on a sec, kiddo," Olivia said, as she retrieved his leash, a couple plastic bags, and her own sweater from a shelf behind the sales counter. As an afterthought, she slipped into the store kitchen, where she picked up an envelope containing the check she'd written to Sadie Briggs, profit from the sale of a dozen of her hand-embroidered aprons. She filled a Gingerbread House bag with half a dozen decorated cookies and rejoined Spunky. The impatient little Yorkie stood on his hind legs and pawed at the front door while Olivia tried to snap the leash on his collar. "Keep your fur on," she said. "Honestly, you'd think I hadn't walked you in a week."

Bothered by the noisy activity in the town square, Spunky wanted to head in another direction, but Olivia tucked him under her arm and headed south. "We're off to see Aunt Sadie," she said. Spunky did not object.

At the southwest corner of the square, Olivia took a shortcut Maddie had taught her, through the grounds of the Chatterley Heights Library to Cherry Blossom Lane, the short, curvy street where Sadie Briggs lived. As she walked past the back door of the library, usually kept locked, she saw the head librarian, Heather Irwin, with Matthew Fabrizio. Olivia remembered hearing they were dating, which would explain the lingering kiss they were sharing. She picked up her pace and was almost off library property when Spunky decided to comment on the couple's behavior. He disapproved with gusto. Heather and Matthew pulled apart and turned to stare. Olivia couldn't help herself. She laughed. When it was clear that Heather and Matthew didn't share her lighthearted reaction, Olivia waved and picked up her pace until she reached the entrance to Cherry Blossom Lane.

"We're almost there, Spunks," Olivia said to her overexcited pet. As they followed the curvy road, Olivia felt a compulsion to look back at the library. Heather and Matthew were still there, too absorbed in each other to notice her curiosity. Matthew bent forward, his head in his hands, while Heather stroked his back in a soothing way. Olivia couldn't be sure, but he appeared to be sobbing. Olivia spun around and walked briskly toward Sadie Briggs's house. Whatever issue Heather and Matthew were hashing out, it wasn't her business. Thank goodness.

Olivia was delighted to see Sadie, whose infirmities often kept her housebound, sitting on her porch. Maddie looked more like her curvy, curly-haired aunt than her own mother, who had died, along with Maddie's father, in an automobile accident over twenty years ago. Though not in the best of health, Aunt Sadie refused to give up what she referred to as her handwork. She could carry on a conversation and knit or embroider at the same time. Olivia often tripped when she tried to walk and talk at the same time.

As Olivia neared the house, she saw that Aunt Sadie was talking with someone hidden behind the high latticework decorating the side of the porch. Aunt Sadie laughed and paused in her knitting to flap her hand at her guest. Olivia could almost hear her say, "Oh, you're such a joker," which she said to Maddie on a regular basis. Maybe Maddie was taking a break from her baking? She rarely felt the need for a break, but perhaps . . . Olivia rounded a curve in the road that gave her a full view of the porch. Sadie's amusing guest wasn't Maddie. It was Paine Chatterley.

Aunt Sadie smiled and waved when she saw Olivia walk toward the porch. Paine turned toward her with a smile, which disappeared as he recognized her. His animation dissolved as well. Intrigued, Olivia placed a porch chair between Sadie and Paine, forming a semicircle. Plunking Spunky on her lap, she studied Paine's patrician profile. Though he appeared distant, removed, Olivia noticed his jaw tighten as if he were uncomfortable.

"Oh, you've brought your sweet little boy," Aunt Sadie said, reaching out her arms. "May I hold him?" Spunky leaped to her lap, licked her face, and settled into a happy ball of fur. "I do miss having a pet," Aunt Sadie said, "but I couldn't take proper care of one." She glanced toward the porch railing, where her walker stood within arm's reach.

"Spunky and I have brought you something, Aunt Sadie." Since Olivia had grown up calling her Aunt Sadie, that's who she would always be. "Your embroidered aprons are stunning," Olivia said as she reached into her sweater pocket and withdrew a substantial check. She handed it over. "They've been quite a hit with our customers. I've raised the price, but they keep flying off their hangers."

Paine shifted in his seat. "I'd better toddle on home," he said, rising to his feet.

"Oh, no you don't, Paine Chatterley," Aunt Sadie said. Spunky's ears perked up at her gently commanding tone. "You'll stay right here and meet Olivia Greyson. Livie's like part of my family, so you just put that shyness in your hip pocket and join in the conversation. If you're going to live in Chatterley Heights, you need to be friendly. Now sit."

Paine sat. Olivia thought she saw a corner of his mouth twitch. Aunt Sadie had that effect on most people.

"Paine, I must tell you my exciting news. You never met my niece Maddie, but I brought her up from the age of ten, and she is so dear to me. Well, she is engaged to be married. Isn't that wonderful?"

Paine hesitated. It was only for a heartbeat, but Olivia noticed. She also noticed that Aunt Sadie left out the fact that Maddie hadn't yet accepted Lucas's proposal. If it were anyone else, Olivia would chalk it up to hopeful thinking, but not Aunt Sadie. Aunt Sadie was observant; she would have her reasons for assuming Maddie was inching closer to the altar.

"I hope she will be happy," Paine said quietly.

Aunt Sadie studied Paine's face, a worry wrinkle between her eyebrows.

"How are you and Mrs. Chatterley settling in?" Olivia asked. "Are you managing without your belongings? When do you expect them to arrive?"

Paine's glance flicked toward Olivia for a moment. "Not for a week or two," he said. "The house is tolerably well equipped, however, so we will be comfortable enough for now." Paine had slipped back into the persona Olivia observed on Tuesday evening — distant and superior.

"Livie," Aunt Sadie said, "Paine has brought me the most lovely gift, all the way from England." Aunt Sadie reached toward her side table and picked up a teacup and saucer decorated with a gray fleur-de-lis motif. Olivia loved all antiques but wasn't an expert on china. It was a Spode design, no longer available, she knew that much. The silver rim of the cup was worn in one area. Olivia imagined a right-handed lady holding the cup to her lips in precisely that spot.

The china rattled in Aunt Sadie's hand.

"My tremor is beginning to act up," she said. "You'd better take it, Livie."

Olivia accepted the cup and saucer with both hands and lowered it to her lap. Inside she saw a small metal cookie cutter. She picked it up for a closer look. It was a teapot shape attached to a backing, made from several smaller pieces of tin soldered together. She turned the cutter over to look at the backing. By the porch light, Olivia could clearly see the outline of the teapot pressing through the tin from many years of hard use. This teapot cutter had passed through many generations of bakers before landing in a Spode teacup. And though she and Maddie had yet to check their inventory for missing items, Olivia knew the cutter had not come from The Gingerbread House.

"This is an extraordinary piece," Olivia said to Paine. "Do you mind telling me where you found it?"

"A little shop in London," Paine said without hesitation. "To be precise, that's where Hermione said she found it. I know little about antiques, nor do I care, but when I saw the teapot, I was reminded of the time I spent here at this house. It was the happiest part of my childhood." Paine's thin lips curved into a faint smile as he added, "Whenever I stayed here for the afternoon, Aunt Sadie brewed a pot of tea and served it with iced cookies."

"At first I used Lipton's tea bags," Aunt Sadie said, chuckling. "Paine informed me that his parents had brought him along on their last trip to England, and — I'll never forget his words — he said, 'The liquid in that pot is *not* tea.' He was all of seven years old. I nearly fell over laughing."

His smile widening, Paine said, "I was being quite serious."

"Yes, lamb, I know. Your little nose was out of joint, that's for sure. But I did take you seriously, once I caught my breath. Why, I called all over the place and finally found a little store in Baltimore that imported tea. I ordered some real British tea leaves from them, and I kept on ordering as long as you came to spend time with me, didn't I?"

"You did."

"I doubt that store exists anymore," Aunt Sadie said, shaking her head.

"Never mind." Paine unfurled from his chair with smooth grace. "I shall bring you a packet of good tea when I visit next." He bent over Aunt Sadie and dropped a light kiss on her forehead.

"I'm so glad you are back," Aunt Sadie said.

"Olivia." Paine gave her a quick bow. He was gone before Olivia could tell him to call her Livie.

"Be honest, Aunt Sadie. Was that the same man I met Tuesday evening in The Gingerbread House? The arrogant one who managed to insult everyone? The cranky fellow who ordered me and Spunky off his property the next morning?"

Aunt Sadie plucked the teapot cookie cutter from its teacup nest and smoothed her hand over the metal backing. "Paine was such a serious little boy. I loved him like a son, but I saw his flaws. Not that I blamed him; his parents treated him like a burden, as if he had chosen to be born solely to interrupt their lives. Whenever I saw Paine with his parents, he acted like a little adult. I made it my goal to help him be a little boy."

"Which is why he loves you," Olivia said.

"I'm afraid it wasn't enough. I hoped he would learn how to be a friend. From what I've seen and heard, he has only his wife, and . . . well, I wonder if she was the best choice for him."

"Or he for her," Olivia said. "On the other hand, who am I to judge? I'm divorced."

"And I never married," Aunt Sadie said with a light laugh. "But that doesn't seem to have kept me from analyzing the marriages of others. Normally, I find it a pleasant way to while away the hours. But not this time."

CHAPTER SIX

As commanded by Mayor Karen Evanson, Olivia arrived at the Chatterley Mansion by seven thirty a.m. Friday morning to find a small crowd gathered across the street. Del and his deputy, Cody Furlow, stood several yards away from the group. Both wore their official uniforms. Not that Olivia had put much thought into her own costume. Following a last-minute inspiration, she had selected her favorite from among Sadie Briggs's aprons and tied it over light brown linen pants and a pale peach sweater. She'd been pleased with how the colors blended with the darker peach and burgundy of the embroidered Chatterley Mansion.

"Love your costumes," Olivia said to Del and Cody.

Cody glanced down at his deputy sheriff's uniform, faint lines of puzzlement furrowing his young brow.

"Thank you," Del said with a half smile.

"I decided to play a sheriff." Del looked Olivia up and down. "Is that the closest you could come to a serving wench costume?"

With a slight curtsy, Olivia said, "I didn't want to disappoint you."

"It's a bit modern," Del said, "though the colors look nice on you. Wait, isn't that . . . ?" He turned for a quick look across the street. "That's the mansion on your apron, isn't it? Who is that in the upper window?"

Cody had moved out of earshot, so Olivia said, "Maddie told me it's supposed to be Paine Chatterley as a little boy. Her aunt Sadie used to babysit him. Only we're thinking about having a contest to guess who it is, so if you tell, I'll have to kill you."

"Fair enough," Del said.

A van pulled up to the curb and four equipment-laden strangers emerged. Olivia assumed they represented some of the weekly newspapers from small towns in the area. So far, they were the only press to arrive. Karen would be furious if the DC and Baltimore papers didn't bother to send anyone.

Olivia noticed that all the celebration committee members were present, though only one, Mr. Willard, had taken seriously Karen's order to arrive in costume. A barrister's cloak hung from Mr. Willard's gaunt shoulders, and a white wig covered his sparse hair. Olivia assumed Bertha had made the outfit for him. A card-carrying Daughter of the American Revolution might object to the British style of the costume, but it was probably the only pattern Bertha could find at short notice.

The mayor herself wore a tailored, pale gray suit and rose blouse. The jacket flared gently at Karen's hips to draw subtle attention to the perfection of her figure. Only the habitual sternness of her expression kept Karen from being a beautiful woman. As she explained her rules to the visiting small-town reporters, Karen reminded Olivia of her first-grade teacher, to whom all children were uncivilized monsters until proven otherwise.

Quill Latimer stood apart from the others, dressed in full academic regalia with cloak, PhD hood, and a mortarboard on his head. An odd choice of costume. Olivia remembered Paine Chatterley's comment about Quill's "well-deserved position" in life. Quill taught at a nearby community college. Olivia knew he had a PhD in history, but she didn't remember hearing where he'd attended graduate school. If he had graduated from a first-rate university, Quill, being Quill, would surely have told everyone. Often.

Olivia noticed Binnie Sloan was now missing from the group. Olivia remembered having seen her just moments ago, mixing with the other editors of weeklies. Predictably, Binnie had ignored Karen's order to appear in costume. She'd worn her usual attire: men's cargo pants, a flannel shirt, and a man's jacket. All three items provided numerous pockets for Binnie's array of small cameras, recorders, notebooks, and pens. Olivia was sure Binnie's jacket had been red and black plaid, her pants and shirt beige. She peeked around the collection of reporters to get a view of the street and the mansion grounds. A squarish red-black-beige figure was passing the Chatterleys' wraparound porch, heading toward the back of the house.

Olivia touched Del's arm to get his attention. "Binnie's going in for a closer look," she said in a low voice, nodding toward the mansion. "She's at the wraparound porch."

Del muttered something curselike and took off at a run, with Cody close behind. Binnie had already disappeared behind the mansion. As Del and Cody raced across the street, Olivia caught Karen glaring in her direction. Olivia shrugged her shoulders, denying all responsibility for this glitch in

Karen's perfect plan.

As two more vans pulled to the curb, Karen's stern expression melted into delight. She waved an enthusiastic welcome and strode toward the first van. Olivia was impressed by the mayor's speed, given she was wearing spike heels and walking through grass.

Young, bored-looking crews emerged from the vans bearing microphones, cameras, and other equipment Olivia couldn't name. She assumed they were junior staff representing major papers in DC or Baltimore, or both. They ignored Karen as she chattered at them. Olivia sympathized with their lack of enthusiasm. She longed to be back in The Gingerbread House sorting through that package of vintage cookie cutters she was expecting to arrive any minute or helping customers find the perfect gel icing color.

As Olivia watched, Del and Cody rounded the mansion porch, holding Binnie Sloan firmly between them. Binnie was no lightweight, but her feet barely touched the ground. As they drew closer, Olivia could see Del's expression, tight and angry. His young deputy grew redder in the face with each step. At six foot three, Cody was probably doing much of the carrying. Binnie dragged her toes in the grass and grinned.

Del and Cody delivered their captive to the mayor, who looked furious enough to sentence Binnie to death. As soon as her feet hit solid ground, Binnie wriggled free of her captors and made straight for the newly arrived news crews, who'd scored a prime spot to set up their equipment. They clustered around Binnie as she scrolled through photos on her digital camera.

While Binnie soaked up everyone's attention, Olivia glanced back toward the mansion. She thought she saw a light flick on and off in a turret window. Sheer curtains covered the window, so she couldn't be sure. She was certain, though, that it was the same window a grumpy, disheveled Paine Chatterley had poked his head through when Olivia had visited two days earlier.

As Olivia watched, the bottom corner of the curtain twitched. She wondered if Paine was keeping an eye on the activity across the street from his newly reclaimed home. The curtain rippled, and she realized the window might be slightly open. Maybe the light she'd seen had been no more than the sun striking a sliver of exposed glass. Olivia was glad she hadn't said anything. Not that anyone would have listened. She seemed to be the only person neither fascinated nor angered by Binnie Sloan's adventure.

Olivia decided her presence wasn't necessary. Karen was busy chastising Binnie, who was barely listening as she continued playing show-and-tell with her colleagues; it was a perfect time to slip away. Olivia had gone only a few steps when she heard an unfamiliar voice nearby say, "Look, something's happening. Start the camera rolling."

Olivia spun around to see the mansion's front door creep open. Hermione Chatterley stood motionless in the doorway. She wasn't dressed to receive company. From what Olivia could tell, Hermione wore a frilly pink negligee and matching peignoir. Her white hair fluffed in loose curls around her plump face.

Cameras clicked and whirred, while muted voices relayed reports about the dramatic appearance of Chatterley Mansion's new mistress. With everyone's attention riveted on her, Hermione reached out with her right hand and opened her mouth as if to welcome her audience. Instead, she leaned against the doorjamb and slid to the ground in an apparent faint.

The visiting press snatched up their equipment, but they weren't quick enough. Del shouted an order to Cody to keep everyone back. "Mace them if you have to," he added, loud enough for all to hear. Del had reached the mansion door before it occurred to anyone, including Binnie Sloan, that Cody wasn't holding a can of mace.

The press belatedly surged forward, but not before Karen rushed to Cody's side and faced the group. In her deep, authoritative voice, she said, "Stay where you are. There's nothing to see. Mrs. Chatterley is an elderly woman with medical problems. I'm sure you don't want your readers to think you invaded the privacy of a sick and vulnerable woman. If there's anything newsworthy to report, Sheriff Jenkins and I will prepare a statement, and you will be the first to hear it." Karen's plea gave Del enough time to pull Hermione's inert body inside the mansion and shut the door behind them.

Olivia was impressed by Karen's quick action. Maybe she would make a decent congresswoman, after all. Then she wouldn't be Chatterley Heights's mayor anymore, so there was definitely an upside.

Staff from the DC and Baltimore papers, looking frustrated, began to check their watches and call in for instructions. Reporters from the small-town weeklies chatted with each other. Olivia assumed they'd be more inclined to stick around. Hermione Chatterley represented local celebrity to them, so her public faint qualified as news. Even Chatterley Heights's own Binnie Sloan seemed content to keep an eye on the mansion rather than sneak closer. Olivia was thankful that Nedra, Binnie's niece and photographer, was still in Baltimore taking a journalism course. Two Sloans qualified as a herd.

Olivia felt her cell vibrate in her pocket. She opened it to a text from Del: "Need you here. Use back door. Don't be seen." *He's always warning me not to get involved, and now he needs me? Interesting.* Olivia texted back that she had brought her key to the mansion and could let herself in the alley door. As she edged away from the group, she saw Cody answer his cell, glance in her direction, and nod once. He parked his tall, lanky frame on a tree stump and announced that he had information about Hermione's recovery from her faint.

While Cody held everyone's attention, Olivia sauntered south, as if she were returning to the store. Once she was out of sight, she circled around the block to the mansion's back door. She half expected to see Binnie waiting for her, but the alley was empty when she slid her key into the lock. Del entered the kitchen as Olivia locked the door behind her. "What's up?" she asked.

"Prepare yourself," Del said. "Hermione is conscious, but she's hysterical and incoherent. That's why you're here, because Hermione trusts you. If you can, get her to calm down and explain what happened."

"What happened . . . ?" Olivia's peripheral vision registered the chaotic state of the kitchen. Someone had removed all the antique pans and cooking utensils from the cupboards, originally set up as museum display areas, and dumped them on the floor. She followed Del into the mansion's formal dining room, which had suffered the same fate. Silverware lay in heaps on the newly scratched surface of a walnut table inlaid with rosewood. The leaded glass doors of the built-in cabinets all hung open, revealing empty shelves. Olivia cringed at the sight of precious nineteenth-century dishware, some broken or cracked, piled in careless heaps on the dining room rug. The rug itself, hand hooked in the early 1800s, depicted a variety of green leaves and blue flowers that reminded Olivia of cookie-cutter shapes. Now china chards pierced the delicate two-hundred-year-old fabric.

"Who could have done this?" Olivia remembered her conversation with Hermione about her husband's state of mind. "Did Paine have some sort of breakdown?"

"Possibly, but we'll never hear about it from him. Paine is dead," Del said, his expression grim. "Watch it." He reached out to steady Olivia as she nearly stepped on a broken plate.

"Del, are you saying Paine might have killed himself?"

"Right now I have no idea. I've called the crime scene unit. We'll know more once they've done their work, and the autopsy should help, too. Paine's death might have been an accident, though the state of this house makes me suspicious."

"You mean . . . *murder?*"

Del shrugged. "Could be an accident or suicide, I don't know. Looks like he drowned in the bathtub." He took Olivia's hand and led her around a mound of silverware. "We'd better get upstairs. Do I need to remind you not to mention any of this to anyone?"

"You just did." Olivia reclaimed her hand.

Del shot her a quick look but otherwise didn't react. "I've shut Hermione in her own bedroom. I don't want her disturbing the scene any more than she already has. If you can get anything helpful out of her, I'd really appreciate it."

Olivia decided to forgive him. They'd had more than one talk recently about her role in solving previous crimes. Del was trying to control his protective tendencies, and she'd been making a genuine attempt to stay away from murder scenes. If this was indeed a murder scene, Olivia was here now only because Del had asked her. And he knew it. Olivia indulged in a moment of smugness.

She followed Del through the house, weaving to avoid random piles on the floor. She wondered what it would be like to move into a museum. Maybe Hermione was simply emptying cupboards and closets to make space for the couple's belongings once they were delivered. That would explain the disarray. The broken plates and scratched furniture were another matter. Most of them had been owned originally by the Chatterleys, and some dated back to the mid-nineteenth century. Did Hermione care so little for family antiques? She was British, so maybe a plate had to be older than a mere century and a half for her to consider it interesting or valuable.

When Del stopped suddenly, Olivia almost slammed into him. He put a finger to his lips and pointed to a closed door. All the other doors they'd passed had been wide open. Olivia heard faint sounds coming from inside the room. Del held up his hand to indicate Olivia should stay where she was.

She nodded her assent. Del drew his revolver and turned the doorknob gently.

Olivia watched Del's jaw tighten as he eased open the door and looked inside the room. He plunged inside, gun drawn, leaving the door ajar. Olivia flattened against the wall. Over the next few seconds, she heard only grunts and shuffling sounds coming from inside the room. She assumed Del had subdued the intruder, but she couldn't be sure. She slid along the wall to the edge of the door frame and risked a quick peek inside the room. It was a mistake. Her appearance distracted Del for a split second, enough for the intruder to break free. Acting on sheer impulse, Olivia slammed the door shut. She braced her foot against the frame and held on to the knob with all her strength, expecting powerful arms to pull in the opposite direction. Nothing happened.

From inside the room, Del's voice called out, "It's okay, Livie. I've got her."

Her? Olivia pushed the door open and looked inside at the intruder's back as Del snapped on handcuffs. She saw a squarish red-black-beige figure. Binnie Sloan.

After depositing Binnie in an upstairs bedroom, handcuffed to a four-poster, Del

131

explained that the back parlor, where they'd found Binnie, once opened out on a garden in the northwest corner of the grounds. Binnie had used her key to sneak in and take photos. "Explain to me why everyone seems to have a key to Chatterley Mansion?" Del did not sound happy.

"Don't blame me," Olivia said. "It was Karen's idea. She wanted all of us, the celebration committee members, to keep tabs on the mansion renovation. As if we didn't all have jobs. Karen didn't trust the workers."

"But she trusted Binnie Sloan?"

"Point taken," Olivia said.

When they reached Hermione's bedroom, Del removed a chair he'd wedged under her doorknob. "Apparently, the mansion's room keys are lost to history," he said. "This was the best I could do."

"Looks like it worked," Olivia whispered as she followed Del into the bedroom.

Hermione Chatterley sat in a green velvet armchair near her window. She had changed from her pink nightclothes into another of her shapeless housedresses, this one white with red dots. She looked none the worse for her dramatic faint in front of the cameras. Her brown eyes had a golden tinge, perhaps in contrast to the redness that implied she'd been weeping for her dead husband. When she saw Olivia, she held out a limp hand. "Oh, I'm so glad you've come. I know we haven't known each other long, but I feel so terribly alone, and you've been kind to me."

Olivia gave her a sympathetic smile as she sat on the end of Hermione's tousled bed. "I'm so sorry about your husband," she said. "It must have been an awful shock."

"Oh, it was, it was. He hasn't been in the best of health, of course, so this is not unexpected, but . . ." Hermione pressed two fingertips against her lips as if she couldn't bear to say more. Olivia would have written the gesture off as staged except for the tears trickling down Hermione's rouged cheeks.

"Livie will stay with you awhile, Mrs. Chatterley," Del said with kindness in his voice. "I do understand your reluctance to talk with me at the moment. We can put that off a bit." He briefly met Olivia's eyes. She understood. A sympathetic ear might elicit a coherent story from Hermione. Well, she could try, but she suspected that Hermione, with her flair for drama, would be inclined to embellish.

Del left, closing the door behind him. Hermione dabbed at her eyes and didn't seem to notice a faint scraping as Del, ever the careful cop, slid the chair back under the bedroom doorknob. "Dear Olivia," Hermione said, "I wish I had the strength to make us some tea, but I'm so very upset."

"I can only begin to imagine how you must feel," Olivia said, patting Hermione's arm. "I was wondering . . . downstairs I couldn't help but notice family antiques scattered about, some of them broken. Do you have any idea how that happened? Perhaps you heard something?"

Hermione blinked rapidly as her lips formed a silent "Oh."

Olivia waited in receptive silence.

"Well, I suppose . . . I mean, I didn't actually go through the house, only down the stairs to the front door to get help. Paine sometimes walked in his sleep, so I suppose . . . he didn't have a terribly happy childhood, you know. Perhaps he saw a dish or a bowl that reminded him of that sad period of his life, and he simply snapped. He did have a bit of a temper. Why, once we were having a slight disagreement, and Paine flung one of my favorite crystal decanters against the drawing room wall." Hermione's fleshy face pinched as she began to cry again.

"I didn't mean to upset you," Olivia said. "I shouldn't have brought it up."

"I was so blinded by grief I'm sure I wouldn't have noticed anything out of place, even if I'd tripped over it. It was such a dreadful shock to find dear Paine in the bath. He looked so peaceful, I thought he was asleep, but then I realized his face was in the water, so he couldn't possibly be . . . be . . ." Hermione covered her face with her hands and sobbed. Olivia noticed several small cuts on her fingers. Hermione dropped her hands and took a tissue from a box on the table next to her chair. Sniffling, she said, "He must have had a heart attack. Or else he simply fell asleep in the bath. He'd been so tired lately. And then, of course, he did like to have a little drink before retiring."

"Is it possible your husband had more than one drink? I mean, if he lost track and drank more than he was used to, maybe he became sleepy and forgot he was in the tub?"

"Dear me, no, I don't think so. Although . . ." Hermione took another tissue and touched it to the tip of her nose, rather than do something so unladylike as to blow it.

Olivia forced herself to maintain a neutral expression.

She wanted the truth, but she suspected

Hermione would play to an eager audience.

"I suppose I might have been confused myself," Hermione said with a slight shake of her head. "I thought the bottle was new because . . . well, we've only been in town for such a short while, after all."

"The bottle? I'm afraid I don't understand," Olivia said.

Hermione reached over and patted Olivia's knee. "I'm sorry, I'm not being clear, am I? I meant the whiskey bottle. I couldn't help but notice, you see, when I saw Paine in the bath . . . I couldn't help but see that the whiskey bottle was nearly empty. Paine didn't usually drink so much in such a short period of time. But he felt weak from all the traveling, so I suppose he might have spilled some and not wanted to tell me." Hermione stared toward the table next to her bed, where Olivia saw a color photo of Paine Chatterley. His solemn, slender face and graying hair made him look perhaps a decade older than he had in the wedding photo Olivia noticed during her previous visit. The tilt of his chin expressed a hint of arrogance.

"I truly did love him, you know," Hermione said. "I never stopped. No matter what."

■ ■ ■ ■

Olivia and Del paused on Chatterley Mansion's front porch after a female deputy, borrowed from a nearby town, arrived to keep watch over Hermione Chatterley. The press had scattered after Mayor Karen Evanson delivered a terse statement, dictated by Del, and Paine's body had been removed by the coroner.

"Did Karen believe you? About Paine's death being accidental, I mean," Olivia asked.

"I doubt it," Del said. "Our mayor informed me that if I suspect suicide or murder, I am to keep it to myself until Monday morning."

"She really wants to go on with this celebration? What am I saying, of course she does. What did you do with Binnie? Please tell me you gave her the third degree. It would give me such pleasure."

With a smug grin, Del said, "Even better. I arrested Binnie on suspicion of breaking and entering, although she insists she used the key she was given as a member of the celebration planning committee. I explained that, key or no key, she had entered a private residence illegally. She is currently being held in the Chatterley Heights jail, minus all electronic modes of communication with the outside world. Will that do?"

"Del, you have made me a happy woman."

"Happy enough to dress as a serving wench this weekend?"

"Don't push it."

"Okay, how about lunch? It's well past lunchtime, and I'm starving."

Olivia's stomach had been rumbling for a couple of hours, but she did need to get back to The Gingerbread House. "Let me call Maddie. She might need help in the store." She dug out her cell phone and speed-dialed Maddie.

"Livie, tell me everything, instantly."

"Are you inundated with customers?" Olivia asked. "I feel guilty I haven't been there to help."

"Not to worry. I called in Bertha to work, and your mom showed up about five minutes later. She'd heard you were babysitting Hermione at the mansion."

"How on earth did she . . . never mind. Mom has her ways, which I will never understand." Olivia glanced at Del, who was staring back at the mansion. It crossed her mind that he was looking for how an intruder might have entered the house, if not with a key. "Del asked me to lunch," Olivia

138

said, "but I know I should get back to the store."

"No, you don't," Maddie said. "We are currently overstaffed and have no need of your services. Go to lunch with Del, and don't come back until he gives you every morsel of information about Paine Chatterley's death. I'm betting it was murder. He was not a popular guy."

"I'll be back in an hour," Olivia said.

"Oh, and let's have a late dinner this evening," Maddie said. "Aunt Sadie told me an interesting story last night, involving cookie cutters and the Chatterley dynasty. Lucas and his guys are doing inventory until late, and I'll need a couple hours to make sure the gingerbread houses are ready for unveiling tomorrow morning. So maybe about eight?"

"My place at eight," Olivia said. "I'll pick up macaroni and cheese from Pete's Diner, if you can come up with a salad. See you at the store in an hour. Or so."

"Don't hurry," Maddie said. "We can manage just fine without you."

"So comforting to know."

The Chatterley Café, located at the north-west corner of the town square, was usually crammed to overflowing during the lunch hour. Del and Olivia arrived shortly after two p.m. and found two tables open. They chose a booth in a back corner, a quiet place to talk.

"My treat," Del said.

Olivia eyed him over the top of her menu. "Bribery is useless. I will not dress as a serving wench."

Del shrugged. "You can't blame a guy for trying. But I owe you lunch, at least, for giving up your morning to watch over Hermione Chatterley."

"Watch over and *grill,* you mean. Which makes me crave grilled Maryland crab cakes with a heaping bowl of clam chowder. Oh look, it's the most expensive meal on the menu."

Del's hearty laugh felt like a warm arm around Olivia's shoulders.

"Olivia Greyson," Del said, "I do enjoy your company."

"Me, too." Olivia's response came out squeaky. She reminded herself to take little steps. Her divorce was much more recent than Del's. If ever there was a time to change the subject, this was it. "So if it turns out that Paine was murdered, would you suspect Hermione?"

Del looked startled but recovered quickly. "The spouse is generally pretty high on the

140

suspect list," he said, handing Olivia the bread basket. "We'll know better how to proceed after we get the autopsy results. We can get through the celebration weekend assuming Paine's death was accidental. Which it probably was."

When the waiter arrived to take their orders, Olivia said, "I'll have the crabs cakes and clam chowder."

"Excellent choice," the waiter said.

Del coughed.

Olivia gave him a sweet smile. "What? Did you think I wasn't serious?"

Del turned to the waiter and said, "I'll have bread and water."

"Very good, sir," the waiter said, without skipping a beat. "I assume you would like the bread medium rare, as usual? I'll be right back with your water."

Olivia watched the young man glide off to another table. "You know that kid, don't you?"

"His name is Ted," Del said. "He's been talking to me about going to the police academy. He's a quick study. I think he'll make a good officer."

"And speaking of police work," Olivia said, "what's your own sense about Paine's death? I know you want to hear what the medical examiner says, but did it really look like an accident to you?"

Ted the waiter arrived with two coffees, a new bread basket, and one large water. With a flourish, he deposited the water and bread in front of Del. Without so much as a twitch at the corners of his mouth, he turned and left. Olivia saw his shoulders shake with laughter as he headed toward the kitchen.

"Have some bread," Del said.

"Oh no," Olivia said. "I wouldn't want you to starve." She poured a dollop of cream into her coffee. "Now how about answering my question? You want to know what I learned from Hermione, so it's only fair."

Del ripped open a warm dinner roll and spread butter on it. "Nothing I saw at the scene suggested murder, if that's what you're really asking. There was a nearly empty whiskey bottle within reaching distance of the tub. If Paine drank too much, then yes, it's possible he passed out and drowned accidentally."

"Hermione mentioned the whiskey," Olivia said. "She insisted it was a new bottle. If Paine was drunk, it might have been easy for a woman to push him under the water."

With a thoughtful nod, Del said, "It's possible. I didn't see any signs of a struggle, though that could have been cleaned up. If

Paine was sleepy enough, he might not have been able to struggle much. However, this is all sheer speculation."

"You say that as if it's a bad thing."

"I'm more interested in facts," Del said.

Olivia drained her coffee cup with appreciation. The Chatterley Café was known for its rich, smooth Italian roast. "Okay, then, here's a factual question: was there any evidence that someone might have sneaked into the mansion during the night and murdered Paine? I'm not yanking this out of the air. As you know, everyone on the celebration committee, including me, has a key to the mansion. We all visited on occasion to inspect the restoration, so we were all familiar with the house. From what I saw at our meeting Tuesday evening, at least two members of the committee were acquainted with Paine, and not in a friendly way."

Now she had Del's attention. "Which two members?" he asked in a clipped voice.

"Quill Latimer and Karen Evanson," Olivia said.

Ted the waiter returned with a full tray. He delivered Olivia's chowder and crab cakes with steamed broccoli and fresh lemon wedges. "And for you, sir." Ted placed a small steak with baked potato in front of Del.

When Ted had left, Del grinned at Olivia. "Medium rare, just the way I like it."

Olivia rolled her eyes. "Okay, fine, you got me."

"I hope so."

Caught off guard, Olivia couldn't think of a retort.

Del's anxious eyes darted to Olivia's face. When she smiled at him, he relaxed. "Anyway," he said, "to answer your question, there is no solid evidence that anyone broke into the house during the night. Paine's bathroom window was latched from the inside. The bedroom window was tightly closed, although the latch is broken. None of the mansion rooms have locks."

"How did Hermione behave when you arrived?"

Del put down his knife and fork. "She was agitated. I told her to stay downstairs, but she followed me to Paine's bathroom. The door stuck, and I didn't realize Hermione was right behind me while I was forcing the door open. My fault, I should have paid more attention."

"You mean Hermione followed you into the bathroom?"

Del ran his fingers through his sandy hair, a gesture Olivia had come to recognize as frustration. "More like she pushed her way past me, almost as if she needed more confirmation that her husband was dead. Then she got hysterical. Cody wasn't there, so I had to calm her down and get her out of the bathroom before I could get a good look at the scene. I should be sent back to the academy."

"I don't know, Del. Did her behavior feel staged to you? I ask because I've noticed at times I feel like a spectator with Hermione, like she's putting on a show."

"Are you saying Hermione might not be who she says she is?"

"I don't know, maybe I'm being unfair, but . . ." Olivia absently poured cream into her coffee cup as she struggled to put her perceptions into words.

"Livie, you realize there's no coffee in that cup, right?" Del signaled Ted the waiter, who added coffee to Olivia's cream without comment. "Would you care for dessert?" he asked. Del and Olivia declared themselves stuffed.

"I trust your instincts about people," Del said once Ted was out of earshot. "But I have to add that I've seen bereaved people behave in some pretty odd ways, especially when a loved one has died violently or suddenly. Having said that, I'll keep your observations in mind if Paine's death turns

145

out to be murder. Not that I'm expecting it to be."

"I hope it isn't," Olivia said. "By the way, how long do you plan to hold on to Binnie? Not that I'm feeling sorry for her or anything."

Del chuckled. "Nor should you. I'll probably release her this evening. She did get into the mansion with a key, so the breaking and entering charge is dicey. Besides, Cody should soon be finished downloading her photos and checking for anything suspicious. He probably won't find anything, but I'm curious about why Binnie was photographing that little room so thoroughly."

"And why she couldn't have taken the photos through all those windows," Olivia said. "I know the back parlor was originally designed to offer a view of a large garden. She didn't have to go inside. She must have seen something. If Cody finds anything interesting in those photos, any chance I can con you into sharing with me?"

With a smile and a shrug, Del promised nothing.

"Fair enough. Binnie will undoubtedly post everything on her blog, anyway."

"Not after Cody copies and deletes her shots, she won't." Del slid a credit card from his wallet and placed it on top of the bill.

"Remind me never to cross you," Olivia said. "Thanks for lunch, by the way. Next time it's on me."

"Great," Del said. "How about taking me to Bon Vivant after the celebration ends on Sunday evening?"

Bon Vivant was the newest and priciest restaurant in Chatterley Heights. Olivia figured Del was teasing her, although she could afford to take him there. Her dear friend Clarisse Chamberlain had left her a generous inheritance, as well as her entire cookie-cutter collection. Olivia had invested much of the inheritance in her business and her mortgage, but she had put aside a bit for emergencies and special occasions. The cookie-cutter collection, which she and Clarisse had spent many happy hours poring over, would be far more difficult to part with, ever.

Olivia had a better idea for an evening with Del. "I am but a poor shopkeeper," she said. "How about dinner at my place instead?"

"Even better. Although . . . were you planning to cook this dinner yourself?"

Olivia's decorated cookies were every bit as delicious as Maddie's, but otherwise her cooking repertoire consisted of frozen pizza and takeout. Maybe the occasional salad.

She couldn't seem to work up the proper enthusiasm for anything except cutout cookies. "You know, one of these days I might surprise you by cooking a perfectly respectable meal that doesn't involve pepperoni. I think you should give me a chance."

"Agreed," Del said. He slid from the booth and offered Olivia a hand. "I'll bring the wine. Lots of it."

CHAPTER SEVEN

After her lunch with Del, Olivia arrived back at The Gingerbread House to find Maddie, Bertha, and her mother, Ellie, inundated with customers. Some of them, unfortunately, were in the market for gossip rather than cookie cutters or pearlized sugar sprinkles. At least three women, Olivia was pleased to note, were cooing over Sadie Briggs's hand-embroidered aprons. One of the women put aside an apron as if she were planning to buy it.

Maddie had finished helping a customer choose a gingerbread house kit, so Olivia waved her over. "Any chance you'd have time to talk Aunt Sadie into parting with more aprons? I think they'll sell well over the weekend. At this rate, we'll have to raise the price again before the festivities begin."

"Already done," Maddie said. "I hung twenty more in the inventory closet. I hate to say it, but a mysterious death in Chatterley Mansion probably won't hurt weekend attendance. Any chance Paine was murdered?"

"I'm sure you meant that in a sensitive way," Olivia said.

"You know what I mean. I'm betting you and Del discussed Paine's death, so what's the scoop?"

Olivia hesitated, remembering her agreement with Del that if he revealed to her any details about a crime, she would keep it to herself. She had acquiesced easily because she'd assumed future crimes were unlikely to involve her in any way. On the other hand, Del didn't seem to think Paine's death was murder. "It's way too early for those questions," Olivia said. "We'll have to wait for the autopsy, and the results will probably appear in Binnie's blog before I hear anything. Assuming Del lets her out of jail soon."

"Binnie can be useful," Maddie said. "But you were inside the mansion, Livie. At least tell me what you saw. I mean, did Paine fall down the stairs or what?"

To Olivia's relief, her mother waved to her from the sales counter, where customers were lining up. "Gotta go. Mom needs my help," Olivia said.

"You'd better fill me in during dinner this

150

evening," Maddie said. "Because if you don't, I might forget to pass on Aunt Sadie's story about the Chatterleys and cookie cutters. If that doesn't work, I'm sure I can think of other ways to blackmail you into talking."

To Olivia, moving back to Chatterley Heights after her divorce had sounded like a good idea. Small-town life looked idyllic . . . from a distance. Now she wondered if her apartment in Baltimore was still available.

Olivia joined her mother behind the cash register, where they whittled down a long line of customers. As the last one headed for the front door, Ellie said, "My yoga class is due to begin in ten minutes. If I miss it again, I can't be responsible for my behavior."

"I wouldn't want that on my conscience," Olivia said. "And thanks for helping. We hired temporary help for the weekend."

As Ellie opened the front door to leave, Mayor Karen Evanson strode through. Ellie sent Olivia a smile and a wave before making her escape.

Could this day get any more complicated? Catching a determined glint in the mayor's eyes, Olivia composed herself as best she could.

"We need to talk," Karen said loudly enough to turn heads in her direction.

"We're awfully busy at the —"

"Now. In private." Karen bypassed the sales counter and headed toward the kitchen door.

Olivia shot a glance at Maddie, who tried to look sympathetic but couldn't pull it off. Olivia took a deep breath, then another, and followed Karen into the kitchen.

Karen leaned back against the kitchen counter, her arms tightly crossed. "I know you are dating the sheriff," she said.

"Okay." *Doesn't everyone know that?* "Is there a problem with my dating Del?"

"Here's the deal." Karen's eyes narrowed to slits. Olivia was reminded of a wolf on the prowl for dinner. "I will not allow our celebration to be canceled for any reason. Certainly not because a drunk drowned in his own bathtub, which I'm still convinced is what happened."

"How do you know — ?"

"Not relevant. I'm the mayor, I know things. The celebration is my highest priority at the moment, but Sheriff Jenkins wants us to 'dial it down,' which means no parade, no interviews with the press. . . . Basically, he doesn't want to call attention to the fact that a Chatterley died under questionable circumstances." Karen began to pace, which in such a crowded kitchen meant about five high-heeled steps in either direction.

"I'm confused, Karen. That doesn't sound like Del. He knows that rumors are bound to crop up, especially since reporters were right there when Hermione Chatterley fainted. I just had lunch with Del, and he said he thought Paine's death was most likely an accident."

"Well, now Sheriff Jenkins suspects Paine was murdered. He wants me to cancel any weekend events near or at the mansion. Something about strangers trampling all over the grounds and interfering with an investigation. He even said he'd call the newspapers, if he had to, and tell them the whole weekend has been canceled out of respect. Ha. He doesn't know the press like I do. They'd smell a story. However, to be on the safe side" — Karen shot her wrist from the sleeve of her tailored blazer and checked her watch — "you must convince the sheriff to back off."

"Why would I do that?" Olivia had an uncomfortable feeling she wasn't going to like the answer.

In high heels, Karen was a shade taller than Olivia's five foot seven. The mayor straightened her spine, emphasizing the temporary height advantage, and said, "Because if you don't talk the sheriff into backing off, he will no longer be sheriff. I will make that happen, believe me."

Olivia believed her. She also knew that Del would be undeterred by the threat, which put Olivia in a sticky spot. "I'll deliver your message, Karen, but you're mistaken if you think I can convince Del to push aside his professional judgment."

"Do so immediately," Karen said as she brushed past Olivia. "I have a meeting in five minutes at the town hall. It shouldn't take more than half an hour. I'll expect a call from you then." Her last few words were tossed over her shoulder as the kitchen door swung shut behind her.

Olivia's cell vibrated as she bit the head off a gingerbread baker. She'd already devoured a gingerbread girl in a bright orange sundress. When she saw it was her mother calling, she grabbed the phone and answered with an incoherent grunt.

"Livie? I have no idea what you just said. Anyway, my yoga class just finished, and I saw your message to call."

"Sorry, Mom. Cookie."

"Oh dear. What has happened?"

"Karen happened." She told Ellie about

154

the mayor's threat to ruin Del's career if he insisted the celebration weekend be altered.

"That is distressing," Ellie said. "Luckily, yoga has restored my mental balance, so it occurs to me that if Karen approached you with such determination, it most likely means she is desperate. She probably already threatened Del to his face and didn't change his mind. Karen does tend to become forceful when she . . ."

"Doesn't get her way?"

"Unkind but true. I'm fond of Karen," Ellie said. "She is ambitious, yes, but she has a strong desire to serve as well. She has given up a great deal to follow her path."

"I bow to your wisdom, Mom, but could we talk about Del? I can't get hold of him. Cody isn't at the police department, or at least he isn't answering the phone, and the officer on duty said he didn't know their whereabouts. Del's cell goes right to voice mail. That isn't like him, not when he's on duty."

"You sound worried, dear. I doubt that Karen is slicing him in half as we speak. As it happens, I do have another yoga-induced thought. Del might turn off his cell when he's in an important meeting with other law enforcement personnel, such as —"

"The medical examiner," Olivia said. "Of

course. I was so upset by Karen, I didn't stop to wonder why Del was so insistent about protecting the mansion grounds. He must have gotten the results of the autopsy."

"So glad to be of help, Livie. Now have another cookie and relax. I'm sure Del will fill you in when he can."

"If he doesn't, I'll — hold that thought, Mom. I've got another call coming through. I'll check in later." Before answering, Olivia confirmed the call was from Del and not Karen.

"Livie, got your message. I'm glad you called. I'm going to need your help with something. It involves our esteemed mayor, so it'll be a challenge."

"Ooh, don't tell me, let me guess," Olivia said. "You've just left the medical examiner, who told you that Paine Chatterley was murdered. You want to keep people away from the mansion grounds until further notice, in case some evidence was missed. Which means you want me to convince Karen to cancel any planned tours in the vicinity of Chatterley Mansion."

"Uh . . . Karen already talked to you, didn't she? Did she mention her threat to get me — ?"

"Fired, lit up, and burned at the stake? Actually, she tried to make it my responsibility to convince you to back off. But enough of Karen. First, I want to know what the ME told you."

"I don't know. . . ."

"Didn't you mention wanting my help dealing with Karen? Is that a sigh I hear?"

"Why do I bother? It'll be all over town soon anyway. Okay, yes, the ME is convinced Paine was murdered."

When Olivia heard silence instead of elaboration, she asked, "How was he murdered? Shot? Stabbed? Poisoned?"

"Other," Del said.

"What's left? Electrocution by blow-dryer? Come on, give me something."

"Later," Del said. "I need to meet up with Cody. When you talk to Karen, remind her that a screwed-up investigation won't look good for her, either. She needs to cooperate with the police, not hinder us."

"Good point. I'll tell Mom."

"Ellie? Why?"

Olivia heard a revving sound. Del must be about to start driving. "Karen won't listen to me. But Mom might be able to talk some sense into her. And if Mom can't, no one can."

"Cheater," Del said. "Now you still owe me."

"I'm sure we could think of some-

157

thing. . . ."

With a chuckle, Del said, "I'm sure we could, but you are going to be too busy. Not only do you have a store to operate and lots of customers about to descend, but you will be spending more time with Hermione Chatterley as well."

"Hermione? But isn't she —" Olivia heard the blast of a car horn.

"Should have driven a squad car," Del muttered. "Folks drive like idiots when they don't think a police officer's around. What were you saying, Livie? Oh yeah, about Hermione. We haven't arrested her."

"But isn't she the obvious suspect?"

"Yes, but —"

"But what? You haven't found the weapon? You're asking me to babysit a possible murderer; I think I have a right to know." Olivia was edging toward irritation, and she let her voice show it.

"Okay, you've got a point," Del said. "Paine did not drown, which is why we think he was almost certainly murdered. He was found with his head underwater, but there was no water in his lungs. The ME said he suffocated. Tests revealed a high level of barbiturate in his system. Paine had a prescription for a barbiturate sleep aid. He'd filled the prescription right before

158

leaving England, and the bottle was almost empty. Yes, he could have taken too many by accident or as a suicide attempt, but how did he suffocate? And how did he get to the bathtub? If he'd merely been unconscious, there would be water in his lungs — and he couldn't have gotten to the tub on his own."

"Hermione is fairly sturdy," Olivia said. "Couldn't she have dragged him? He was a slight man."

"Not if she was telling the truth about the state of her health, and it seems she was. She told us she has congestive heart failure and a bad back. Cody took her to Johns Hopkins for tests and a thorough checkup; that's where I'm going now. He called a while back and confirmed it's unlikely Hermione could have lifted or dragged a grown man and then gotten him into the bathtub. It's one of those old tubs — you know, the tall ones with claw feet."

"Maybe she had help."

"Maybe." Del sounded frustrated. "But we can't arrest her with what we've got. That's why I want you to visit her. She's unlikely to reveal anything accidentally when a police officer is around, but she might start chattering with you. The officer will be within yelling distance, in case you wondered. I don't want to find you facedown in a bathtub."

"Good to hear."

CHAPTER EIGHT

Maddie reached toward the bowl on Olivia's kitchen table. "Macaroni and cheese is never as good the next day," she said. "Or so I've heard."

"Be my guest," Olivia said. "You load up on cholesterol, and I'll start the dishes."

"I think cholesterol must be a French word because I don't understand it." Maddie slid the macaroni and cheese toward her and ate the last few bites. As she scraped the cheese off the sides of the bowl, she said, "Now let me get this straight. Del said that Paine Chatterley was dosed up on sleeping pills, and he suffocated. Except he somehow undressed, got into the bathtub, drank a large amount of whiskey, and actually died before his head slid underwater. And Hermione couldn't have carried or dragged him into the tub. I'm confused."

"I know," Olivia said. "That bothered me, too." She fitted the empty macaroni and

161

cheese bowl into the dishwasher and started it running. "It'll get noisy in here," she said. "I'll start the coffee and scrounge some cookies for dessert. You head for the living room. And take this mutt with you." Olivia swept back the silky hair that had fallen over Spunky's eyes. Sensing an opportunity, he tilted his head and whimpered. "My little con artist," Olivia said with affection. "As if you didn't just finish eating half an hour ago." She handed two dog treats to Maddie. "He'll follow you to the living room," she said, "but only give him one treat. He can have the other when we've settled on the couch. Otherwise, he'll come trotting back to tell me he hasn't eaten in a week."

Olivia arranged a plate of decorated cookies — gingerbread men and women, all wearing crowns atop hair colors not found in nature. She placed the plate on a tray along with the coffee carafe and cups. Cream and sugar for both of them, of course. When she arrived in the living room, Spunky sat motionless on the sofa, his limpid eyes fixed on Maddie.

"Thank God you're here," Maddie said. "I think he was planning to kill me."

"Nonsense," Olivia said as she placed the tray on the coffee table. "Spunky is almost entirely nonviolent. Aren't you, boy?"

Spunky's ears twitched, but his concentration never wavered.

"Please tell me I can give him his tre— his t-r-e-a-t," Maddie said. Spunky yapped and jumped onto her lap. "Hey, when did he learn to spell?"

"My little boy," Olivia said fondly. "He wants to go to Harvard, but I told him, Mommy can only afford in-state tuition. He'll have to get a scholarship. Anyway, you'd better throw his treat onto the rug. It's your only hope."

Maddie threw the treat so hard it hit the living room wall and broke in half. Spunky hit the rug running and crunched his way through both pieces.

"Two seconds," Olivia said. "A personal best." She selected a gingerbread queen with violet hair and settled back on the sofa. "About Paine Chatterley's death," she said. "I think Del left out some details about the order in which Paine was drugged, drunk, dragged, drowned, and/or suffocated."

"As I understand it," Maddie said, "Paine didn't drown. The pills apparently didn't kill him, either. Maybe he got really zonked on pills and alcohol, then suffocated accidentally? I can imagine someone in that condition getting dangerously tangled up in the bedclothes."

"Except how did he get into the tub? According to Del, the medical examiner insisted it was murder. So there has to be something else, something technical that Del didn't think we needed to know."

"Geez, it almost sounds like Paine wouldn't die, and his killer was desperate." Maddie dunked her gingerbread king's green hair into her coffee and got it to her mouth before the cookie dissolved. "Maybe Del didn't think you needed all the details. As he keeps telling you, we aren't police officers."

"Which reminds me," Olivia said, "I'm not telling you any of this."

"Understood. Maybe Paine was already in the tub when someone came up behind him and strangled him."

Having gnawed through his own version of cookies, Spunky leaped onto the sofa and nestled between Maddie and Olivia for a warm nap. Gently stroking his ears, Olivia said, "When Del called to tell me Paine was murdered, his last words to me were 'I don't want to find you facedown in a bathtub.' I might be overinterpreting, but I'm wondering . . ."

"You're wondering," Maddie said, "why Paine would be facedown? If he was in the tub when he died, wouldn't he have slid underwater faceup?"

"Exactly. Although maybe Del wasn't being literal."

"Livie, when have you known Del to be imprecise about his work?"

"Point taken," Olivia said. "Although Paine might have been trying to get out of the tub while he was being suffocated. I'd like to hear Hermione's story."

"And isn't it convenient," Maddie said, "that Del wants you to babysit Hermione. Maybe you can get her to spill a few clues."

"I suppose we have to assume that Johns Hopkins School of Medicine knows what it's doing," Olivia said, "which would mean that the perfect suspect, Hermione, wouldn't have the strength to get Paine into the tub after he was dead."

Maddie reached for another member of the gingerbread royalty, this time with cobalt blue hair. "What would be her motive? I mean, aside from the fact that Paine wasn't the ideal husband. So far, the last of the Chatterleys have behaved like bankrupt freeloaders. Hermione is a thief. Paine drank, took pills, and slept a lot. I'm not confident there's an inheritance for Hermione, except maybe the mansion and its contents."

"That's something," Olivia said, "though

I don't see much evidence that she cares about the house." Spunky complained as his mistress left his side to get paper and pen from the little Queen Anne desk under the front window. She settled back on the sofa and began to jot down notes. "Del wants me to spend some time with Hermione, and I want to know what to listen for."

Maddie divided the last of the coffee between their two cups. "You know, we've been concentrating solely on Hermione Chatterley, but what about Quill Latimer and Karen Evanson? I'd love to learn how Paine knew them and why they seemed to dislike him. They had keys to the mansion, too."

Olivia wrote down the two names. "I wonder if anyone on the celebration committee would know about Hermione's heart and back problems. We need to find out if any of the others had past connections to Paine, good or bad."

"Ooh," Maddie said, "wouldn't it be nice if we found out that Binnie Sloan hated him? Maybe she was taking pictures of that back parlor to set up someone else as a suspect. Sounds like Binnie, doesn't it?"

"Now, now."

"Okay, fine, but you have to admit she's a

better suspect than Mr. Willard."

"I think we can safely leave Mr. Willard off the suspect list," Olivia said.

"Although he did screw up by not recognizing Paine's death certificate as a forgery. I mean, I love the guy, but we should think about whether he gained anything by Paine's death."

"I suppose so," Olivia said without enthusiasm. "I think I'll chat with him. His memory goes back a long way. I know he's trying to track down information about Paine's alleged death certificate; maybe he'll turn up something interesting. . . ."

"Speaking of information sources, we should start with your mom," Maddie said.

"My mom, like everyone else in Chatterley Heights, is completely booked for the weekend. Us, too, much of the time. I'll work on Hermione, with Del's blessing, but otherwise we really have no business doing more than speculating and listening to gossip."

"Luckily, we do both well," Maddie said. "Now, while we devour the last two cookies, I shall relate a fascinating cookie-cutter story Aunt Sadie told me."

"A perfect way to end the evening." Olivia offered the cookie plate to Maddie, who selected a gingerbread girl with teal pigtails, leaving Olivia a boy with tangerine locks.

"He clashes with my hair," Maddie explained. "So about the Chatterley cutters . . ."

"If this is about the legendary cookie-cutter collection that Amelia Chatterley allegedly began in 1765 or so and that succeeding Chatterley wives allegedly added to until the alleged collection allegedly disappeared —"

"Enough with the legalese," Maddie said. "Of course you've heard of Amelia's famed collection, and I'm here to tell you there's no allegedly about it. You have to keep this to yourself, though, because Aunt Sadie told me in the strictest confidence . . . although the central character is deceased."

"Are you talking about Paine or Amelia?"

"Aunt Sadie is heartbroken about Paine's death. She's been talking about him a lot. I think she's wondering what in his life could have led to such an end. She really loved him as a little boy."

"I saw a different side of Paine yesterday evening when I walked to Aunt Sadie's house to deliver her first payment for her apron sales," Olivia said. "Paine was visiting. He was almost . . ."

"Human?"

"A different person," Olivia said.

"Maybe he always was different with Aunt Sadie. Anyway, suddenly I'm hearing all these stories from her about Paine and his parents and the mansion, which is how I learned about the cookie-cutter collection." Maddie curled her legs underneath her and nestled Spunky on her lap. "When Paine was a young boy, he used to prattle to Aunt Sadie about everything that went on at the Chatterley Mansion. One day he arrived at her house all excited, with his pockets bulging. He said he'd found out a secret. He'd heard his folks talk about a treasure they were looking for, something they thought was hidden in the mansion. Sally, his mom, was excited because she'd found some pieces of the treasure. Paine heard her tell his father that she'd hidden them in an old, empty coal bin in the cellar. She wanted him to put them in their safe-deposit box right away."

"But if Paine's father —"

"Don't interrupt, Livie. Aunt Sadie said that Harold was a Chatterley man through and through, which I'm guessing meant he had outside interests of the extramarital kind, and he must have thought that Sally was just trying to keep him home. Anyway, he blew her off and said he'd take a look when he got back from his 'important meeting.' Which gave Paine time to sneak downstairs and check the coal bin. And guess what he found."

"Um, cookie cutters?"

"Cookie cutters. But not your average, run-of-the-mill cutters. Paine had stuffed two of them in his pockets to show Aunt Sadie. She knows her antique cutters, and she'd never seen any this old or rare. She still remembered exactly what they looked like, too. One was a rearing horse with a rider who looked like he might be carrying something on his back. Aunt Sadie wondered if it might be a quiver for arrows, but it could have been a sack of potatoes for all she could tell. That piece was signed, but Aunt Sadie couldn't make out the name because the tin was so worn. The second cutter Paine showed her was a cat with its tail in the air. It was fairly crude and unsigned, Aunt Sadie said, and it was so worn it probably wouldn't cut well anymore. She said Paine really liked animals when he was a kid."

"Hard to believe we're talking about one person," Olivia said. "He wasn't thrilled to see Spunky with me when I visited the mansion Wednesday morning." At the sound of his name, Spunky stirred in Maddie's lap. Olivia reached toward him and softly stroked his ears.

"Maybe Paine was an impostor?" Maddie said. "Except if he was, he sure fooled Aunt Sadie. Anyway, if those cutters were part of the Chatterley collection, I'm guessing Harold and Sally sold them off. That was back when vintage and antique cookie cutters were starting to become popular with serious collectors. And legend has it that Harold and Sally were inclined toward unrestrained spending. They probably needed the dough. So to speak."

Olivia made it a rule to ignore puns, even if perpetrated by a best friend since age ten. "Did you see the teapot cookie cutter Paine brought Aunt Sadie? It makes me wonder if the collection really was sold off. If there was a collection to begin with, which is yet unproven."

"Livie, you are so skeptical, so . . . so *businesslike.*"

"We can't all be creative geniuses," Olivia said as she gathered up their empty plates and cups. "One of us has to balance the books."

"For which you have my fervent thanks."

Olivia swept some cookie crumbs off the coffee table and onto a plate. "What, for recognizing your artistic talent?"

"Mostly for balancing the books," Maddie

said as she shifted a groggy Spunky off her lap and onto the sofa. "But, yeah, the genius thing, too." She checked her watch. "It's almost midnight, and tomorrow will be nonstop madness. It's time we —" The phone in the kitchen began to ring, and Spunky's head shot up.

"That could be Del," Olivia said, heading toward the kitchen. "He probably wants to touch base about my visit with Hermione Chatterley tomorrow." Spunky leaped off the sofa and trotted behind. Before Olivia could reach the phone, her new answering machine kicked on. A woman's voice said, "Livie? Are you there? It's me, Heather Irwin. I — I've got to talk to you. I'm right outside, and I can see your light on . . . though maybe you leave it on all night, I suppose. But if you're up, please, could I talk to you? It can't wait till morning. I'm desperate. They've arrested Matthew for murder."

Olivia opened a bottle of merlot and gathered three glasses while Heather Irwin sobbed. She'd admitted she rarely drank alcohol, but Olivia decided she needed a calming beverage, and coffee wasn't it. Hoping she and Maddie could get some coherent details out of Heather before she got

172

too relaxed, Olivia handed her only half a glass of merlot. Heather poured the wine down her throat. Then she coughed for a good minute. Olivia brought her a glass of water and exchanged a rueful glance with Maddie, who shrugged.

The coughing fit interrupted Heather's sobs, but she still looked miserable. Her straight brown hair hung in tangled strings, and her generous mouth quivered. She did not offer her glass for a wine refill, so Olivia left it empty. "Okay, Heather, fill us in. Are you quite sure that Matthew has been arrested for murder? Are you sure he wasn't, perhaps, drunk? We all know that's something of a problem for him." Maybe she'd been too blunt, but Olivia hoped to get the story out as fast as possible.

Heather's round young face flushed with anger. *Good,* thought Olivia, *better anger than more tears.* "He isn't . . . it isn't as big a problem as everyone around here thinks," Heather said. "I mean, Matthew drinks maybe a bit too much sometimes, but only when he's really, really upset. He's sensitive. It's because he's so artistic. He's been adding the most wonderful Victorian gingerbread to the library exterior in honor of Chatterley Heights's birthday, and . . . and now . . ."

Sensing the return of storm clouds, Olivia poured Heather another half glass of merlot. When Heather ignored the glass, Olivia said, "Let's start with who Matthew is supposed to have murdered. Did the sheriff tell you that, Heather?"

"Paine Chatterley," Heather said. "Only Matthew didn't do it, I know he didn't."

"Can you prove it?"

Heather's plump shoulders drooped. "No. I'd lie for him, only it wouldn't work. Thursday night my horse, Raven, got sick. I stayed with him in the barn to keep an eye on him. He kept getting worse, so I called the vet around one a.m., and she came right out. Raven was really sick. He kept throwing —"

"Those details are probably unnecessary," Maddie said, pushing the wineglass toward Heather. "When did the vet leave?"

"Not until about five thirty in the morning, when Raven was out of danger. And I stayed in the barn with Raven until it was time to leave for the library. Oh, Livie, can't you talk to Sheriff Del? Try to get him to understand, Matthew would never do such a terrible thing."

Olivia sipped her own wine and recalled what she'd heard about the falling out between Matthew Fabrizio and Paine Chat-

174

terley. Matthew was, as Heather had indicated, a temperamental artist who had a reputation for drinking too much. Olivia had heard stories of his temper, especially when he'd been drinking. He was also, in Olivia's estimation, a self-absorbed dreamer. But she had difficulty imagining Matthew as a cold-blooded killer. If Paine had been killed in a bar fight, then yes, she'd be able to envision Matthew as a viable suspect. From what little Del had told her, though, she knew Paine's murder had required a cooler head than Matthew possessed.

"All right," Olivia said, "I'll call Del and —"

"Oh, thank you, thank you, Livie." Heather bolted from her chair and threw her arms around Olivia. "I knew I could count on you. I'll stay right here to hear what the sheriff says." She plunked back down and sipped her wine. "I don't suppose you have a cookie?" she asked.

"Heather, you didn't let me finish. I'll call Del in the morning, but I can't promise anything. I'll just try to find out what I can."

"No, you have to call *now.* Matthew can't spend the whole night in jail. He's so very —"

"Sensitive," Maddie said. "Yes, we get that. But it's past one in the morning, and poor Del is surely in bed. Give the guy a break; he has to keep the peace nonstop all weekend while the hordes descend. The Chatterley Heights jail doesn't keep prisoners chained to the wall. Matthew will be fine for the night. It'll give him a good chance to sober up and get through the nasty hangover coming his way."

"But you don't understand. . . ."

"I do understand," Maddie said, slipping an arm around Heather's plump shoulders. "If it were Lucas in jail, I'd be just as upset as you are, and yeah, I'd be beating down Livie's apartment door to get her help. And she'd tell me exactly what I'm telling you. Do not roust Del from a good night's sleep. A cranky sheriff is an uncooperative sheriff. Let Livie handle this in her own calm, collected way, and it will go better." Maddie pushed Heather in the direction of the apartment door. "I'm off home myself. I'll walk you to your truck."

"My truck has a flat tire," Heather said. "I didn't want to take the time to change it, so I rode to town on Raven. He's feeling himself again, and he needed the exercise."

"Then I'll walk you to your horse," Maddie said, turning to roll her eyes at Olivia. "Lord save us," she muttered. Or at least that's what Olivia thought she heard.

CHAPTER NINE

The sky barely hinted at dawn when Olivia descended the stairs to The Gingerbread House, Spunky under her arm. The little Yorkie would find himself banished upstairs to her apartment before the store opened to the public, but for now he could have the run of the sales area. Spunky still had trouble with chaotic days, which this was destined to be. Maybe someday soon, he'd settle down. But not yet. When the Chatterley Heights High School marching band passed by the store, attempting "The Stars and Stripes Forever," Spunky would make a run for the distant hills. Even hearing the band from the quieter safety of Olivia's upstairs apartment might tempt the little guy to think more fondly of the puppy mill. Or not, Olivia thought as she watched Spunky whiz around the store, sniffing every corner for threats to his domain.

Olivia strolled around the dimly lit store,

allowing the faint gingery scent to fill her with a warm sense of pleasure. Cookie cutters hung from every available hook and wire. She reached up and tapped a mobile as she passed. The metal flower shapes rippled and shone as if ruffled by a breeze in the moonlight.

Olivia settled onto Spunky's favorite chair, an antique with a carved straight back and a needlepoint padded seat. It was surprisingly comfortable and afforded her a view of the town square. Around the perimeter, old-fashioned lamps dotted the park with warm circles of light, revealing colorful banners swaying in the early morning breeze.

Spunky finished his rounds and clicked across the sales floor to Olivia. He jumped onto her lap and stared through the window, where dawn was announcing its imminent arrival. "Well, Spunks, this is going to be one heck of a weekend," Olivia said as she massaged his ears. "Trust me, you'll be happier out of it." The Yorkie's ears perked at the sound of Olivia's voice, then relaxed for a moment. When his small body stiffened, Olivia followed his gaze. In the early dawn light, she could make out a figure in a raincoat walking north on Park Street. It wasn't surprising, even at such an early hour. Shopkeepers would want to get an early start before the weekend celebration began.

As the figure neared, Olivia realized the walker was a woman. The woman most likely to be out patrolling on this particular morning was, of course, Karen Evanson. And she was heading right toward The Gingerbread House.

"I suspect we're about to get a visit from our forceful mayor," Olivia told Spunky. "Mind your manners." She wrapped her arm around Spunky's middle, in case he didn't obey her order.

Sure enough, a few minutes later the outside doorbell rang with irritating insistence. Spunky yapped fiercely and squirmed to free himself of Olivia's tight grip. "Hush, Spunky. Be civil. If she doesn't behave herself, I promise to let you chase her off. Deal?" The frustrated pup complied with a grumbling growl. Olivia rewarded him with a quick ear scratch.

Olivia unlocked the door to The Gingerbread House and reached for the dead bolt on the outside door just as the doorbell rang again . . . and kept ringing. She imagined Karen smashing the innocent button through the door. By the time she'd fumbled the lock open, holding her squirming dog, Olivia was not in the best of moods.

"It isn't necessary to be so —" Olivia's objection died on her lips, along with her anger. The woman in her doorway was not the demanding Karen Evanson. She was Rosemarie York, the normally easygoing administrator of the Chatterley Heights Community Center. Rosemarie's red, swollen lids highlighted the green in her troubled hazel eyes.

"Livie, I'm so sorry, I didn't mean to be strident, but I have to talk to you. I don't know where else to turn."

While Olivia stocked and decorated The Gingerbread House before opening time, Rosemarie followed along, clutching a mug of coffee to her chest as if it were keeping her heart from leaping out. "I raised Matthew from the age of four," she said. "He's my sister's child. Annmarie married the father but left him before Matthew was born. She divorced him, refused to let him see the baby. She wouldn't even take money from him. I thought she made the right decision."

Olivia hung a macramé banner from a wire above the front window and stepped back to make sure it was straight. Her mother had created the hanging using purple and silver metallic yarn. She'd added silver beads knotted into the pattern to form the year Frederick P. Chatterley first wandered into what later became the town of Chatterley Heights. According to dubious yet persistent legend, Frederick P. had become lost on the way home from his newest mistress's abode. He later dumped the mistress but claimed the unsettled land for himself and his future dynasty.

"Why did you think it was a good idea for your sister to raise Matthew alone without financial support from the father?" Olivia asked.

"That man was bad news," Rosemarie said. "He hit Annmarie when she told him she was pregnant. He really wanted Annmarie to get rid of the baby, and she was afraid he'd hit her again to make her miscarry. When she divorced him, he didn't fight for shared custody, just took off. Annmarie couldn't go to our parents; they were very religious and would have criticized her endlessly for divorcing her child's father, never mind how abusive he was. So she came to me for help. I was thirty-three and married at the time."

"I didn't realize you'd been married," Olivia said as she selected a smaller purple and lavender macramé to hang from the sales counter. "But if you raised Matthew

181

from age four, where was your sister?"

"She lived with us," Rosemarie said. "Of course, our parents figured out what happened and wouldn't speak to either of us, but at least Annmarie and the baby had a place to live that wasn't with the father. My husband and I worked full-time, so we all lived fairly comfortably. Then my husband got sick. Matthew was about three, too young for Annmarie to go to work, and I had to quit my job to take care of my husband. For a while, we were all hopeful, but the cancer was aggressive and, well, my husband lived less than a year." Rosemarie ran her fingers through her short brown hair, drawing Olivia's attention to gray roots. She knew Matthew was about twenty-five. If Rosemarie was thirty-three when her sister was pregnant with him, she would be about fifty-eight now. She'd never remarried, which meant she'd raised Matthew on her own.

"I know what that's like," Olivia said, touching Rosemarie lightly on the shoulder. "My dad died of pancreatic cancer when I was a teenager. It took him very fast."

Rosemarie took a gulp of her coffee. "It got worse," she said. "I was heartbroken, but with Annmarie and Matthew there, I had something to live for. I went back to work. When Matthew started preschool, Annmarie got a part-time job. We were doing okay." Rosemarie's voice trailed off. Olivia knew there was more, so she arranged a display of party-themed cookie cutters and waited. "One morning, Annmarie dropped Matthew off at preschool and headed for work. She never made it. Some kid out joyriding slammed into her car on the driver's side. She was gone by the time the police arrived."

Olivia tried to swallow the lump in her throat. "I can't even imagine. . . ."

Rosemarie plunked her cup down on the sales counter and took a deep breath. "It was a long time ago," she said. "I raised Matthew, of course. I couldn't love him more if he were my own son. Maybe I spoiled him a bit, but . . . anyway, I know he's high-strung and moody. I guess he inherited that much from his father. But he didn't inherit his father's meanness, I swear he didn't. My sister was a good person, and so is Matthew. I know with absolute certainty that he didn't kill Paine Chatterley. I just can't prove it."

Olivia felt a sinking feeling that stretched from her chest to her stomach. She knew what was coming.

"That's why I've come to you, Livie."

"Rosemarie, I can't —"

"Now hear me out." Rosemarie sounded commanding, more like the successful, middle-aged administrator she was. "You're so smart, Livie, and you've done this sort of thing before — you know, helping an innocent person who is accused of a crime he could never, ever have committed."

"But —"

"*Please,* Livie. I need your help. The sheriff won't tell me anything, and you and he . . . well, maybe he'll talk to you. Livie, I'm desperate. I have to help Matthew. He'll clam up and get stubborn and make things worse." Tears dripped off Rosemarie's chin and plopped onto the collar of her raincoat.

"I suppose I could talk to Del," Olivia said. "Only I can't promise —"

"Oh, thank you, thank you, Livie. I'd better run; there's still so much to do to prepare for this dreadful weekend." Rosemarie squinted up at the store's Hansel and Gretel clock, a gift from Olivia's mother. It was lovely but so intricate that even Ellie couldn't read it accurately.

"It's somewhere around seven to seven fifteen," Olivia said. When she saw the mute plea in Rosemarie's eyes, Olivia added, "I can't force Del to share anything with me, but I will talk to him."

■ ■ ■ ■

Once Rosemarie had left, Olivia took Spunky on a quick outdoor bathroom break in the side yard. For once, the little guy was efficient. According to her watch, Olivia had thirty-nine minutes before opening time. The town square teamed with people, many of whom she did not recognize. She hoped the visitors had come for the festivities and not merely to gossip about Chatterley Heights's sensational murder and arrest.

As she and Spunky reentered the front yard, Olivia recognized the back of a distinctive wheelchair making its way up the newly finished ramp that skirted the steps leading to The Gingerbread House porch. The wheelchair — half state-of-the-art motorized vehicle and half antique rocking chair — as well as the dark blond hair showing above the backrest belonged to Constance Overton, owner of the Chatterley Heights Management and Rental Company. The two were becoming friends, despite their high school tussle over a boyfriend.

Spunky welcomed Constance with a friendly bark. Constance stopped her wheelchair and turned her head. "Is that you, Spunks, old buddy? I see you've been taking Livie for some much needed exercise. No offense, Livie."

"Very little taken." Olivia unlocked the front door and held it wide. "Does the ramp pass inspection?"

"It's perfect," Constance said as she guided her chair into the store. "I'm grateful."

"Some of the other shopkeepers on the square are dragging their feet," Olivia said. "I'm hoping the Victorian look will ease their concerns."

Constance shrugged her slender shoulders. "Well, Lady Chatterley's got their ramp set up in time for this weekend, so I've got cookies and clothes. My two highest priorities." Her teal cashmere sweater and the matching blanket on her lap were undoubtedly special ordered by Lady Chatterley's. "Matthew did a nice job with the Victorian gingerbread touches for both ramps," Constance said. "He's why I'm here."

Olivia poured a cup of coffee from a large urn she'd set up in the cookbook nook, near two easy chairs and a table supplied with cream, sugar, and a large tray piled with decorated cookies. "Does everyone in town know Matthew has been arrested, and will all of them be pumping me for details?"

Olivia handed the coffee cup to Constance.

"The rumor is going around," Constance said. "I guessed it was true because Matthew didn't show up to work on my building at six thirty a.m., like he usually does. I wasn't sure until I saw Rosemarie York leaving your store this morning. There's only one reason she'd be here so early on such an important day: she wants you to rescue Matthew from the sheriff's clutches."

"Why does everyone believe I can make murder charges go away?"

"Down, girl," Constance said. "Not everyone thinks you can work miracles. I certainly don't, and I say this with newfound sisterly affection. That being said, I want Matthew exonerated as much as the next person. I recently bought out the dentist who owned the other half of my building, so I could expand the M & R Company. Matthew is in the middle of renovating the facade. Call it enlightened self-interest. Matthew is a self-involved hothead, probably because Rosemarie spoiled him, but he is supremely talented. Also, I don't think he's controlled enough to murder Paine Chatterley without waking up Hermione and several surrounding neighborhoods. Now I want a cookie." Constance wheeled herself toward the cookbook nook.

Olivia followed her and flopped down in one of the stuffed chairs. The store opened in twenty minutes, but final preparations would have to wait for Bertha to arrive. "Constance, let me ask you this: what if Hermione manipulated Matthew into helping with Paine's murder?"

Constance nibbled on a cookie shaped like a waving banner. Pink writing on maroon icing read **"Eat Me!"** "Here's what I think," she said. "If Hermione got Matthew to kill her husband, she'd have promised him something that would further his career. More work on the mansion, maybe, I don't know. Anyway, if there was such a promise and Hermione lets Matthew rot in jail, he will sing like a birdie."

"But, Constance, how does that help Matthew? He would still be charged as an accessory, at the very least. And he'd need some proof that Hermione was complicit."

"Well, I don't have any proof, but I do have some interesting information," Constance said with a grin that displayed her perfect former-cheerleader teeth. "Yesterday just before closing time, I had a visit from Hermione Chatterley. She wanted to put Chatterley Mansion on the market. Yep, less than twenty-four hours after Paine's death, his wife is making plans to get out of town."

"Which means," Olivia said, "out of the country. Though I presume Del has her passport since he considers her a suspect. Or at least he did yesterday when he suggested I babysit Hermione sometime this weekend. He hasn't mentioned if he's changed his mind."

"Hand over another cookie." Constance held out a perfectly manicured hand. "I need the calories."

"I hate you," Olivia said as she passed along a balloon cookie with mauve and white stripes, specially ordered by Mayor Karen Evanson to match the banner stretched across the band shell.

"Yes, of course you do." Constance savored a ladylike bite before saying, "I doubt Del has decided to trust Hermione. He's too good at his job, which means he is always suspicious. You need to tell him about Hermione's urgent desire to exit Chatterley Heights."

"Me?"

"Well, I can't tell him," Constance said. "It's a professional ethics thing. I took her on as a client, or at least I pretended to do so. I promised her I'd do a quiet search for a buyer who doesn't live here in town. So obviously she wants to arrange an exit as soon as possible, and she's trying to avert suspicion. Anyway, I've done my duty, and we both have work to do." Constance executed a smooth wheel-around and headed toward the front door, snagging another cookie on the way. "The sooner Matthew gets back to work on my building makeover, the happier I'll be," Constance said over her shoulder. As Olivia hurried to open the door for her, Constance added, "By the way, I'm taking a risk by sharing this information in possible violation of professional ethics. I'm doing it for the good of the town and the success of the celebration. Not to mention it'll look good for Del if he can wrap up this investigation himself. I think my taking such a selfless risk merits several dozen cookies at, say, half price?"

"Constance, you're doing this to get Matthew back to work on your building."

"That, too, but mostly for the cookies."

"Geez, you're a cheapskate," Olivia said. "You're rolling in dough."

"Yeah, but not the kind that turns into cookies. And I didn't get rich by paying retail."

CHAPTER TEN

On the first day of Chatterley Heights's two-hundred-fiftieth birthday celebration, The Gingerbread House filled up within minutes of opening, though not entirely out of eagerness to buy cookie cutters. Hometown customers knew that the store's front picture window offered a panoramic view of the town square. Since the Queen Anne that contained The Gingerbread House was built on a small hill — better described as a mound, really — folks inside the store would be able to watch the morning parade over the heads of the crowds outside. A few onlookers chose to sit on the front porch or the steps. However, anyone who dared to stand outside, blocking the view from inside, ran the risk of being run out of town on a sharp-edged rail. Several out-of-towners had already abandoned the porch after receiving this warning from townsfolk.

Olivia was happy to stay inside for the

simple reason that the plate glass would mute the sound of the Chatterley Heights High School marching band. She would never admit this openly since many of her customers had school-aged children in the band. Of course, many of those same parents were currently inside The Gingerbread House and likely to stay through the parade. After enduring home practice sessions, they had done their duty.

With commerce suspended in deference to the parade, Olivia joined her staff and customers at the window. Her mother, being four foot eleven, had secured a spot in front. Bertha, who shared Olivia's height advantage, stood with her behind the onlookers.

"Aren't they lovely," Bertha said as three majorettes passed into view. "And so limber." Bertha was in her sixties and always on the go, but she was far from athletic. Since becoming involved with the widowed Mr. Willard, Bertha had slowly whittled down to a pleasant plumpness. Olivia's mother, on the other hand, could probably keep up with those majorettes without breaking a sweat.

As three young trumpeters passed, one of them struggling to get back in step, Olivia asked, "Couldn't Mr. Willard join us to watch the parade?"

"Oh, the poor dear is in his office, working. He feels terrible about the mix-up over Paine Chatterley being declared dead." Bertha put her fingers to her lips. "I didn't mean that to sound so cold — now that he's actually dead, I mean."

"Bertha, you couldn't be cold if we encased you in ice. I knew what you meant. Does Mr. Willard have some new information about Paine Chatterley's death certificate? I mean the one he received years ago."

"Here comes the piccolo," Bertha said. "I do love the piccolo. It sounds so brave, high above the rest of the instruments. Although . . . are those the right notes?"

"Not a one." Olivia was so glad for the thick plate glass. She didn't have the best musical ear in town, but something was going very wrong with the piccolo part. Luckily, the girl passed out of sight, to be followed by the softer flutes.

"Willard is so upset with himself for not noticing a problem," Bertha said, her eyes following the clarinet players as they marched by. "Though really, how could he have known? It was sent from England, looking all official with a stamp and a signed letter."

"Of course he couldn't have known,"

Olivia said.

"Well, he insists it was plain as plain could be, if he'd only done a little checking. But, well, at the time he didn't see any reason to be suspicious. Of course, it was many years ago, and he was less experienced then, which is what I told him in no uncertain terms. Also, that was right when his wife got so sick."

The lone tuba straggled by, taking up the rear of the marching band. Next came the parade banner — mauve, as Karen Evanson had decreed during the planning committee's fateful last meeting. The mayor herself followed, head held high and smile tight. Olivia lost interest in the parade. She backed away from the group at the window, followed by Bertha.

In the cookbook nook, as they started more coffee and replenished the cookie supply, Olivia asked, "Did Mr. Willard happen to mention why he should have recognized the death certificate as a forgery?"

"Oh my, he was so mortified. And the mayor was quite irritated with him, although the sheriff couldn't have been nicer about it. But Willard insisted he was at fault because he did have several papers in his files that Paine had signed."

Olivia almost dropped a plate of cookies.

194

"Are you saying that Paine Chatterley signed his own death certificate?"

"Well, not exactly," Bertha said as she snapped the lid on the coffee urn. "Some other document in the package from England, I think. Anyway, it makes you wonder, doesn't it?"

"It certainly does."

With Ellie, Bertha, and the temporary help — two high school girls — handling the sales floor, Olivia slipped into the kitchen to make a quick call to Del.

"Hey, Livie, good timing," Del said. "Just a minute, let me . . ." Del's cell went quiet for a few moments. "Okay, it's quieter in here. I'm going a little nuts. Karen wants me and Cody everywhere at once."

"And you with a murder to solve."

"Exactly. Listen, Livie, could you break away for an hour or so to visit Hermione Chatterley this afternoon? All I can get from her is a blank stare and a lot of mumbled nonsense."

"I'll make it work," Olivia said. "What do you need from her?"

"Any reference to Matthew Fabrizio, no matter how inconsequential it sounds. I can't hold him any longer with what I've got even though Hermione is absolutely certain he is guilty. I've got no witnesses who can swear Matthew threatened to kill Paine Chatterley. That doesn't mean he is innocent; he's still my best suspect after the run-in he had with Paine about his questionable lineage. But I need more to go on."

With one hand, Olivia poured herself some coffee and retrieved the cream from the refrigerator. "Del, were you aware that Hermione Chatterley wants to sell the mansion as soon as possible? She approached Constance about putting it on the market. Constance doesn't want it generally known that she's the source of the information. Professional ethics or something. I haven't had a chance to call you; it's been so chaotic here."

As if to prove her point, the kitchen door burst open to reveal one of the high school girls she'd hired for the weekend. "Ms. Greyson, I don't know what to do. We had five of those pretty aprons on display, and they sold in, like, five minutes, and there's all these ladies who want to buy more of them."

Olivia held up one finger and pointed to her cell. "Del, I —" A demanding knock on the alley door interrupted her. She opened the door to find Rosemarie York, her fist poised for another knock. "Um, could I call you back later, Del? Life is getting complicated at this end."

"There's a lot of that going around," Del said, chuckling. "I'll follow up with Constance and promise to say it's a rumor going around. Small towns and gossip, that sort of thing. Call me when you've had a chance to talk to Hermione."

As Olivia signed off, Rosemarie marched into the kitchen and sat at the worktable. Her hair needed brushing, her raincoat was missing a button, and she looked every minute of her fifty-eight years.

The young clerk eyed Rosemarie uncertainly before saying, "Everyone else is so busy. . . ."

Olivia grabbed a set of keys from the kitchen counter. "Here, this key opens the storage room. Do you know where that is? Good, then right inside there's a hook on the wall. There are ten more aprons hanging on it, already tagged. Put them all out on the coatrack. Go."

The young clerk snatched the keys and scurried off.

Olivia sloshed some coffee into a clean cup and pushed it toward Rosemarie. "You look like you've got something important on your mind." Olivia didn't mention that Del wasn't sure he could hold Matthew in jail much longer. Better to wait and see if Rosemarie was about to spill important information.

Rosemarie took a swig of her coffee. "I've never told this to anyone." She squirmed in her seat as if she were physically uncomfortable. Normally, Olivia would have produced some cookies to lighten the mood. This time it didn't feel right.

"I should have," Rosemarie said. "I should have told. It wasn't right, what he did."

"He?"

Rosemarie's hazel eyes met Olivia's. "Paine Chatterley," she said. She lifted her coffee cup and put it down again. "It was more than thirty years ago. Going on forty, actually. I was twenty, not yet married. I was in college studying to be a high school teacher. But after what I experienced . . ."

Again, Olivia forced herself to stay silent, though her thoughts were racing. Did Rosemarie have an affair with Paine? He would have been seventeen or so. Would Paine have tried to blackmail her, then or since his return to town? *Chill, Livie. Just listen.*

Rosemarie straightened her spine with an air of resolution. "I confess that I have an ulterior motive for revealing this now. I'll do anything to save Matthew, and this might help. So you have to promise me that you will tell my story to the sheriff. I just can't face doing it myself. I feel so guilty. . . . Promise me, Livie."

Olivia nodded. "I promise."

"It was fall semester, and I was student teaching at Chatterley Heights High. Paine was starting his senior year. So was Quill Latimer."

So that's how Paine and Quill knew each other. If Olivia hadn't been so busy, she could easily have figured that out. She missed Maddie's magic computer fingers. She risked a question: "Are you saying that Paine and Quill were friends? Or enemies?"

"Yes and yes," Rosemarie said. "They seemed to be good friends when I began my student teaching. I was working with the history and social studies teachers. Paine and Quill were in two of the classes where I was assisting, and I got to know both of them. They always hung out together. Quill Latimer was a straight-A student, very serious, if a bit pretentious. Paine . . . well, he was hard to read. He was bright, no doubt of that, but his performance was erratic. He could be quite charming, but then he'd turn surly, even nasty. Looking back, I wonder if he had some sort of psychological problem. One hears so much about that in the schools these days."

Olivia cast a surreptitious glance at the kitchen clock. The noon rush would begin soon, after which she hoped to visit Hermione at the Chatterley Mansion. "You mentioned that you 'experienced something' that made you uncertain about becoming a teacher. Did it involve Paine and Quill, and how would that help Matthew?"

"Paine's class work started to improve dramatically. At first I assumed it was because he and Quill were studying together, which might have helped Paine buckle down. Then I noticed a pattern. The two boys usually sat together in class, but sometimes they couldn't find seats together. Whenever that happened, Paine did badly on tests. So I began to wonder if —"

Olivia heard the kitchen door open behind her. She didn't turn around. No one spoke, and the door closed again.

"I wondered if Paine might be cheating, copying from Quill's paper," Rosemarie said. "I mentioned this to the teacher, but he didn't take it seriously. The school tended to go easy on Paine because of his family connections. Quill's family was working class."

"I'm assuming it didn't end there?" Olivia asked.

"Nope," Rosemarie said with a mirthless laugh. "I had to go and stick my fingers in the blender. I almost got them sliced off. You see, I was pretty earnest in those days. I wanted to be the best teacher I could be, so if Paine really was cheating, I couldn't simply overlook it. On my own I devised a little experiment. I was in charge of typing up the tests and making copies. I created two versions, which contained the same multiple-choice questions but in a different order. On test day, Paine and Quill sat next to each other, and I made sure they got different versions."

Olivia felt her heart rate quicken. "And was Paine copying Quill's answers?"

Rosemarie heaved a deep sigh. "I wish it had been that easy. Yes, at first my trick seemed to have worked. The answers weren't identical; Paine was too clever for that. My guess is he copied most of Quill's answers but not all of them. But I could tell when I graded the tests that Paine had copied from Quill. For many of Paine's wrong answers, he'd picked the same letter choice that Quill had — a, b, c, or d. Only Paine's questions were in a different order, so Quill's answers were incorrect for Paine's test. Quill's answers on his own test were almost all correct."

"That sounds like fairly solid evidence to me," Olivia said.

"I felt confident about it, but when I told the teacher what I'd found, he . . . well, he acted strangely. First he seemed flustered, then he got mad at me for 'perpetrating a hoax,' as he called it, without running it past him. Finally, he ordered me to bring the test papers to him, and he'd take care of it. So I did."

"I'm guessing nothing happened?"

"Oh, something happened, all right," Rosemarie said. "Quill Latimer was accused of cheating on the test. Somehow the names wound up switched around on their answer sheets. At least, that's what I assumed. I never saw those tests again. And Paine insisted that Quill had been copying his answers all along. Never mind all the previous times Paine did worse when he couldn't sit next to Quill. And the real kicker is, Quill never defended himself. That's when I decided I didn't want to be a teacher."

"Not surprising," Olivia said. "There's got to be more to the story. The teacher must have been complicit."

"I heard later, after I'd left, that he'd been involved with a married teacher. They both resigned abruptly. Paine must have known about the affair and threatened to tell. But I could never figure out how Paine got Quill to go along. Quill paid dearly. The accusation went on his high school record, which meant he ended up going to a community college instead of a really good school, like he deserved. After that, he hadn't a chance to get into a first-rate graduate school."

"Quill must have hated Paine," Olivia said.

"Exactly." Rosemarie stood to leave. "Please, please, tell the sheriff everything I've told you."

"Why not tell him yourself?" Olivia asked. "Del will listen."

Rosemarie shoved her hands into the pockets of her raincoat. "I'd break down and sound hysterical. The sheriff might think I was making the whole thing up to protect Matthew." She lowered her gaze. "I feel guilty about Quill. I let him down all those years ago, and now I've made him a murder suspect. I wouldn't have said a word if it were anyone but Matthew in jail. I guess that makes me a real jerk. And I don't care."

CHAPTER ELEVEN

Once The Gingerbread House finally cleared of lunchtime customers, Olivia checked her cell and found a text from Del asking her to call before she headed over to the Chatterley Mansion. When Del didn't answer, Olivia left him a brief message that there might be another suspect for Paine Chatterley's murder. "I'm leaving soon," she added, "to visit Hermione." As she filled a small Gingerbread House bag with decorated cookies, her cell rang.

"Glad I caught you," Del said when Olivia answered. "What's this about a suspect?" Olivia gave him a quick summary of Rosemarie York's story. "Well, it's worth throwing in the hopper," Del said, "but nearly forty years is a long time to carry a grudge."

"I agree," Olivia said, "although Quill's entire future was affected by the incident, and not in a good way. I'm not sure how I'd have dealt with being accused of cheating."

"You'd have fought to clear your name," Del said. "From what Rosemarie said, Quill simply accepted his fate. Call me a suspicious cop, but to me that screams guilt."

"I bow to your greater experience with guilty consciences," Olivia said. "Paine's murder required some planning, or at least some thought went into covering it up. For that, Quill Latimer fits the bill better than Matthew Fabrizio."

"Almost anyone does. Listen, Livie, the reason I called is about those photos Binnie Sloan took of the back parlor. I'm emailing one of them to you along with one of the crime scene photos. See if they mean anything to you, okay? Just first impressions, don't spend a lot of time on them. I'm really hoping your personal expertise will notice something helpful. Check them on your computer so you can see the detail better. Thanks."

"My laptop is upstairs," Olivia said.

"No big hurry. I'd better go — got a meeting with the medical examiner."

"One question, Del. Do you know for sure that Paine was really Paine? Bertha told me Mr. Willard figured out Paine's death was faked. I need to know what to listen for when I talk to Hermione."

"News sure gets around fast," Del said.

"The medical examiner ordered an expedited DNA test to settle the identity of our victim. Expedited or not, it'll take some time to ascertain that our Paine Chatterley was the original Paine Chatterley. I'm inclined to think he was, given that several folks recognized him. We may never know how or why he faked his own death. Either way, he's dead now, and he was murdered. I doubt Hermione will say anything helpful or self-incriminating, but keep your ears open. And Livie, don't take any chances, okay? Just observe and listen. No pointed questions."

"Understood." Olivia almost meant it.

Spunky hurled himself at Olivia the moment she opened her apartment door. "I love you, too, Spunks." She caught the excited Yorkie before he could escape down the staircase. "We are going to see Hermione — remember the meat lady? Of course you do. Don't tell Del, but we're going to pick up Maddie on the way." Spunky squirmed out of Olivia's grasp and ran into the kitchen. "Oh, all right, I'll buy your silence with a treat." Her laptop was on the kitchen counter. She could take a look at the pictures Del said he'd emailed to her.

Before checking her email, Olivia gave

Spunky two small doggy treats to keep him occupied. She'd forgotten to close her email program the night before, so it sprang to life when she lifted the laptop lid. A string of messages downloaded. She opened the one from Del and clicked on the first attachment. Binnie's cell phone photo appeared small and blurry on Olivia's aging little MacBook. When she enlarged the shot, she barely recognized the back parlor of the Chatterley Mansion. She knew Binnie had taken the picture before her tussle with the sheriff, yet the room looked as if it had endured a bar brawl. Olivia made out two brocade armchairs toppled onto their sides, a delicate carved side table broken in two, and what looked like part of a lamp on the rug. Several items on the floor had fallen from the broken table, including a plate broken in half. Near the plate Olivia saw some puzzling blobs of blue, green, and yellow.

Olivia clicked on the second attachment, which Del had identified as from the crime scene. Olivia was surprised to see a bedroom instead of the bathtub. The professional photo showed a tall four-poster bed with the top sheet and blankets tossed over the side, as if the sleeper might have thrown them off to . . . go take a bath?

Clutter covered Paine's bedside table. Though the quality of this photo was far better than that of the previous one, Olivia could barely make out several shapes that looked like pill bottles and a glass. A spot of color next to the glass intrigued her. It almost looked like . . . She enlarged the photo until it practically covered her tiny screen. The photo became grainy, but Olivia was able to recognize a small plate holding the remains of a decorated cookie. She couldn't make out the shape, but the icing was red and pink. "Huh. That must be what Del wanted me to see. Interesting." Olivia didn't realize she'd spoken aloud until Spunky whimpered and tried to jump up onto the counter.

"Forget it, Spunks," Olivia said, scooping him into her arms. "Face it, you aren't a cat." She gave his ears a rub. Before closing down her laptop, she forwarded Del's email to Maddie's newer and more powerful PC laptop. Olivia unplugged her freshly charged cell phone and grabbed a leash from a hook in the kitchen. Spunky wriggled and yapped with excitement as she hooked the leash onto his collar. "Time to consult Maddie," Olivia said as she locked her apartment behind them.

Olivia didn't even glance into The Gingerbread House to see if all was well. With her thumb, she punched her speed-dial number for Maddie, who was at the Chatterley Heights Community Center. After two unanswered rings, Olivia was sent to voice mail. "Hey, Maddie, it's me. I'm on my way to the community center. Hope you're there along with your laptop. If you get this in time, check your email."

Olivia and Spunky cut through the town square, skirting around booths and platforms at various stages of completion for Sunday afternoon's birthday fete. Wielding buckets and mops, Chatterley Heights citizens scrubbed the rarely used band shell for an evening concert of early American songs, to be performed by the Chatterley Heights High School choir with the assistance, thankfully, of the excellent St. Alban's Episcopal Church choir. Olivia's cell phone rang as she approached the buffed and polished statue of Frederick P. Chatterley attempting to mount his horse.

"It's me," Maddie said. "I'm looking at the pics now, with intense fascination. Can't wait to hear what's up. If you're going on an adventure, I'm coming. Because, frankly, with the gingerbread houses finished and on display, I'm bored. I mean, I love all the 'oohs' and 'aahs,' but it's fair to say that my ego is sated. Where are you?"

"Just past Fred and Trigger," Olivia said, referring to their childhood names for Frederick P. and his horse.

"Come right to Rosemarie's office," Maddie said. "I don't have my laptop, but I'm using the community center's nice, big desktop computer."

"I thought only Rosemarie could log on to that computer."

"Oh please, Livie. I can hack into your computer, and your password is in French."

"You hacked —" Olivia interrupted herself as she neared a group putting up a kissing booth.

"Livie, my naive friend, I keep telling you to mix in some numbers and symbols, but will you listen? All I had to do was look up the French phrases you throw around most often — the Internet makes it easy, you know. Then I tried them one by one, and, um . . . voilà?"

"Sadly, you are correct," Olivia said.

"I'm only doing it for you. I'm determined to force you to use stronger passwords."

"Right."

"Well, there's also the fun of it. Anyway, we can be private in Rosemarie's office because she left me her key. She's pretty distracted right now, what with Matthew in

210

the clinker and all. Although I heard a rumor he might be released. Is it true?"

"Maybe," Olivia said. "I'll explain later. Right now we have an assignment. I'll be there in five."

Olivia held Spunky in a tight hug as she wound through the impressive crowd in the community center's large public meeting room. The gingerbread houses created by Maddie and her team formed a small village that filled a third of the room. A volunteer herded visitors through a line that started near the front entrance. Olivia paused for a longing gaze toward the gingerbread houses. Through a gap in the line of visitors, she saw a flash of peach and burgundy, the same shades Aunt Sadie had used to embroider the Chatterley Mansion on Olivia's apron. She was glad she'd decided not to use the apron as a costume today.

Worried that Maddie might have given away the identity of the little boy in the mansion window, Olivia veered toward the display to get a closer look. The peach and burgundy gingerbread house represented a small Victorian cottage, not unlike The Gingerbread House. No little boy appeared in a window. Olivia looked down the row of gingerbread houses and saw the Chatterley

Mansion showcased in the middle of the display. The gingerbread mansion's colors matched the freshly repainted Chatterley Mansion. She wasn't close enough to see the cookie window scene Maddie had created, but she remembered the little boy had dark hair, and his clothing was vaguely nineteenth century.

Spunky was starting to squirm in Olivia's grip, so she slipped past the line and headed toward Rosemarie York's office. She glanced inside the kitchen as she passed and saw several women cleaning up after their baking marathon. No wonder Maddie was so eager to leave. Cleaning bored her, and Maddie did not tolerate boredom with good humor.

"Hey, you two," Maddie said as Olivia appeared in the office doorway. "Heard you coming." Spunky yipped and reached out his front paws toward Maddie, who held out her arms. "Come to me, my little tiger."

Olivia handed him over. "He never appreciates me. It's a mother's lot."

"Close the door, we have much to discuss." With Spunky in her lap, Maddie swiveled Rosemarie's chair around to face a blank computer screen the size of a large television. She hit a key, and the photo of Paine Chatterley's four-poster popped up.

"I'm assuming Del wanted us to take a look at those cookie bits next to Paine's bed." Maddie pointed to the photo, now enlarged but still fairly clear.

"I couldn't tell what the shape was," Olivia said, "but I did bring a bag of cookies to the mansion when I visited Wednesday morning. Most people snarf them up right away. I suppose Hermione might be the type to dole them out, though. . . ." Olivia shook her head, remembering the steak Spunky had liberated from the mansion's garbage can.

"Hermione is the type to waste," Maddie said. "And steal. I still think she killed her husband. If she did it by poisoning one of our cookies, I'll . . . Wait a minute." Maddie squinted at the computer image. Her fingers traveled around the keys at warp speed, and the plate of cookies grew larger. More key tapping, and the image sharpened. "Huh," Maddie said, stroking Spunky's ears. "I don't think that's one of our cookies. Take a closer look and see what you think." She held Spunky in a cuddle and relinquished her seat to Olivia.

"I see what you mean," Olivia said. "It looks sloppy. Also, unless my twenty-twenty vision deceives me, it's a sugar cookie. The cookies I brought on Wednesday were all gingerbread. We have plenty of sugar-cookie dough in the freezer, but I haven't used any for at least two weeks."

"Nor have I," Maddie said. "And that sloppy icing job certainly isn't my work. Or yours."

"Thanks for the afterthought." Olivia sat back in the roomy office chair. "You know, I just remembered . . . when was it? Thursday? The last week is a blur."

"You're starting to sound like your mother," Maddie said. "What did you remember?"

Olivia laughed. "Ironically, it's a comment Mom made in her dithery yet brilliant way. She was in the store to pick up emergency supplies for your baking team. I started to fuss about where all these supplies were going, and she mentioned something about the supplies disappearing from the community center kitchen. Did you notice that?"

"No, but then I might not," Maddie said. "I was in creative-genius mode. As long as I have my paints and my canvas, I'm in my own little art studio. I trust your mom on stuff like this, though. She was probably keeping an eye on the supplies, trying to make sure everything went smoothly. Hey, you don't suppose . . ." Maddie hooked her foot around the leg of a metal chair and pulled it next to Olivia. "If Hermione Chatterley stole from some of the stores on the square, maybe she also took the baking supplies. She visited at least once while we were in the midst of maniacal baking. No one paid much attention to her."

Maddie's attentiveness to Spunky had waned, so he crawled onto Olivia's lap and curled into a ball. "Which might indicate," Olivia said, "that Hermione baked that cookie. Maybe that's why the kitchen was such a mess, because Hermione had to dig through the displays to find baking equipment. Although it doesn't explain the dining room." Olivia reached over Spunky's snoozing body toward the keyboard. She opened Del's second attachment, the photo of the Chatterley Mansion's back parlor. "What do you think of this?" she asked. "Del didn't have time to discuss what he was looking for in these photos; he just asked for a first impression."

"My first impression," Maddie said, "is that somebody has no respect for antiques." She pointed to the overturned chairs. "Those are genuine Victorian parlor chairs, although reupholstering their backs and seats lowered their value. Now one of them has a broken leg. And that poor little parlor table — also Victorian, ordered from Europe by one of the Chatterley ladies, can't remember which one." Maddie stroked the image on the screen, as if she were comforting it. "I might never be able to visit the Chatterley Mansion again."

"That's unfortunate," Olivia said, "since that's where I'm heading next. I was hoping you'd go along."

"Of course I'll go," Maddie said. "I refuse to wallow in grief."

"So brave," Olivia murmured. "Now my first impression when I saw this photo was that it looked angry — or staged to indicate anger."

"So maybe someone broke in? Someone very angry with Paine? That sounds a lot like Matthew Fabrizio," Maddie said. "Or maybe someone else set up the scene to make it look like Matthew had had an outburst of rage. If that's the case, the perpetrator could be anyone who knew how much Matthew wanted to insinuate himself into the Chatterley clan. Which could be just about anyone in Chatterley Heights, given Matthew's penchant for high drama."

Olivia stared at the image on the screen for several moments, trying to make sense of an idea that hovered in her mind. "There's another explanation," she said, "but it might be far-fetched. Several rooms in the mansion are in chaos, maybe for unrelated reasons. But what if someone has been tearing rooms apart looking for something? Maybe, and I'm just spinning ideas here, but maybe Paine Chatterley came back to town to get even with someone, to settle a score. If he threatened his victim with damning evidence of some sort . . ."

Maddie leaped from her chair so quickly that Spunky jumped to his feet and wobbled on Olivia's lap. She held his middle to steady him.

"Remember when Paine and Hermione came to the store Tuesday evening? Paine made a point of hinting that he knew both Karen Evanson and Quill Latimer," Maddie said, hoisting herself onto Rosemarie's desk.

"Yes," Olivia said, "and I now know the story behind Paine's relationship with Quill, at least according to Rosemarie." She filled Maddie in on Rosemarie's tale of having caught Paine cheating on a test.

Maddie ran her fingers through her wild hair until the tangles defeated further progress. "So Quill has a reason to hate Paine, if Rosemarie is telling the whole story. Maybe Quill was cheating, too, and Rosemarie didn't catch him. Maybe Paine and Quill were in cahoots, helping each other with test answers, but Paine fixed it so only Quill got blamed." Maddie's shoulders drooped. "No, that doesn't make sense. Not if Rosemarie is sure Paine was the one who benefited."

"Maybe Quill had a guilty secret that Paine knew about," Olivia said. "Otherwise, why would Quill take the blame without protest?"

"You know," Maddie said, "this might explain why Hermione has been stealing. If she and Paine came back here because they were broke, maybe Paine turned to blackmail to fatten the family wallet. Isn't it the blackmailer who usually gets murdered? Come to think of it, I'll bet Paine had something juicy on Karen, too."

"This is a whole lot of conjecture," Olivia said.

"Party pooper." Maddie slid off the desk and began to shut down Rosemarie's computer. "This is our cue to visit her ladyship, Hermione Chatterley. If the docs at Johns Hopkins are right — and really, what are the odds those guys would be wrong? — Hermione probably isn't the one who's been tearing up the mansion. Aunt Sadie has congestive heart failure, and she'd keel over if she started flinging furniture around. But I'm betting Hermione is involved, or at least she knows a lot more than she's letting on."

As she watched the photo and email program disappear from the screen, Olivia said, "There is one other possible explanation for the condition of Chatterley Mansion. It's a long shot but worth thinking about."

"Tell," Maddie said. The sparkle in her eyes matched her emerald ring as it caught the overhead light.

"What if someone, or more than one someone, believes the Chatterley cookie-cutter collection is more than fantasy. A whole collection has never been found, but from Aunt Sadie's description, Paine's parents might have unearthed a number of genuine pieces. Paine saw them, too."

"You're thinking Paine was searching the mansion before he died? Maybe he had some reason to believe his parents hadn't found all the cutters and sold them. Hermione had to be in on it, even if she couldn't do much searching. But someone killed Paine, and it probably wasn't Hermione."

"At least not alone," Olivia said. "Unfortunately, if the motive involves the famed Chatterley cookie-cutter collection, the suspect list gets longer."

"It does indeed," Maddie said. "One

particular name comes to mind: Rosemarie York. She's a cutter fanatic."

Holding Spunky, Olivia got up to check the corridor. "Empty," she said, shutting the door behind her. "Why didn't I know about Rosemarie's interest in cutters? And why wouldn't she have visited The Gingerbread House more often?"

"Because she's only interested in truly antique cutters, and we mostly sell vintage ones. Not to denigrate vintage cutters, which I love with all my heart and soul."

"As do I. How come you know about Rosemarie's passion?"

"Two reasons," Maddie said. "Shortly after you inherited Clarisse's cookie-cutter collection, Rosemarie asked me if you were planning to sell any of the older pieces. She didn't want to ask you because it might seem insensitive. I told her you were unlikely ever to part with those pieces. I might even have hinted you'd be buried with them, which, in retrospect —"

"We do need to leave for Chatterley Mansion before winter arrives."

"The second reason is . . ." Maddie opened the bottom drawer of Rosemarie's desk. "Take a gander at these. They ought to look familiar."

The drawer was stuffed with magazines,

catalogs, and articles printed off the Internet, all relating to cookie cutters. Olivia picked up a copy of *Early American Life* magazine, featuring an article on the history of tin cookie cutters. "I have this," she said. "It's fascinating. And look at all the books from the Cookie Cutter Collectors Club. Oh, and I love this one." Olivia picked up a dog-eared copy of *300 Years of Kitchen Collectibles* by Linda Campbell Franklin.

"The whole drawer is full of research materials on cookie cutters," Maddie said. "I would never have guessed Rosemarie was so interested in antique cookie cutters. I mean, she never helped with the baking for the celebration, except for picking up supplies when we needed them. So here's what I'm wondering: what if she's really interested in the Chatterley collection? Matthew Fabrizio is her sister's son, and he is descended from Frederick P. Chatterley. So Rosemarie is, too, right?"

Olivia replaced the magazine on top of the stack of materials and closed the desk drawer. "Given all the materials Rosemarie has gathered, she's been studying antique cookie cutters for some time. Her interest might have nothing to do with the Chatterley cutters." Olivia absently stroked her thumb across her sleeping pup's head. "I'm inclined to think the Chatterley collection is either a myth or was found and sold off long ago. That's what Clarisse used to say. It's hard to believe there'd be any hiding places left after all the renovation on the mansion."

Olivia's cell vibrated, and she flipped it open. "Del, glad you called. I'm about to head over to the mansion."

"Livie, I wanted to let you know, we released Matthew Fabrizio. Thanks for the info from Rosemarie York. I questioned her and talked to some folks at the school. Her story checked out. I just finished questioning Quill Latimer. He admitted he was accused of cheating but insisted Paine was the real culprit."

"Does Quill have an alibi for Thursday night?" Olivia put one finger to her lips to warn Maddie not to squeal with excitement.

"Until midnight," Del said.

"On a school night?"

"He doesn't teach on Fridays, so he got together with a couple of friends for an 'intellectual discussion' involving several bottles of wine. His companions confirmed he was sloshed when they left his house at midnight. Not a perfect alibi but better than Matthew's, which is nonexistent. They both have motives, both had keys to the mansion, and both were under the influence."

"So no arrest, then?"

"Not yet."

"There's a murderer roaming the streets," Olivia said. "Goodie. I'm heading over to the mansion now for my baby-sitting assignment. I'll sneak into a closet and call at once if Hermione gives herself or anyone else away."

"There's something odd about that woman," Del said. "If she gives herself away, get out fast."

CHAPTER TWELVE

Struggling to catch her breath, Hermione Chatterley opened the heavy front door of Chatterley Mansion after five rings. "Oh how . . . how lovely," Hermione said when she saw Olivia and Maddie on the front stoop. "And your little dog, too!"

Maddie giggled at Hermione's repetition of a line from *The Wizard of Oz*. Olivia tried to envision Hermione Chatterley as a wicked witch. The best image she could come up with was a plump version of the gingerbread house witch in the Brothers Grimm fairy tale, "Hansel and Gretel."

"Do come in and visit," Hermione said, holding the door wide. "Oh, and you've brought cookies, how lovely. I'm so glad your friend has come, too. Maddie, is it? My memory isn't what it once was, I'm afraid, but I do remember we met in The Gingerbread House. My poor Paine so enjoyed your cookies." Hermione kept up her prattle as she led her guests down the hallway and into the front parlor.

"I was just about to make tea," Hermione said. "I'll see if I can find a treat for the little one." She gave Spunky a light pat on the head. Spunky perked his ears at the word "treat."

"We'd be delighted to help," Olivia said as Hermione paused for several deep breaths.

"Now you stay right here and make yourselves comfortable," Hermione said. "I'll put these cookies on a plate, and we can have a proper tea." Her shoulders heaving, she plodded toward the kitchen. Olivia remembered her first visit, when Hermione's gait had been brisk and lively. Either grief had weakened her condition or . . . "I wonder if she's having as much trouble breathing as she seems to be," Olivia murmured.

Maddie jumped up and peeked into the hallway.

"What are you doing?" Olivia said, louder than she'd intended.

"It's okay, she's out of earshot," Maddie said in a low voice. "Aren't you planning to search the room or something? Come on, let's get cracking."

"Honestly, I can't take you anywhere." Spunky yipped and leaped onto a velvet

225

sofa. "Or you, either." Olivia picked him up and stroked his head to quiet him. "Sit down, Maddie. When am I ever without some semblance of a plan?"

"Hold that thought," Maddie said. "I'll be right back." She disappeared into the hallway.

Olivia buried her face in her little Yorkie's fur. "So much for planning." She lifted her head and took a centering breath, the way her mother did when life threatened her inner peace. In a few seconds, Olivia came up with a reasonable explanation to give Hermione if she returned first. She'd say that Maddie needed the loo, information that didn't invite follow-up questions.

To Olivia's relief, Maddie reappeared a few minutes later. "I wanted a peek into the back parlor, where Binnie took the photo Del sent us," Maddie said.

"But that's right near —"

"Yes, Livie, I know it's near the kitchen, but that meant I could hear Hermione making tea. She kept huffing and puffing, by the way, so apparently that isn't an act. Anyway, the back parlor door was closed, with crime scene tape hanging down one side. I figured the police finished with the room, or they wouldn't have let Hermione stay in the mansion alone. I opened the door and slipped inside. The room still looks like it did in Binnie's photo, at least as far as I can tell. Hermione hasn't so much as picked up that sweet little Victorian parlor table, which I'm sure she could do without having a heart attack."

"I shouldn't encourage you," Olivia said, "but did you get a look at the dining room?"

"Yeah, it's still a mess, too. Plates and cups and shards all over the floor. Hermione has to walk through it to get to the kitchen. It's weird . . . like she doesn't care in the least that she's surrounded by chaos."

The sound of rattling crockery halted their conversation. Olivia leaned close to Maddie's ear and whispered, "I really do have a plan, of sorts. Follow my lead." She plunked Spunky on Maddie's lap and handed her the leash.

Hermione entered the parlor carrying a tray laden with tiny sandwiches, store-bought gingersnaps, and a thin slice of turkey, in addition to a large pot of tea, three cups, cream, sugar, small plates, and napkins. The tray shook in her hands. "Here we are," Hermione said. "A lovely tea for all four of us."

Olivia hopped up and reached for the tray. "Let me take that. You shouldn't be carrying such a load." As she'd guessed, the tray

227

was quite heavy. She wondered how Hermione had managed to carry it, as well as pick her way through the mess in the dining room, without tripping.

"Oh, nonsense," Hermione said. "I'm certainly able to tote a tea tray. I took one of my little pills to help me breathe, and I'm right as rain. Now, I'll be Mother, shall I?"

As Hermione prepared tea and handed plates around, Olivia said, "I'm glad you're feeling better, but it's hard to lose a loved one. Maddie and I want you to know we'd be glad to help you in any way we can. The police left your things in such disarray. . . . Perhaps we could help you tidy up or pack everything away for when your own belongings arrive from England?"

"So kind," Hermione murmured into her teacup. "You have such busy young lives with that sweet little store to take care of. I'm sure I can manage." Hermione's teacup clattered as she placed it on its saucer. "Where are my manners," she said, smiling at Spunky. "You haven't had your treat, little one." She put the plate of shaved turkey on the rug near her feet, and Spunky lunged for it. "There is one thing you could do for me," Hermione said. "Would you tell me if the police are certain they've identified the awful person who made me a widow? I did rather like that young man — Matthew, as I recall — though he upset Paine terribly by bringing up poor old Frederick's shocking behavior."

"I don't think they are certain," Olivia said. "I believe they are looking at other suspects as well."

"Oh my, that's so unlikely, isn't it? It must be that young man. He has such a temper; he quite terrified me. We've only been here a few days, hardly time enough for so many suspects to pop up out of nowhere."

"That makes the situation . . . difficult." Olivia took a long sip of tea, allowing the silence to grow. She put down her cup and said, "You see, when there are no other suspects, the police turn their attention to family members."

"Well, there you are, then," Hermione said. "That boy claimed to be a Chatterley, though really, when one comes from the wrong side of the sheets, one is expected to keep quiet about it."

"Livie, haven't there been others in town who've discovered they're related to Frederick P.?" Maddie asked. "What about them?"

"I think they all had alibis." Olivia had no idea if this was true. "I did hear a rumor that Matthew Fabrizio was being released for lack of evidence."

"How monstrous!" Hermione's plate slid off her lap, and Spunky lunged for it. Maddie leaped up and grabbed him around the middle. He didn't object when she plunked him on her lap — he'd had just enough time to determine the plate was empty. Hermione ignored the commotion. "Such incompetence would never be tolerated in England." Her voice had assumed an aristocratic tone.

Exchanging a quick glance with Olivia, Maddie said, "Paine grew up in Chatterley Heights. Maybe someone from his youth has a grudge against him?"

"Of course," Olivia said. "Mrs. Chatterley, didn't you mention that your husband was upset when he recognized two individuals from his past in our store Tuesday evening? I noticed he seemed to remember both Quill Latimer and Karen Evanson, our mayor."

Hermione's plump face hardened. "I believe Paine and the professor were at school together. Paine wasn't one to wallow in unpleasant memories, but he did mention to me that — Quill, did you say? Such an odd name to give a child. Anyway, Paine once mentioned that Quill had copied his schoolwork. That's all I remember. But that woman . . ." Hermione began to gather the empty teacups.

"Oh, let me do that," Maddie said. "You need to consider your health. You know how it is in a small town," she added apologetically. "By now, everyone has heard about your visit to Johns Hopkins Hospital."

"How very considerate of you," Hermione said. "I grew up in a tiny village in England, so of course I'm not surprised in the least that you know of my heart condition. It is tiresome, but there you are. I try not to let it rule my life." Without protest, Hermione allowed Maddie to clear away the tea things and take the tray to the kitchen.

"Did your husband say anything about Karen Evanson?" Olivia asked.

With an unladylike snort, Hermione said, "He didn't have to say a word. I knew all along what that woman was like. Of course, it isn't my place to judge your mayor. Who knows, perhaps she turned her life around, although from the little I've seen, she's as self-indulgent as ever."

"It sounds as if you actually knew Karen," Olivia said. "If there's something in her past you think the town should know about . . ."

"Well, for the good of Chatterley Heights . . . after all, the town *is* named after Paine's family." Hermione patted her fluff of white hair and settled back in her armchair.

Olivia wished Maddie would return to hear Hermione's story. It might be helpful to have a second pair of eyes and ears, especially when those eyes and ears belonged to Maddie Briggs. Olivia suspected she was conducting a quick search of the kitchen and nearby rooms.

"I'm not a gossip," Hermione said, "never have been. However, little Miss Karen Evanson hasn't always been as respectable as she wants the town to believe. About twenty-five years back, maybe more — when Karen was, oh, nineteen or twenty years old, I'd say — Paine and I had the misfortune to cross her path. I'm only a few years older than she is, but at that time, Paine and I had already been married for several years, so I was far more mature."

Olivia estimated that Hermione's "few years older" equaled at least ten. Spunky lifted his sleepy head at a rustling sound from the hallway. Maddie appeared in the parlor doorway, about to speak. With an infinitesimal shake of her head, Olivia warned her not to interrupt. Maddie quietly sank into her chair.

Hermione continued as if she hadn't noticed Maddie's return. "This was back in the eighties, of course, so morals were quite loose. Karen was studying art, I believe, somewhere in France. I have little interest in frivolous pursuits such as art — except for the old masters, naturally. In the early spring, Karen came to London and stayed for several months. I presume she'd become bored with art and decided a fling would be more fun. She became entangled in a most unfortunate and inappropriate affair with a wealthy — and married, I might add — gentleman of our acquaintance. His wife Ariana was a dear friend of mine. She was so heartbroken. I tried to comfort her, but . . ."

Hermione's story had so mesmerized Olivia that she hadn't thought about what information she ought to elicit. Luckily, Maddie was quicker on the uptake. "Did Karen break up their marriage?" Maddie asked.

"Oh, far worse," Hermione said. "Poor Ariana tried to kill herself. Well, that created quite an uproar, I can tell you. Sir Laurence, Lady Ariana's husband, he was the one who found her, barely alive. She was terribly ill for some time. Bundled off to the country to recover, she was. Well, with her out of the way, Sir Laurence and that selfish little blonde, they thought they'd carry on as they had before. Well, I wasn't about to let that happen, I can tell you. I called the tabloids." Hermione nodded with self-satisfaction.

Olivia was taken aback. In the United States, tabloids were popular but wielded little real power. She reminded herself that British tabloids had operated for many decades with fewer controls. They had successfully intruded into the lives of the wealthy and powerful, until recently without repercussions. "I'm intrigued," Olivia said. "That was a clever way to punish the people who hurt your friend so badly."

Hermione grinned like a feral cat with a feather in its mouth. "It worked, too. Sir Laurence was humiliated. He ended his affair with that woman and moved to the country to be nearer his wife during her recuperation. Karen, of course, was outraged. She's an American, so she didn't understand why Sir Laurence took the tabloids so seriously." Hermione leaned toward Olivia and Maddie, her hands neatly clasped in her lap. "You see, Karen believed that Sir Laurence would divorce his wife and marry her. She couldn't understand why a few tabloid pieces ruined her dream of becoming the wife of a rich lord. And ooh, she was so angry with me. Because she knew I was the instrument of Ariana's revenge." Hermione sat back in her chair and smiled.

Acting on a hunch, Olivia asked, "Did Karen by any chance try to take revenge on you? I ask because I see her as someone who doesn't easily accept defeat. I suspect she wouldn't have been that . . . mature." Olivia almost said "passive," but Hermione might have interpreted that as a compliment to Karen.

Hermione waved a dismissive hand. "There really wasn't much she could do. The reporters wouldn't leave her alone, you see. They parked themselves outside her flat, took photos every time she left the building. . . . If she went to the shops, they photographed her buying biscuits or bottles of wine. If she talked to anyone, especially a man, we'd read an interview with him the next day. She left London in less than a fortnight."

Olivia shivered as she imagined what it would feel like to be hounded daily. Seeing herself in Binnie Sloan's irritating blog was the closest Olivia had come to feeling publicly exposed, and it hadn't been comfortable. She had a hard time believing Karen would have slunk away without lashing out at her tormentor. There was more to Hermione's story; Olivia was sure of it. She was willing to bet the vintage Hallmark cookie-cutter collection she'd inherited from Clarisse that the rest of Hermione's story involved her husband. Had Karen run into Paine in London? If so, she would know that his death certificate was a fake. Yet she'd raised no objections to the town's ownership claim to Chatterley Mansion. What if Paine was the man with whom Karen had a fling? That would explain why Hermione's anger with Karen sounded personal. And why else would Paine have greeted Karen as if he'd once known her well?

CHAPTER THIRTEEN

Wielding a pastry bag filled with fire engine red royal icing, Maddie swirled a crooked grin on the face of a running gingerbread man. *"C'est magnifico!* I just get better and better."

"Well done." Olivia glanced up from the gingerbread girl she was decorating. "That was two languages in one exclamation."

"Drat," Maddie said. "I'll never get the hang of French. What did I do wrong this time?"

"Not a thing. It's just that *c'est* is French and *magnifico* is Italian, which makes you multilingual." Olivia squeezed two drops of icing to create baby blue eyes for her gingerbread girl. "Besides, I continue to feel impressed and horrified that you managed to guess my email password. Now I have to change it to another French phrase, one I never use but might have a shot at remembering." She moved her finished cookie to a drying rack and selected another. "How many more dozens do we have left to decorate?" Olivia asked, glancing up at the kitchen clock. "It's already eight p.m. Aren't you and Lucas going to the dance in the park?"

"At least five dozen, and Lucas flaked out," Maddie said. "He's tired, so he decided to go home and to bed. I think the real reason is he thinks he can't dance. I've been teaching him."

"Maybe that's what wore him out." Olivia decided on aqua for her gingerbread man's hair and beard. After all, Maddie wasn't the only one allowed to veer beyond the limits of reality.

"Nonsense," Maddie said. "Lucas is nearly ready for *Dancing with the Stars.* He's shy, that's all. But no matter. We have work to do, you and I, and I don't mean mere cookie decorating."

"Good," Olivia said. "I didn't want to keep you away from the dance, but I wasn't looking forward to traveling the Internet on my own."

"That's why I brought my laptop. I'll crank it up while you tell me your plan. Because I know you have one." Maddie finished decorating a gingerbread man with black eyes and red fangs. She dribbled a few drops of icing blood down his chin and placed him with the growing collection of finished cookies.

"My plan is more like a list of questions." Olivia counted the remaining cookies with misgiving. They were destined for The Gingerbread House's booth at the Sunday afternoon fete, so they had to be designed with skill and imagination. When it came to decorating cookies, Olivia was excellent, but Maddie was superb. Maddie was also superb at navigating the Internet. Olivia wasn't even in the running.

Olivia stretched her back, loosened her shoulders, and reached for a gingerbread boy. "First, I'm dying to know if that story Hermione told about Karen Evanson has any truth to it. Hermione said it happened sometime in the 1980s. Would something that far back be on the Internet?"

"We can but try," Maddie said. "Members of the British nobility can be tracked down through a number of avenues, especially when they've been involved in a scandal. What were the names again?"

"Sir Laurence and Lady Ariana." Olivia squeezed her pastry bag too hard and left a red glob at the corner of the gingerbread boy's mouth. She added more icing and formed clown lips. "I wish we'd gotten their last name. Hermione said they lived in London and then moved to the country after the scandal. It might be someplace with a private hospital or rest home."

After several minutes of rapid clicking sounds, Maddie sat back and grunted.

"No luck?" Olivia asked.

"Not yet, but not to worry. I've come up with lots of Arianas, with one 'n' or two, and Laurences in numerous spellings, but not the two together, except . . . I wonder . . ." After more tap-tapping, Maddie said, "I've returned to a site that I dismissed earlier because I thought it wouldn't be relevant. Sir Laurence and his wife Ariana are listed as characters in a London play called *Malice and Teacakes* that tanked in 1986. It lasted about three weeks. I don't recognize the playwright's name, probably for a good reason."

Olivia longed to pull a chair next to Maddie, so she could see the site for herself, but the silent cries of naked gingerbread people kept her working. "Are the actors' names listed? Anybody we might know?"

"Good idea." Maddie clicked through several screens. "Here they are. Nope, don't recognize a one. I was hoping to see Hermione's name; if there's anyone who screams failed actress, it's Hermione. She could have used a stage name, of course. There's one character in the script that also reminds me of Hermione — a betrayed wife in her thirties, named Doris. Let me see if I can find a photo of the cast."

As Olivia began decorating a gingerbread clown, a familiar longing for a cookie made her reach toward a small gingerbread boy dressed in a sea green sailor suit. She mentally slapped her own hand and drew it back.

"Here's a cast photo," Maddie said. "It labels the character names and the actor playing the role, which undoubtedly caused endless embarrassment, given the snotty reviews." Her finger on the screen, Maddie twisted her head toward the worktable. "Livie, come look at this, will you? It's the actress who played Doris, the betrayed wife. Tell me what you think."

Olivia capped her icing bag and scrunched next to Maddie on the roomy kitchen chair. "Way too tall to be Hermione Chatterley," Olivia said. "Hermione can't be more than about five foot two. This actress is closer in height to the other female cast members, so she's got to be at least five foot six. She looks like she's in her midthirties."

"Ah, the wonders of greasepaint," Maddie said with a grin. "Get this, the actress's name is Karin Evensong."

"No."

"Yes." Maddie tapped the screen at a list of actor names. "Our mayor in a New Age moment. I will enjoy having this information."

"You wouldn't —"

"Only if pushed beyond human endurance," Maddie said. "Anyway, this actress might be Karen Evanson, which would indicate that she was in London in the 1980s, as Hermione claimed. Karen couldn't have been more than nineteen or twenty then."

"If this is Karen, it means Hermione might have had some connection with her, at least through this play. Hermione used the names of the main characters in her story about Karen's alleged affair. Why would she make up such a story?" Olivia reluctantly returned to her mammoth cookie-decorating task. "Does anyone else in the cast look familiar to you?"

"Nope," Maddie said. "None of the male characters is small enough to be Paine Chatterley. It's always possible that Hermione worked backstage, I suppose. I can't imagine Paine doing manual labor, especially volunteer." Her fingers bounced over the computer keys. "I'll check a few more sites."

To speed up her decorating progress, Olivia placed three gingerbread men side by side. She gave one of them yellow hair, the second got a yellow shirt, and the third acquired yellow shoes.

"Hey, this is interesting," Maddie said. "It's a British tabloid article from about five years ago. Someone posted it recently because one of the people in the article died. The names are different, but the story is exactly the same as the one Hermione told us. Young American woman leaves art school in Paris, visits London, has affair with much older member of the aristocracy, wife has stroke, and so on. Only there's a photo of the young woman, and she wasn't Karen."

"So Hermione lifted her story from a tabloid exposé," Olivia said. "Then she changed the names, using characters from a play in which Karen performed? That's a lot of work. Hermione must have prepared that story in advance."

"Maybe Karen and Hermione knew each other, and not in a friendly way," Maddie said. "Hey, what if the man Karen had an affair with was —"

"Paine Chatterley!" Olivia squeezed her

pastry bag, inadvertently squirting a ribbon of magenta icing into the air. It landed on the table, less than an inch from a row of decorated cookies. "Oops."

"Put the pastry bag down, Livie, and no gingerbread people will get hurt. Remind me not to get you a firearm for your birthday."

"Duly noted." Olivia dragged a chair over to the computer. "Break time. Let's look up Paine and Hermione."

"Excellent." Maddie typed in their names and hit return. "Huh. Not much there, except recent articles about their arrival in Chatterley Heights and Paine's untimely departure." She checked several pages of listings. "I don't see anything from the UK here." Maddie pulled up a site that promised to find anyone, anywhere. She added "London" to their names and requested an address. No reference popped up. Since Paine had been reported dead, Maddie tried Hermione's name alone. "Nothing," she said. "That's weird. Maybe they were using assumed names. They did have passports, right?"

"Del confiscated them," Olivia said. "He'd have said something if they were using different names. How accurate are these sites?"

"I wouldn't bet Clarisse's cookie-cutter

collection on them. With a little time and hacking, I might be able to locate an official site; that would be more accurate. Still, it's odd that Paine and Hermione don't show up anywhere except here in Chatterley Heights. I'd assume they were impostors, but Aunt Sadie totally recognized Paine."

A stray lock of auburn hair fell across Olivia's eye, and she smoothed it behind her ear. "I meant to ask you," she said. "When I visited Aunt Sadie and Paine, or his evil twin, was there, she complained about a hand tremor. I hate to even think this, but could she have something neurological going on?"

"Not Aunt Sadie," Maddie said with certainty. "That tremor is a nerve thing caused by excessive embroidery, or that's what the doctor says. She's supposed to lay off for a while, but you know Aunt Sadie. She insists that the tremor goes away when she embroiders, so now she's doing even more of it. I told her, we'll have to sell all her aprons to get enough money for the whopping surgery she'll wind up needing. But did she take me seriously?"

"I'm guessing not?"

"Good guess." Maddie squinted at the computer screen. "Here's something interesting." She pointed to a listing that read

"The legendary Chatterley cookie-cutter collection . . ." Maddie clicked on the link and up popped an article by a collector whose name Olivia recognized. As she remembered, the woman had passed away two or three years earlier.

"When did the article first appear?" Olivia asked.

"2007."

"I'd better get back to decorating," Olivia said, "but I'm curious. Read the article out loud."

"Excellent, a command performance," Maddie said. "Okay, here's the text:

"The legendary Chatterley cookie-cutter collection might be more than a legend. The Chatterley family died out years ago, and their nineteenth-century home, located in the quaint little town of Chatterley Heights, Maryland, is now a historical landmark. The small mansion has seen better days, both inside and out, and few visitors make it a destination spot. Of course, most avid cookie-cutter collectors have made the pilgrimage to the Chatterley Mansion at least once. None has found so much as a single battered biscuit cutter, not one item worthy of the famed Chatterley collection. Legends die hard, though, and some collectors still believe that generations of Chatterley wives and mothers brought cutters from Europe; acquired more cutters from itinerant tinware peddlers; and, during periods of prosperity, commissioned cookie cutters in unique designs from tinware artists.

"To find out more, I spoke with two knowledgeable individuals from the cookie-cutter-collecting world.

"Livie, listen to this," Maddie said. "The two collectors she interviewed were Anita Rambert and Clarisse Chamberlain. Clarisse insisted the Chatterley collection was a complete myth, that it never really existed."

"Clarisse said that? But . . ." Olivia's pastry bag was aimed at a gingerbread man's chin, where she'd planned to put a red beard. Instead, several beads of fire engine red icing dripped on the man's neck. She decided to change him into a woman with a necklace and short skirt. "That article was published before I moved back to Chatterley Heights," Olivia said, "but still, Clarisse and I talked endlessly about cookie cutters, and I never heard her deny the Chatterley collection ever existed. She did think it was long gone, maybe even thrown away, piece by piece, over the generations. She said many housewives were more practical than sentimental."

"Maybe she wanted to protect her town

from hordes of fanatic collectors," Maddie said. "Anita Rambert hedged a bit, too. When it comes to local antiques, no one knows more than Anita. All she said was the Chatterleys probably acquired some unique cookie cutters during their wealthier periods, but they wouldn't have thought of them as potentially valuable. If they got bent or broken, Anita agreed that Chatterley wives would have tossed them or perhaps given them to the servants."

"Anita is a shrewd antiques dealer," Olivia said. "She's always thinking ahead. If anyone ever does find a collection, she'll want to acquire it quickly and quietly. It's in her best interest to dampen expectations. I could give Anita a call and ask her, but I'm afraid she'd think I'd learned something that might lead to —"

Olivia was interrupted by a series of explosions, like spitting gunfire. "What was that? Oh right, fireworks." A louder boom was followed by an unearthly howl coming from The Gingerbread House sales area. "Oh no, I left Spunky in the store." Olivia bolted toward the kitchen door. "He's fine with thunder, but fireworks terrify him, as we discovered last Fourth of July." As she opened the door, a brindled streak flew into the kitchen. He came to rest in a quivering ball inside the tiny kitchen bathroom. Olivia sat down on the bathroom floor next to Spunky, and he slunk onto her lap. "Poor little guy," she said. "Tell you what. You stay in here, and the health department need never know."

Maddie poked her head into the bathroom. "Pathetic," she said, "and yet somehow adorable. We're down to about three dozen naked gingerbread people, so we're in good shape. I'm going out to the sales floor to watch the rest of the show."

A series of firecrackers exploded. Spunky yelped, bolted out of Olivia's lap, and hid behind the toilet. "I won't be joining you back there, kiddo. Stay as long as you need to; I'll tell you when it's safe."

Olivia stood up, brushed the dust off her jeans, and hurried to join Maddie at the store's front window. They kept the lights out to better appreciate the flashing, sparkling colors in the night sky.

As a huge "Happy 250th" firework — mauve, naturally — splashed through the darkness, Maddie said, "I'm impressed. The celebration committee came up with some creative fireworks."

"Expensive, too," Olivia said. "It might be another two hundred and fifty years before Chatterley Heights retires the debt for this shindig. That's something Karen might want to keep quiet about if she does run for Congress."

"Good luck to her," Maddie said. "It's tough to hide sensational information like a possible affair with Paine Chatterley once the Internet gets hold of it. Anyone who knows Karen could find that cast photo and link her to Paine's presence in London. I'm thinking of our Binnie Sloan, of course. She wouldn't care if it's true, as long as it's juicy. I almost feel sorry for Karen."

"Maddie, look out there on Park Street. Does that look like a squad car parking in front of our store?" As the final barrage of fireworks turned the sky into multicolored daylight, Olivia watched Del get out of the driver's side and sprint in her direction. Deputy Cody Furlow's tall, skinny body unfolded from the passenger's side of the squad car. Cody opened the back door, and his large black Lab leaped out, nearly knocking him over. With a firm hold on the leash, Cody was able to restrain Buddy, and the two of them set off toward the town square park.

Del crossed The Gingerbread House lawn, heading toward the alley behind the store. Olivia flipped on the sales-floor lights to get his attention. She could no longer see Del until he appeared right at the front window and waved. He pointed toward the alley. Olivia sensed from his grim expression that this wasn't a friendly call.

"Something has happened," Olivia said. She dimmed the sales-floor lights and led Maddie into the kitchen. Spunky ran to them, whimpering for comfort. Maddie cuddled him while Olivia unlocked the alley door for Del.

"What's wrong?" Olivia locked and bolted the door behind him.

"How did you . . . ? Never mind. I wanted to warn you two that we've started a manhunt, so keep your doors locked. I'll give you a call when it's over." Del gave her a peck on the cheek and turned to leave.

"Oh no you don't, Del Jenkins. Tell me what this is about. I'll settle for the short version, at least for now, but we need to know who you're looking for, in case he or she decides to break down The Gingerbread House door." Olivia planted herself in front of the alley exit. "And no impatient, manly sighing, either. Talk."

Del spread his hands in a gesture of defeat. "Fair enough. Besides, at some point I might need your help again with Hermione Chatterley. We're looking for Matthew Fabrizio, and he might be armed. At least, that's what Hermione said, that he threatened her with a gun."

"Did Hermione say what type of gun?"

"All she said before she passed out was that Matthew waved a gun and threatened to shoot her." Worry pinched the corners of Del's normally warm brown eyes. "This has been one hell of a weekend, and it's only half over."

"Do you want me to stay the night with Hermione? I might be able to get more details. I'm assuming you've arranged for protection for her until you've captured Matthew?"

With a faint shake of his head, Del said, "I wish it were that easy. I've sent out a call for reinforcements, and a couple state troopers are on the way to the hospital to protect Hermione."

"Hospital?" Maddie squeezed Spunky too tightly, and he yelped.

"The Chatterley Heights Hospital," Del said. "She needed immediate care, so it was too risky to take her out of town. Looks like she's had a serious heart attack. If Matthew Fabrizio's behavior didn't trigger it, I don't know what did."

CHAPTER FOURTEEN

Olivia felt as if she and Maddie had decorated millions of gingerbread cookies, and still more awaited. When the kitchen phone rang, Olivia glanced up at the clock. It was eleven p.m. "This might be Del," she said as she lifted the receiver. "Maybe he found Matthew." It wasn't Del, though, and the female voice was so agitated it took Olivia some time to recognize Heather Irwin. "Slow down, Heather. Take a deep breath and start over. All I got was something about Matthew?" Olivia met Maddie's questioning gaze and shrugged as she listened to Heather repeat her message in a calmer tone.

When Heather paused, Olivia said, "Let me get this straight. You're saying Matthew is under arrest again, even though the sheriff hasn't found a gun? No, I'm not assuming Matthew hid the gun, I'm just . . . Got it: Hermione claimed he had a gun and threatened to kill her, but no gun has been found. And Del refuses to release Matthew because some folks who were out walking said they heard gunfire. Yes, of course, they might have heard fireworks and mistaken them for gunfire, but Heather, was Matthew by any chance . . . was he sober? He wasn't. Okay, calm down, I had to ask. I really can't second-guess Del; I'm sure he had good reasons for . . ." Olivia couldn't help herself; she rolled her eyes at Maddie, who snickered. "Heather, I can't intercede with Del. He's the sheriff, and I won't tell him how to do his job."

Olivia finally managed to extricate herself from the conversation by agreeing with Heather that Hermione might have made the whole thing up. "At least I didn't promise to convince Del to let Matthew out of jail," Olivia said to Maddie. "My guess is he was drunk and threatening, which is more than enough reason to keep him off the streets for a time. Now, hand me the bag of green icing, will you? No, I need the darker —"

The kitchen phone rang again. "No way am I answering that," Olivia said, aiming the forest green icing at a gingerbread man's chest. After several more calls, she gave in. "Hello." The greeting did not sound welcoming.

"Livie? I woke you up, didn't I?" It was Rosemarie York's voice. "I'm so sorry, but I really need to talk to you about Matthew."

"I know he's in jail," Olivia said, "and I'm assuming he isn't sober. And the sheriff hasn't found a gun but apparently believes there was one."

"Heather called, didn't she?" Rosemarie said. "Well, you're right on all counts, including the drinking. I love that boy so much. I don't know, maybe I tried too hard to make up to him for his mother's death and his father's . . . never mind that now. Del didn't believe Matthew's version of the incident. Yes, Matthew is not the most reliable of sources when he's been drinking, but I believe him, and I need to tell someone."

"And you're hoping I'll get Del to listen."

"That's up to you, Livie," Rosemarie said. "I'll keep it short, so you can get back to bed. Matthew said that when Hermione opened her front door, she was holding a small-caliber pistol. I don't know what that means, but anyway, Hermione ordered him off her property and pointed the gun at him. When he didn't leave fast enough, she fired it twice. Not straight at him, Matthew said, just into the air. He said she looked startled and unsteady afterward. Matthew was in shock, so he took off running. After a while, he stopped running and sat down under a tree to pull himself together. He should have kept going, but it didn't occur to him that the police might get involved. He wasn't thinking too clearly."

"In other words," Olivia said, "Matthew had a little too much to drink."

"Matthew wasn't too drunk to understand and remember what happened, if that's what you're getting at." After a moment's pause, Rosemarie spoke more calmly. "Livie, all I can say is I believe Matthew. I don't think Del looked for a gun in the mansion, at least not very hard. Hermione probably kept it hidden."

"I'm confused," Olivia said. "When did Hermione have the heart attack? I had the impression she collapsed during the confrontation with Matthew." As she thought back, Del had been vague about the sequence of events.

With a moan, Rosemarie said, "This is such a horrible mess. It's all Hermione's word against Matthew's because no one else was there. Matthew said he was gone before Del showed up. The only thing Matthew got from Del is that Hermione made the 911 call herself from inside the house. I guess she really was having a heart attack, only it happened after she closed the front door. Matthew is sure she took the gun back inside with her. Del said he didn't find a gun, but I don't know how hard he looked."

"Rosemarie, you sound exhausted," Olivia said. "I'll talk to Del. He might already have searched the mansion more thoroughly for a gun."

"He hasn't. I talked to him right before I called you. He just doesn't trust Matthew. Anyway, thanks for listening, Livie. The decision is up to you." She hung up without waiting for a response.

"Well?" Excited curiosity shone from Maddie's eyes. "Are you going to call Del and ask about the gun? Or should we go look for it ourselves?" She put the final violet touches on a gingerbread woman's high heels before capping her pastry bag.

"Give me a break," Olivia said. She waved her hand toward the racks of undecorated gingerbread cookies.

"We'll be finished with those in half an hour," Maddie said.

"Not a chance. Besides, remember what happened to Binnie Sloan when she made an 'unauthorized' visit to Chatterley Mansion?" Olivia commandeered the violet icing bag and gave a gingerbread man a lurid mustache.

"Oh, Livie, you can be such a poop head." Maddie grabbed a finished gingerbread boy in striped shorts and bit off his head. A spot of icing on the table seemed to fascinate her as she nibbled her way through the entire cookie. Her silence meant she was thinking, which made Olivia nervous.

Brushing the cookie crumbs off her hands, Maddie said, "I feel refreshed and re-invigorated. It must be the ginger."

"Or possibly the sugar," Olivia said.

"Livie, what do you think about the Chatterley cookie-cutter collection?"

Olivia found the sudden change in topic highly suspicious. "Could you be more specific?"

Maddie examined the available pastry bags for a new icing color to use on her next gingerbread man. Reaching for tangerine, she asked, "Did a collection ever exist? Has it been swooped up, a few cutters at a time, by various collectors?"

"I have no idea."

Maddie pouted. "You are seriously no fun sometimes. Look, Livie, remember that story I told you from Aunt Sadie about the two cookie cutters that little boy Paine brought to show her years ago, the ones he said his mother hid in the mansion's coal bin. Aunt Sadie thought they were genuine antiques."

"I believe her," Olivia said. "Aunt Sadie is a good judge of antiques, especially cookie cutters and china. Were they part of a larger collection? That we may never know. From what Paine overheard, his father believed the collection had been hidden in a number of spots around the mansion. I can't believe that at least some of them wouldn't have been found by now."

"Especially with the renovation," Maddie said. "Lucas kept a close watch over the process. He was always popping in unannounced to make sure the work was being done right. He'd have known if any cookie cutters turned up. And before your suspicious mind turns against the love of my life, it would never occur to Lucas to use the mansion renovation as a cover for a treasure hunt. That man is guileless, innocence in human form, not a devious bone in his hunky —"

"I get it," Olivia said, laughing. "Lucas would save kittens from a burning building."

"Without a thought for his finely chiseled features." Maddie put the final tangerine touches on the gingerbread man in front of her, set him aside, and moved on to the next cookie. "Hand me the magenta and violet, will you?" With quick, smooth movements, Maddie gave a gingerbread girl violet curls and magenta cheeks. "What do you think, Livie? Should she have rose eyes, or would that look diseased? Livie?"

"Hm?" Olivia had drifted into a pleasurable fantasy, where she was wandering through a Chatterley-free Chatterley Mansion. She was finding secret cubbyholes and hidden doors in every room, all stuffed with antique cookie cutters.

"I know that dreamy look," Maddie said. "What clever, fiendish plan are you hatching?"

"No plan at all," Olivia said. "I was just wishing we'd thought about searching the mansion ourselves a week ago, before Paine and Hermione showed up. Now we might never get the chance to see if a cookie cutter or two might still be hidden somewhere in the building, especially since it's now sort of a crime scene."

"Cheer up; maybe Hermione will be convicted of murder, in which case the mansion would probably revert to Chatterley Heights. Or was that mean of me?"

A colorful array of cookies covered the cooling racks on the kitchen table when Olivia stood to stretch and check the kitchen clock. Midnight. Maddie held a capped pastry bag but seemed too lost in thought to aim it toward a cookie. "No time for dreaming," Olivia said. "We need to finish up soon."

"Personally, I can dream and decorate cookies simultaneously," Maddie said as she reached for an undecorated cookie shaped like a church. "Anyway, we're nearly finished."

"I count at least a dozen bare gingerbread cookies still waiting to be dressed," Olivia said.

"Piece of gingerbread," Maddie said. "We'll be done in ten minutes. After that, we ought to think about how to get into the Chatterley Mansion."

"You're kidding, right?"

When Maddie shook her head, red curls snaked out through the edges of her bandanna. "I've remembered something that might really help us. When Lucas decided to take on the renovation, the first thing he did was draw a blueprint of the entire mansion, inside and out. Lucas studied architecture, you know."

"I didn't know, but —"

"Livie, listen to me. We can kill two birds with one . . . sorry, insensitive metaphor. What I mean is we can satisfy our antique cookie-cutter lust and help Rosemarie and Heather — and maybe Matthew — at the same time because Lucas's drawing will show us where to look."

"But we don't have Lucas's —"

"A minor detail," Maddie said.

"But —"

Maddie grabbed an undecorated gingerbread cookie and stuffed it into Olivia's mouth. "Enough with the interruptions," she said. "Lucas made a really thorough diagram of the mansion, which he proudly showed me, and only me, before he locked it in the hardware store safe. I was a bit bored, but given my almost-fiancée status, I tried my best to pay attention. Now I'm glad I did, which should be a lesson to me, if I can remember it. I do, however, remember what was on Lucas's diagram. The relevant parts, anyway."

Olivia swallowed a bite of chewy, gingery cookie and felt a familiar ping of pleasure. "So you're saying we wouldn't actually have to break into the hardware store and crack Lucas's safe to steal the diagram? Why am I not reassured?"

"Don't be silly, Livie. I have a key to the store, and I know the combination to the safe. But no, we won't have to use them. I remember that Lucas had marked some parts of the house to be blocked off. He said he wouldn't bother renovating those areas. He didn't want to waste time and money, since he didn't expect anyone to be living in the mansion. No one had been in those parts of the mansion for years, even decades, and he worried they might not be safe."

Olivia had finished eating the unexpected cookie, but she no longer wanted to interrupt. She was hooked.

"The attic was one area. Lucas said he'd looked inside and found it empty, plus a couple of floorboards were rotting. He also found two short doorways that were sort of hidden. And here's the really interesting part — Lucas never noticed them before. He'd been in that mansion many, many times, what with his fascination with architecture. He'd wanted to renovate the place for years."

Olivia couldn't help herself. "Did Lucas find anything behind those doors? I'm dying here."

"Investigation is not his thing," Maddie said with fondness. "One door is at the back of a storage closet under the front stairs, and the other is in the root cellar wall. No one goes down there because of the creepy crawlies, but my brave Lucas isn't bothered by a few bugs or snakes or —"

"I get the picture," Olivia said. "I might never get it out of my head."

"Lucas found the door in the root cellar when he tried to move a cupboard filled with old, empty canning jars. The cupboard fell apart. I won't describe the stuff that fell out. Lucas cleaned up the mess and saw the door in the wall. He tried to open it, but it was stuck shut, so he gave up. He wondered if it might be some sort of tunnel for helping slaves escape or something."

"Uh, I doubt that," Olivia said. "The Chatterleys were known for owning slaves, not helping them escape. More likely it's an old hiding place or storage area of some sort. Oh . . . are you thinking the Chatterleys might have used it as a safe for their valuables?"

"Well, it's a thought," Maddie said. "A root cellar seems like a logical place to hide cookie cutters. I mean, cookies are food of the first order, plus who wants to go treasure hunting in a root cellar?"

"Definitely not me," Olivia said.

Maddie slid a lid on a cake pan filled with the last batch of decorated cookies for the fete. "It's only twelve thirty a.m.," she said. "Are you thinking what I'm thinking?"

"That we should finish cleaning the kitchen and get some sleep?"

"Antique cookie cutters? Chatterley Mansion? Come on, Livie, we'll never get another opportunity like this. I mean, I'm truly sorry that Hermione is in the hospital with a heart attack, and I hope she comes through okay."

"But the sooner she recovers," Olivia said, "the sooner she's back in the mansion, and our opportunity will be gone, right?"

"Well, at least until she sells the house, and then who knows?"

Olivia wedged a mixing bowl into the dishwasher, added soap, and pressed the on button. "I forgot to mention, Constance called earlier and left a message on my cell. She said Hermione told her to forget about putting the mansion on the market. She didn't say why she'd changed her mind. Constance was curious, and so am I."

"There you are, then," Maddie said. "Once Hermione comes home from the hospital, our chances go bye-bye. I had a good look around when we were visiting her, and I think she's been tearing the house apart looking for the Chatterley cookie cutters. Paine probably told her about the collection and how valuable it might be. Maybe she decided to do away with him so

265

she wouldn't have to share the profits."

"But, Maddie, how could Hermione manage the search on her own? If Matthew frightened her into a heart attack, all that heavy lifting would probably have killed her." Olivia lifted her pooped pup from his blanket under the kitchen desk. She'd allowed him to sleep in the kitchen due to his recent fireworks-induced trauma. "Time for bed, little guy." Spunky whimpered without opening his eyes.

"Livie, what if heavy lifting is what caused Hermione's heart attack? Did anyone actually see Matthew threaten her?"

"Not that I know of." With Spunky draped over her shoulder Olivia gathered the small bottles of gel food coloring scattered around the worktable and tightened all the tops. She felt torn between her rational, grown-up self and the cookie-cutter hunter bubbling to the surface. Finding even a tiny fraction of the Chatterley cutter collection would be a thrill she'd never forget. However, conducting a secret search of Chatterley Mansion while its mistress was hospitalized with a heart attack struck Olivia as callous . . . and so tempting.

Olivia's temptation went beyond the Chatterley cutter collection. Ever since Paine and Hermione's arrival in town, Olivia had felt she was missing something. Paine had behaved like two different people, which was odd enough, but it was really Hermione she'd puzzled over. Olivia very much wanted to know about Hermione's connection with Chatterley Heights's mayor, Karen Evanson. She didn't believe she'd heard the truth yet from either woman. A search of Hermione's belongings might yield a clue or two.

"If we are caught," Olivia said, "Del will be furious."

"We won't be," Maddie said. "We're only going to pick up some of Hermione's clothes to bring to the hospital. It's a small-town gesture."

"Oh yeah, that'll work," Olivia said. "Del might want me to do that at some point, but not in the middle of the night and without permission."

"There's that," Maddie admitted. "It's a chance I'm willing to take. Livie, it's okay if you don't want to go. I can handle it on my own. There's probably nothing to find anyway, but at least I'll know."

"I can't let you go alone." Snuggling her drowsy pup against her chest, Olivia held open the kitchen door and doused the light. "Let's grab a couple hours of sleep first. By three a.m., the streets will be as deserted as they'll ever be. You can crash in my guest room."

"I'll hang out on the sofa," Maddie said. "I won't be able to sleep, so there's no point in messing up your guest bed. I'll have double-strength coffee perked by two forty-five. If you're not up by three, I'll leave without you."

CHAPTER FIFTEEN

Olivia's alarm awakened her from a disturbing dream in which she was being pursued by a crazed gingerbread man wielding a licorice hatchet. She was trying to run up a staircase made of pearlized sugar sprinkles, which rolled away as she stepped on them. Since Olivia was not prone to nightmares, she figured this one was guilt induced. However, she had no intention of backing out of the plan to search Chatterley Mansion. If she did, Maddie would just go by herself anyway.

The aroma of fresh coffee helped her roll out of bed, fully dressed. Spunky opened his eyes without lifting his head. He saw nothing to convince him it was time to get up. Olivia left quietly, as if she were making a bathroom run.

"Good," Maddie said as Olivia entered the kitchen. "I wasn't looking forward to dragging you out of bed. Spunky might get all protective."

"I should hope so." Olivia drained her coffee. "Let's get going before Spunky catches on. I just need to collect a couple things on the way out." She sorted through a kitchen drawer and found a sturdy screwdriver, which she slipped into her jacket pocket. She also grabbed two flashlights, one of which she handed to Maddie. Her cell phone lay on the small table by the front door of her apartment. She left it turned off and dropped it into another pocket.

Within minutes, they were on the front porch of The Gingerbread House. Olivia scanned the town square for movement and saw none. It had been a full day for the citizens of Chatterley Heights, and she hoped they were all sound asleep. Matthew Fabrizio, incarcerated or not, was probably deep in alcohol-induced slumber. Olivia felt a pinch of sympathy for Heather.

With Maddie in the lead, they followed a circuitous route to Chatterley Mansion and slipped down the alley to the back door. Olivia was pleased to notice that several lights had been left on, perhaps to make the house look occupied while so many strangers were in town. No lights shone in the kitchen or over the alley door, for which Olivia was grateful. She felt confident they

270

had entered unseen.

Maddie aimed her flashlight at the kitchen floor. "Remember there's stuff all over the place," she whispered. "It's easy to trip, even with a light on." They picked their way through the dining room and down the hallway to the front of the staircase, where a door led to a closet under the stairs. "Lucas is so thorough," Maddie said as the closet door opened smoothly. "He actually oiled all the hinges in the house. I could have killed Paine myself when he complained about the mansion being in bad shape."

"I wouldn't repeat that if I were you."

"I'm just saying." Maddie poked her head inside the closet and pulled out a tasseled lamp shade with a rip in the fabric. "We'll have to excavate our way in. At the back, Lucas found a door that went up about to his waist. Luckily, it'll be higher for us." She handed Olivia several more broken pieces of what were once lovely examples of nineteenth-century furnishing. "That should do it." Maddie shone her flashlight on a small door painted the same light yellow as the closet walls. The door stuck when she pulled the wooden knob, but it yielded on the next try. Maddie bent through the open doorway and disappeared into darkness.

"Come on in," said Maddie's disembodied

voice. "I feel so Nancy Drew-ish. I haven't had this much fun since you and I were twelve, and we sneaked into that creepy old farmhouse on the edge of town. Remember that? We thought it was haunted." Maddie aimed her flashlight near the opening so Olivia could see her way.

"That place really was haunted," Olivia said as she scooted through the short doorway. "By a flock of pigeons. I also remember I nearly fell through a rotted floorboard."

"Yeah, good times." Maddie moved her light along the inner walls of the small hidden closet-within-a-closet. "Looks like old papers and books. Probably nothing useful, but it's worth a few minutes." She sat cross-legged on the floor, stirring up decades of dust.

Olivia sneezed twice and decided against sitting. "I hope there aren't any mice in here," she said, kneeling to pick up a small book with a blank, stained cloth cover. Opening to a random page, Olivia saw faded, cramped handwriting. "I wonder if this is a journal of some sort," she said.

"Cool! Read some to me. I've found nothing but boring old receipts and household budget figures. Although I suppose historians might drool over this stuff." Maddie abandoned the papers and began looking for a more promising stack.

Olivia held her flashlight on a page in the little book. "I think the handwriting style is really old. I can't make sense of it."

"Hand it over. Aunt Sadie told me about old cursive writing when we saw the Declaration of Independence at the National Archives Building in DC." Maddie's flashlight cast shadows on her face as she frowned in concentration. After examining several pages, she looked up and grinned. "I think I know what this might be. See that mark that looks like a big '2'? That's a capital Q in old cursive. So '2uarts' is really 'Quarts.' Hey, this is a recipe book! It's written in a run-on style, like paragraphs of description. Not the way we write recipes today." Maddie turned several more pages. "Ooh, and this recipe," she said, tapping the page, "has got to be for some type of gingerbread cookie." She handed the book to Olivia.

"I don't see —"

"I know it's hard to make out," Maddie said, "but I know what I'm looking for. See that word there, with what looks like the letters 'fs'? That's really 'ss,' not 'fs,' so the word is 'molasses.' That's how folks used to write when they used quill pens. I think it was because quill pens left globs of ink on the paper if you lifted them, so people tried to connect letters to keep the pen on the paper." She took the book back from Olivia and leafed through it. "There's no name in this. Or date. I'm guessing it was written by an early Chatterley cook, then brought along when the mansion was built."

"Would a cook have been able to read and write in those days?" Olivia asked.

Maddie shrugged. "Don't know. Maybe she was from an educated family in England and came to the colonies alone. Or her husband died, and she had to find a way to survive." Maddie unzipped her backpack. "I'm taking this with me. It's my duty as a citizen of Chatterley Heights. Hermione Chatterley hasn't shown an excess of appreciation for the historical artifacts in this house. I wouldn't put it past her to sell everything behind our backs or throw stuff away."

"Presuming anything is left unbroken," Olivia said.

"Exactly."

"We've been in here for at least twenty minutes," Olivia said. "Fascinating as all this is, I don't see any sign of cookie cutters. We need to move on."

Maddie rolled to her knees. "Time to

battle the creepy crawlies in the root cellar."

"Before we head downstairs," Olivia said, "I want a look at Hermione's room."

"For anything in particular?"

"Not sure." Olivia crawled back into the larger closet and turned off her flashlight before returning to the hallway. "There's something unreal about Hermione. She's way too good at making up stories, like the one about Karen. I want to know if there's anything else she's fibbing about."

Leaving the mansion lights out, Olivia and Maddie hurried up the staircase to Hermione's bedroom. Once inside the room, they found the shades pulled down. Since the overhead light might show around the edges of the shades, they turned on their flashlights.

"At least this room hasn't been ransacked," Olivia said. "I know the police searched it after Paine's death. They didn't find anything incriminating, or they would have arrested Hermione."

"So what's left for us to find?" Maddie asked. "And how will we know it when we see it?"

"Look for anything personal: photos, newspaper clippings, papers." Olivia shone her flashlight under Hermione's bed, looked under her mattress, and examined her pillows. "If it's important, Hermione would have hidden it carefully. The police were searching for possible weapons or additional drugs that might have been used on Paine. But I want to know about Hermione's past, her secrets. The police probably ignored personal items unless they might tie her to her husband's death."

Maddie tackled Hermione's walnut dressing table, a well-preserved antique with a marble insert. "Wow, Livie, come look at this." Maddie had pushed aside used lipsticks and a half-empty jar of inexpensive facial moisturizer to make room for the table's one drawer. "This drawer is crammed with brand-new, unopened cosmetics," Maddie said. "I wonder what the cops thought of that."

"If they were guys, maybe they thought nothing of it. Or the stores Hermione was stealing from decided not to report the thefts," Olivia said. "I'm not sure I would."

"What happens in Chatterley Heights stays in Chatterley Heights?"

"At least until the celebration is over." Olivia had moved on to Hermione's closet. She picked up a pair of worn leather walking shoes that had new heels. On impulse, she twisted one of the heels. It took some muscle, but finally the heel shifted and slid open. The heel was hollow inside, and empty. Olivia closed the heel, picked up the matching shoe, and tried the same maneuver. It, too, was empty. At least she now knew that Hermione sometimes carried items she wanted to hide.

Olivia searched through the ten or so dresses hanging in Hermione's closet. All were variations of the great-grandmother style Hermione favored. At the far end of the closet hung a canvas coat. Olivia pulled it off the hanger for a closer look. The beige coat looked well worn and was stained down the front with what might have been coffee. It didn't strike Olivia as good enough to bring overseas. She lay it on the bed and examined the pockets, all of which were empty. She spread the coat open. The lining looked new, which struck her as odd. Why reline such a battered old coat. Olivia lifted the lining away from the coat fabric. "Bingo," she said.

"What?" Maddie left her search and joined Olivia. "Two linings," Maddie said. "The hidden lining has stitching in it, see? I'll bet those are hidden pockets. Okay, this is now officially fun."

Olivia turned the coat inside out, revealing the inside of the hidden lining. There were, indeed, four pockets. Two of them were empty.

Maddie reached inside the remaining two and came out with two British passports. Opening one, she said, "This is Hermione's photo, but the name is Portia Carswell. So this is why Hermione and Paine Chatterley didn't show up on the Internet. I would so love to know why they were using assumed names. Ooh, maybe they were international jewel thieves."

"If they were jewel thieves," Olivia said, "they must have been incompetent. On the other hand, Hermione did steal from some local businesses, so the thief part is accurate." Olivia opened the second passport, which contained a photo of Paine and the name Howard Carswell. So they'd swapped first initials. "Hermione and Paine must have been in hiding. Or they were involved in something illegal. Or both." She returned both passports to their hiding places and rehung the coat. "Unfortunately for us, we have to tell Del about this."

"Not right this minute, though," Maddie pleaded. "We have one more hidden storage area yet to explore. Hermione is in the hospital; she's not going anywhere. This information can wait awhile, right? Livie? I know Del will be angry, but I'll tell him I came here alone so he won't get mad at you."

"I guess so," Olivia said. "I'll take care of telling Del. He'd never believe I came here without you."

"Can we go to the root cellar now?" Maddie asked. "I can't wait to see what's behind that door Lucas found. If there's any place left unexplored in the mansion, it would be the root cellar."

"Just a sec." To be thorough, Olivia looked through the remaining items in Hermione's closet. When she came across a second coat, made of fine wool, she removed it from its hanger. "Might as well check out this one, too." Olivia felt inside the pockets. "Aha. This is my lucky night." She extracted a battered envelope, taped shut. Inside she found a collection of photographs in various shapes and sizes. Pausing at a small, square, black-and-white photo of an infant, Olivia said, "Hey, Maddie, take a look at this. Does that look like a newborn to you?"

Maddie settled cross-legged on the floor and shone her flashlight over the photo. "It reminds me of those photos some hospitals take right after a newborn baby is cleaned up. Several of my cousins have sent me pictures like this one. Personally, I wouldn't want one in my portfolio." She turned the print over. "No identification, not even a date. That's weird. My cousins always list names, dates, weight, length, actual minute of birth, duration of labor. . . ."

Olivia joined Maddie on the floor. "When the Chatterleys first showed up at our store on Tuesday evening, I remember Paine saying he and Hermione had never been blessed with children. I wonder if they lost a child. This baby's eyes are closed. That might not mean anything, of course; he or she might have been asleep. I imagine being born is exhausting."

Handing back the snapshot, Maddie said, "It's sort of creepy to think someone would clean up a dead infant to take its picture."

"I can understand it," Olivia said. "People grieve in different ways." She flipped through the remaining photos. "A few of these might be older relatives, probably Hermione's, since Paine apparently cut off contact with his own parents. The rest are pictures of Hermione and Paine in what I suspect were happier days. Look at this one." The dog-eared, faded photo she handed to Maddie showed the Chatterley couple dressed for a special occasion.

"Wow," Maddie said. "I bet they were going to a Euro disco party. Or maybe a costume party; the look is a bit seventies, and Paine wouldn't have arrived in Europe until the early eighties, right? Look at Hermione's dress — the empire waist, filmy fabric, short. . . . She had good legs, too. And her hair! It was a lot like mine only honey blond and better behaved."

"I barely recognize Paine with his hair hanging over his ears instead of brushed back," Olivia said. "They look happy. They're holding hands and grinning at the camera. I'd love to know who took the photo." She turned it over and found nothing. "It's odd that Hermione didn't write anything on any of these pictures. My mom always records as much detail as she can fit in the space available. She says memories fade over a lifetime, so if you want to remember, write it down."

"I suppose we can't keep these photos, can we?" Maddie asked.

"Not a chance. Too risky."

Maddie reached in her jeans pocket for her cell phone. "I'll send them to my computer. They might turn out crappy, but you never know."

While Maddie clicked each photo with her cell phone camera, Olivia finished searching the closet and every drawer in the bedroom. Hermione had brought very little with her. On the top shelf of the closet, Olivia found several items that had come from Chatterley Heights businesses, confirming their accusations that Hermione had stolen from them. Olivia left them untouched.

Checking her watch, Olivia said, "We need to get a move on. It's going on four o'clock."

"I'm good," Maddie said. "Let us adjourn to the root cellar, shall we?"

"If we must." Olivia replaced Hermione's photos in their envelope, which she slid back into the coat pocket. "I hope those pictures weren't in some special order that only Hermione would know."

"I doubt she will dust them for fingerprints," Maddie said. "Come on. The creepy crawlies await."

"This is why I've never ventured down to the root cellar underneath The Gingerbread House," Olivia said as she tried to extricate her hair from a clinging cobweb.

"I didn't know there was one," Maddie said. "Watch it. I believe I hear the scuffling of tiny rodent feet."

"They better not be rats."

"I had a pet rat when I was a kid. I named him Sir Reginald the Rat. He was sweet."

"Your aunt Sadie was always a patient woman." Olivia swept her flashlight across the dirt floor in front of her. So far, she hadn't encountered much insect and animal life, but she suspected that armies of mice, rats, and spiders were gathering in the shadows, waiting for her to let down her guard.

"Here's where Lucas found a door. He wanted to make sure no one got hurt trying to open it." Maddie aimed her flashlight at five rectangular cuts of unfinished wood, each about three by six feet in size and one-half inch thick. They leaned lengthwise in a thick stack against the wall. Olivia ran her finger lightly along the edge of one piece and noticed the edge was smooth, as if it had been intended for use.

"Now I'm really curious," Olivia said. "Let's move this wood aside. I want to see that door."

Olivia positioned her flashlight on a nearby shelf so it illuminated the boards. Maddie did the same. They tackled the first length of wood and found it difficult to slide along the uneven floor. Their combined strength wasn't enough to lift it slightly off the floor, either.

"I keep forgetting how strong Lucas is," Olivia said. "This has got to be solid oak. It's much larger and heavier than a modern door, and there are four more of them." She retrieved her flashlight and swept it around the area. "I think we have enough room to swing them sideways and 'walk' them out of the way."

"Livie, I have known you all these years, and I had no idea you possessed such an impressive spatial imagination."

"Chalk it up to self-preservation," Olivia said. "I'm hoping to avoid wrenching my back moving those suckers."

Maddie gripped one side of the wood with one hand and the top corner with the other. "Ready? Come on, Livie, I can't stand the suspense much longer."

"Ready as I'll ever be," Olivia said as she grasped the other edge. "Let's walk it out from the stack a bit." She managed to slide her edge away from the wall. "Now you slide your side forward. Good. Now you stay where you are, and I'll walk my end around in front of you in a semicircle. See how it works?"

"Cool. I'm sure I could have thought of that," Maddie said. "In about a million years."

"You are the adventurer; I am the planner," Olivia said. "It works for us. Now we walk the board backward and lean it against the wall."

"Why can't we just let it fall against the wall?" Maddie asked as she let go of her grip on the wood.

"Because it'll make too much —" Olivia didn't let go in time, and the wood slammed into her finger, pinning it against the wall. "Ouch!" She flinched as she extracted her finger.

"Oh no! I'm sorry," Maddie said. "Did you break anything?"

Olivia flexed her fingers. "No broken bones or skin. Just a nasty pinch."

"Should we stop?"

"No way. Neither bugs, nor blood, nor broken bones . . ." The maneuver went more quickly and smoothly the second time through, except they both let go a moment too soon, and the wood landed against the wall with a thud.

"We should probably try to be quieter," Olivia said. "Just in case."

The last two boards landed more smoothly. Olivia took stock of the result and determined that they could open the door, if it opened at all, at least halfway. "A job well done," she said. "Are you sure Lucas didn't at least try to peek inside before he covered the door?"

"Sweet Lucas," Maddie said, shaking her head. "He is totally adorable and, of course, manly, but avid curiosity isn't his strongest characteristic. He figured he'd do a more thorough plan of the mansion once the celebration was over, when he'd have more time to work on his video of the restoration work. So yeah, if Lucas said he didn't look behind the door, he didn't look behind the door."

"Well then, let's see if it even opens after all this time and dampness." The door in the wall came up to Olivia's chest. She clutched the small, rusty knob and yanked. It came off in her hand.

"Crap," Maddie said.

Olivia unzipped her jacket pocket and drew out her screwdriver.

"There's that planning gene again," Maddie said.

"Can't help myself."

"Hey, it's a quality I count on." Maddie retrieved her flashlight and aimed it at the edge of the door.

"I'll try not to damage anything," Olivia said, "though we already moved the boards and yanked the knob off, so it will be obvious to Lucas that someone tried to open this door. If he ever gets to finish the restoration, that is." Olivia kept her hurt finger out of harm's way.

"Have I mentioned Lucas's lack of curiosity? He'll assume another worker moved the boards and the knob fell off on its own. I doubt Lucas would notice screwdriver marks, either. If he ever mentions them, I'll distract him. I have my ways."

Olivia chuckled, then swore under her breath as the screwdriver took out a chunk of wall. "I thought this wall would be harder; it's solid wood. I forgot about damp- ness and dry rot."

While Olivia worked on the door, Maddie said, "We're right under the kitchen, but maybe this wall isn't flush with the wall upstairs. That would allow space for a stor- age area. Maybe it's a secret hiding place for valuables. I'm thinking cookie cutters here, of course."

Another chunk of wall fell out, and Olivia said, "We might as well go for it." She wedged the end of her screwdriver as far as she could into the crevice between the door and the wall. As she hit the screwdriver handle with her fist, she felt it sink deeper. "Here goes," she said as she pushed the screwdriver handle toward the wall. The door groaned, then cracked open a fraction of an inch.

Maddie's flashlight bobbed as she gasped with excitement. "Can you open it?"

"Almost." Olivia reinserted her screw- driver and pushed hard on the handle. She felt the door shift an inch or so, scraping the floor. Handing her screwdriver to Maddie, Olivia slid her fingers through the opening, grabbed the edge of the door, and pulled with all her strength. She grimaced at the pressure on her finger.

Maddie squealed with excitement. "It worked!"

Olivia put her fingers to her lips. "You can scream later."

"Yes, ma'am. Can I go in first?"

"With my gratitude," Olivia said. Unlike Lucas, she had plenty of imagination, and she didn't like what she was picturing beyond the door.

Apparently, Maddie had rosier expectations because she eagerly slid through the opening, disappearing behind the door. After several moments, Maddie said, "Crap."

"What? Are you okay?" Olivia envisioned everything from a swarm of rats to a pile of bones.

"I'm fine, but . . . well, take a look for yourself."

Olivia peeked through the opening and saw Maddie's back. "Could you move aside? You're blocking the view."

"I'm coming out. There's not much room to maneuver in here," Maddie said.

As Olivia edged through the narrow opening, her heart climbed up her throat. Maddie had not looked thrilled. As Olivia swirled her flashlight around, she understood why. It was impossible tell what had once been behind the door, even whether it had been a tunnel or a room. There was barely enough space for one person, and she had to crouch to avoid bumping her head against a rotting beam. Inches beyond her toes, dirt piled higher than her head, making further movement impossible. The dirt might have fallen through the disintegrating ceiling, or perhaps the construction had never been completed. Olivia was surprised by the depth of her disappointment.

"What a letdown," Olivia said as she reentered the root cellar.

"Shh," Maddie whispered, her hand on Olivia's shoulder. "I think I hear something." Maddie pointed upward.

Olivia switched off her flashlight. At first she heard nothing but the random creaks that old houses always make. She whispered, "I don't —" But then she heard the distinct tinkle of a glass or plate smashing. Someone was in the house. It was Olivia's turn to say, "Crap."

Maddie leaned toward Olivia and whispered, "What should we do?"

Olivia could barely see the boards against the wall, but she knew they would be a red flag to someone who knew the mansion well. Besides, the hidden door was open. With the lights out, she couldn't bring to mind anyplace in the root cellar that might provide cover. If whoever was upstairs came downstairs . . . Olivia put her lips close to Maddie's ear. "We're probably goners," she said, "but all we can do is be quiet and wait. Maybe whoever is up there doesn't know about the root cellar."

"What are the odds of that?" Maddie whispered.

"Slim to none. But we have no choice." Olivia clutched Maddie above the elbow and edged them away from the open door. The sounds upstairs grew more distant, as if the intruder had left the kitchen and dining room and moved to another area of the mansion. This might be the person who'd been searching the mansion at night. It couldn't be Hermione Chatterley unless she had miraculously recovered from her heart attack and was determined to bring on a second one. A chill quivered through Olivia's body, and it had nothing to do with the clammy air in the root cellar. It was a good bet that whoever seemed to be ransacking the mansion at that moment was also involved in Paine Chatterley's murder.

Olivia risked switching on her flashlight to illuminate their way to a less obvious area of the root cellar. There wasn't much to choose from, but in one corner she saw a chipped ceramic gas stove, a 1950s model. She and Maddie might be able to squeeze behind it without too many limbs sticking out. She guided Maddie's elbow toward the dubious shelter.

There was enough room behind the stove to hide both women if they turned sideways and squatted, which meant being up close and personal with the floor. Maddie used her flashlight to take a quick look and said, "Ick. I propose we stand up unless the danger becomes imminent."

"I second." Olivia slid behind the stove and thought about brightly colored sugar cookies, lots of them, in comforting shapes, like bunnies and puppies.

"Who do you think is up there?" Maddie asked in a low voice.

Olivia hesitated, puzzled by the level of destruction that seemed to be going on upstairs. "I think this is about more than cookie cutters. That's a very angry person, or I'm not the second best baker in town."

"You're tied with Aunt Sadie for second, but I get your point. Matthew Fabrizio is the most obvious candidate, but he's in jail. Again."

"We're assuming he is," Olivia said. "Del didn't say he'd actually found a gun, so he might have released Matthew by now. I wonder how angry Quill Latimer is after all these years. He didn't seem too bothered when Paine Chatterley showed up at the store Tuesday evening, but he controls his feelings well. On the surface, anyway. Karen has been pretty upset with both Chatterleys ever since they arrived, and Rosemarie was beside herself about Matthew."

"I can't blame her," Maddie said. "Paine played a nasty trick on Matthew, letting him think he'd be rewarded for finishing the gingerbread trim."

A scraping sound, like heavy furniture being shoved across a wood floor, startled them into ducking down. "That sounded close," Olivia whispered. "The dining room, maybe."

"Do you really think a woman would be knocking furniture around like that?"

"Sexist," Olivia said. "I'm not sure how strong Rosemarie is. Karen, on the other hand . . . Mom told me Karen can run circles around her — which is not easy, I can tell you. I know Karen works out, too." Olivia shot up and shook her leg. "Ugh, I think something is crawling on my ankle. There, it's gone."

"Shh, listen," Maddie said.

After several moments, Olivia said, "I don't hear anything."

"Exactly. While you were distracted, I heard footsteps overhead, in the kitchen. Then a door opened and closed. I'm thinking our short-tempered visitor has left."

"That seems abrupt," Olivia said.

"Let's get out of here." Maddie headed for the stairs. "I'm totally cured of my longing for adventure."

"Who are you and what have you done with my friend? Okay, let's make sure it's safe up there, and then you go on home," Olivia said. "I want to take another look around the mansion."

"The mansion is probably wrecked even worse than it was before. What more do you need to know?"

"I'm just wondering. . . ." Olivia reached the top of the stairs and peered through the door. "All clear." She listened for several moments before whispering, "I think we're okay."

Maddie followed her into the kitchen. "What were you wondering?"

Olivia led the way through the dining room, using her flashlight to help them avoid obstacles. As they entered the hallway, Olivia said, "I'm wondering if perhaps the intruder found what he or she was looking for." She ran her beam along the wall, where framed paintings of nineteenth-century Chatterleys hung askew.

"Aha," Maddie said. "You're thinking the intruder has been searching for the Chatterley cookie-cutter collection and finally found it?"

"The Chatterley collection . . . maybe."

"What else is there to look for?" Maddie sounded frustrated.

"Let's check the front parlor," Olivia said, "and then call it a night. We can still grab a few hours of sleep before we have to start setting up our booth for the fete."

"Why the front parlor?"

"Because before we examined the contents of the hidden storage area under the staircase, I peeked into the front parlor with my flashlight. I figured those velvet curtains were heavy enough to hide the light from anyone outside. The parlor looked the way it did when we visited Hermione — neat and orderly."

The front parlor's heavy curtains also blocked the moonlight, leaving the room in complete darkness. Olivia switched on her flashlight, and Maddie did the same.

"Whoa," Maddie said in a hushed voice. "This is not how I remember the front parlor from our visit with Hermione."

"Look over there, along the wall," Olivia said. "That long, heavy bureau has been moved away from the wall. There's no carpet under it. I think that's what we heard from downstairs, the bureau being scraped across bare wood." She switched on an etched-glass table lamp. Warm light circled out, illuminating a section of wall that the long bureau had hidden. "Well, well," Olivia said. "What have we here?"

Maddie whistled softly. "It looks like some kind of safe built into the wall, and the door is open." She shone her light on the small enclosure. "It's made of wood." Maddie examined the open door. "This isn't a safe," she said, "just a plain door with a ring pull so it doesn't stick out too far from the wall. It looks old. I know this bureau goes back to the 1800s, and Lucas decided not to bother painting the wall behind it. I bet a Chatterley had the opening created and put the heavy bureau in front to hide it." Maddie shone her light deep inside the compartment. "If this is where the cutter collection was secreted, it isn't here now."

"That space could hold a few cutters, but not many," Olivia said. "The opening is fairly short and goes back a ways, almost like a letter slot. Maybe this is where important papers were kept. What we don't know is whether it has been empty for decades or was emptied in the last half hour."

Maddie ran her hand over the newly refinished wood floor, now freshly scraped in a semicircle. "This is definitely what we heard from downstairs shortly before the intruder took off. I'll bet you a six-quart Pro Line stand mixer with all the attachments that he found something really important and took it with him."

"Or her," Olivia said. "Hermione Chatterley might not be able to move this bureau, but a younger, healthier woman could."

As she turned off the lamp, Maddie asked, "If we knew what was hidden — assuming it was still here — do you think we would know who killed Paine Chatterley?"

"I think we'd be a lot closer to knowing," Olivia said.

At four thirty a.m., Olivia unlocked the front door of her apartment, and Spunky shot past her. He stopped suddenly about halfway down the stairs.

Olivia called to him, "Spunks? It's just me." Whimpering, Spunky ran back up the stairs and into the apartment. Olivia followed, locking up behind her, while Spunky raced around the apartment like a pup possessed. Olivia had never seen him so frantic. She had left him alone in the apartment before, but never so late. Maybe her absence had made him feel trapped again, like he was back in the puppy mill.

When Spunky trotted back into the living room, Olivia sat on the sofa and held out her arms to him. He hesitated for only a second before leaping onto her lap and snuggling close. Olivia realized he hadn't felt trapped; he thought she had abandoned him.

"You funny little creature, I wouldn't abandon you for all the cookie cutters in the world," Olivia murmured, rubbing her cheek against the silky hair on his head. She noticed that Spunky was starting to need a bath. It was a smell she was growing to love as much as the aroma of lemon sugar cookies fresh out of the oven. Well, almost as much.

With Spunky relaxing in the crook of one arm, Olivia headed for her bedroom. The little guy had worn himself out; he barely opened his eyes when she nestled him at the foot of her bed. She dropped her clothes on the floor, pulled on a long T-shirt, and crawled under the covers. Leaning on her pillow, she checked her cell messages. She found one, from Rosemarie York, who said, "Livie, I know it's late, but I wanted to catch you before you tried to talk to Del. It's okay, he let Matthew out of jail about half an hour ago. The poor boy is home with me and really tired, so I sent him to bed. The sheriff said he hadn't found any sign of a gun, at least so far." Olivia heard Rosemarie's voice deepen with anger. "I think Hermione was confused by firecrackers some kids were setting off, so she was expecting to see a gun. I don't think that woman is right in the head. Anyway, thank you, Livie, for saying you'd talk to Del about Matthew, but now you don't have to. Hope I didn't wake you."

Olivia checked the time of the call. One a.m. She'd turned her cell off by then. If Matthew Fabrizio was free by one a.m., he was back on the Chatterley Mansion intruder suspect list. For that matter, so was Rosemarie York. She'd sounded angry with Hermione. Moreover, Rosemarie was passionate about antique cookie cutters. She could easily have copied Matthew's key to the mansion so she could search for the famed collection.

According to Olivia's cell phone, it was four forty-five. Her mother would tell her to hit the off button and get some sleep. Her mother was nearly always right. Olivia set the alarm for eight a.m. and plugged in the charger. Since the store would be closed all day Sunday, she'd have plenty of time to take a shower before she and Maddie had to set up their Gingerbread House booth in the town square park.

Olivia slid farther down between her covers, already imagining herself wandering through a field of decorated sugar-cookie flowers waving gently in the breeze. She found a baby pink daisy with rose sprinkles, balanced on a red licorice stem. As she bent to pick it, Olivia heard a harsh scraping sound behind her. Her eyes shot open, and her heart thumped. Someone must have broken into her apartment. She raised up on one elbow to listen and saw that Spunky hadn't so much as twitched. If someone were in her apartment, her faithful protector, all five pounds of him, would have raced out to subdue the intruder. In a half-dreaming state, she'd remembered the sound of the bureau scraping across the parlor floor, that's all.

Olivia lay back against her pillow but couldn't relax. She knew what was wrong. She felt guilty. She had to tell Del about the intruder in Chatterley Mansion. It hadn't occurred to Olivia that her little adventure with Maddie would encounter so many complications. It wouldn't be easy to make Del see the innocence behind their ill-fated search for the fabled Chatterley cookie cutters. Well, she might as well get it over with. She reached to her bedside table for her cell and punched in her speed-dial number for the Chatterley Heights Police Station. After one ring, she snapped her cell shut. What was she thinking? It was barely past five a.m., an odd time to return from a lighthearted cookie-cutter hunt in someone else's locked home. She would wait until morning to call Del. A few hours' sleep and she'd know what to say. All would be well. She put her phone back on the table, pulled the covers up to her chin, and returned to her field of sugar-cookie flowers.

CHAPTER SIXTEEN

Yanked from a deep sleep, Olivia bolted upright in bed as Julie Andrews belted out, "The hills are alive with the sound of music." Spunky leaped to his little paws and let loose a volley of yaps. When Ms. Andrews repeated her musical observation, Olivia identified the source as her cell phone. Still half asleep, she reached toward her bedside table and fumbled for the light switch. As her phone sang again, Olivia flipped it open and yelled, "I get it, I get it!"

"Olivia? What's happened? I'm coming right over." It was Del, sounding worried.

"Oh, Del, I'm sorry, it's just that you woke me out of a sound sleep. Is something wrong?"

"You tell me," Del said.

"I'm not the one calling at" — she checked the backup alarm clock she kept by her bed — "six thirty. As in morning."

"Livie, you called me." Del was miffed.

Then she remembered. She'd dialed the police station and let the phone ring once before changing her mind. "Are you at work already?"

"It's fete day," Del said, "and the peace in Chatterley Heights hasn't been very good about keeping itself lately. So why did you call me?"

"I'm sorry, Del, I didn't want to call your cell in case you were asleep, and it didn't occur to me at the time that the station phone would have caller ID."

"A police station without caller ID? You're kidding, right?"

"Did I mention I was very tired?"

"Livie, I'll have you know the Chatterley Heights Police Station has the finest secondhand equipment money once bought."

Olivia was relieved to hear a touch of humor replace Del's irritability. He'd need it. She took a deep breath and filled him in on some of what happened in the Chatterley Mansion only a few hours earlier. She left Maddie out of it.

"Let me get this straight," Del said after Olivia finished her summary. "You're claiming it was merely a childlike flight of fancy that sent you to the mansion. It occurred to you that a Victorian house might contain secret hiding places, and you wanted a look while Hermione was . . . otherwise engaged."

Okay, maybe Olivia had left out a few details. "When you put it like that, it sounds a bit cold and crazy."

"A bit."

"Del, I've been working so hard for so long to help get this celebration weekend off the ground. Karen orders me around, the store is really busy. . . . I haven't had much fun for quite a while. I just wanted to enjoy a cookie-cutter adventure. If that makes sense." Olivia heard Del chuckle and hoped that was a good sign.

"From you, it makes sense," Del said. "Only here's the thing: you heard a prowler in the mansion — other than yourself, that is — and you didn't call me or Cody as soon as possible. Why?"

Olivia was ready for that question, and she didn't even have to lie. Much. "I'd turned my cell off, and it plays that irritating little jingle when I turn it on. So I needed to wait until the intruder left, but that took quite awhile, and then I wanted to get safely home first, but by the time I got home it was really late, and the intruder was long gone anyway, and I was so tired I simply fell asleep." *Could I have sounded more frantic . . . and guilty?* Olivia was grateful Del couldn't see her cringe.

"Uh-huh," Del said. "Haven't you left out a few details?"

"Details?"

"Yeah, like about Maddie being there with you. And that you two managed to break open a hidden door in the wall of the root cellar, a door that led to a pile of dirt? Oh, and after the prowler left, you and Maddie discovered the front parlor ransacked, a large bureau pushed away from the wall, and a small wall enclosure left open and empty? Those little details."

Uh-oh. "Maddie told you, didn't she?" It hadn't occurred to Olivia that Maddie would confess to Del, especially so quickly. It wasn't like her. She'd never been a tattletale.

"To be precise," Del said, "Lucas told me. Maddie was with him, and she looked miserable, as well she should. I think she was desperate to call and warn you, but Lucas insisted they come to the station instantly."

"How forceful of him," Olivia muttered.

"What was that?"

"I said, 'How ethical of him.' I guess you can scratch Lucas off the list of suspects for Paine's murder."

"So, did you find anything when you

304

searched Hermione's bedroom?" Del's voice sounded a shade too casual.

"What did Maddie tell you?"

"I asked first."

"Okay, Del, you win. We found a couple passports in what I assume were false names; some stuff Hermione filched from local businesses; a bunch of photos in an envelope, stuffed in a coat pocket; and a pair of shoes with heels that opened up, but there was nothing in them. Oh yeah, and under the staircase, we found what looked like a cookbook from way back, maybe as far as the American Revolution. I didn't recognize anyone in the photos except Paine and Hermione, when they were younger and happier. There was one photo of an unnamed baby, so Maddie and I wondered if they'd lost a child. That can do strange things to a relationship. I couldn't tell from the photo whether it was a boy or a girl."

"Maddie didn't mention the cookbook," Del said, "so you get a point for that."

"Del . . . are we all right? I'm sorry we searched Chatterley Mansion without permission, but really, it was helpful, too. We found a number of things I'll bet the police missed. And I still feel the mansion belongs to all of us. We kept it going and fixed it up, so . . ."

"I should arrest you."

When Del went silent, Olivia asked, "Are you sighing? I hate it when you sigh, but I'm hoping it means you don't plan to arrest me. Or are you?"

"I can't. If I arrested you, I'd have to arrest Maddie. Then there'd be no serving wenches at the fete this afternoon."

Olivia was savoring a cup of coffee at the store's front window, watching booths go up in the park, when she heard someone fumbling with the lock in the front door. Spunky leaped off her lap, yapping fiercely. After last night's experience hiding in the Chatterley Mansion's root cellar with Maddie, Olivia couldn't help but be jumpy; her pulse took off at a trot.

"Livie, are you in there? Could you give me a hand here?" It was Maddie's voice.

"Coming," Olivia called out. When she opened the front door, Maddie stumbled into the store, laden with stuffed canvas bags. "I thought we were only selling cookies at our booth," Olivia said. "What's all this? Decorations?"

"And costumes, my friend." Maddie dropped the bags on the floor. "No fete is complete without the perfect costumes. No, Spunky, get out of there." Maddie reached into the bag and produced a wriggling Yorkie, entangled in a white blouse with a gathered neckline. "You take this creature," Maddie said, handing Spunky to Olivia. "Check this out." Maddie held up the blouse by two spaghetti straps to demonstrate what it would look like. Low cut was what it looked like to Olivia. Puffy elbow-length sleeves were designed to hang off the shoulders, leaving them bare. "This is part one of my serving wench costume. And here is part two." From the same bag, Maddie retrieved a long skirt, gathered at the waist. "I made this myself. I used silk essence, which flows nicely and gathers without adding bulk to the hips. Our curves are fine as is."

"*Our* curves?"

"I made this skirt in emerald green because —" Maddie flashed the emerald promise-to-think-about-it, almost-engagement ring Lucas had given her. "Also it emphasizes my eyes."

"I doubt anyone will be looking at your eyes," Olivia said.

"And the pièce de . . . de . . ."

"Pièce de résistance," Olivia said. "Which makes me worry."

"Ta-da!" Maddie slipped an earthy green top over her head. It laced across the rib cage and was held up by a curved fabric strap that went up each side and wound around the neck. "This is worn over the blouse."

"Is that what I think it is?" Olivia asked.

"Sort of," Maddie said. "It isn't a real bustier, of course. They're expensive to buy and take too long to make correctly. If I'd had more time, though, it would have been fun to try."

"So this is just for show? It won't actually make you spill out of your rather skimpy blouse? Not that you wouldn't look great, but with the cooler weather, you might catch cold. I'm only thinking of your health."

Maddie grinned as she delved into another bag. "And this, my friend, is your costume." She shook out a second gathered skirt in deep teal blue.

Teal was Olivia's favorite color. However . . . "There's only one serving wench lined up for the fete, and she is you. I intend to dress as Livie Greyson in a sweater, linen pants, and comfortable shoes."

"See, I knew you'd blow off Karen's decree that everyone wear a costume, which is why I made you one. And it isn't a serving wench costume."

"What is it, then?"

Maddie dug through her bag and emerged with a white blouse that looked suspiciously familiar. "You will be dressed as a *tavern* wench. There is a difference." Maddie produced a pseudo bustier exactly like hers only in a rich gray with teal laces. "Livie, you will look stunning in this, I promise you. The teal and gray will bring out your eyes. Del will melt. *Please* wear it."

"Well, maybe I could throw a sweater around my shoulders." Olivia had to admit the colors were perfect, and since the bustier wasn't real . . .

"Excellent! Oh, here's one more item for our costumes." Maddie handed Olivia a small, tissue-wrapped package.

Olivia had that sinking feeling she'd gotten when her ex-husband, Ryan, began oh-so-casually to recount conversations with a fellow medical student named Joanie. She opened the tissue paper. "A *push-up* bra?"

Maddie gave her a look of feigned surprise. "Of course. I told you I didn't have time to make real bustiers, but we can get the same effect with a push-up bra. Come on, let's get dressed. This is going to be so much fun." Maddie gathered up her bags and costume and headed toward the kitchen.

It was Olivia's turn to sigh, and she did so

with gusto. "I have a bad feeling about this. I'll probably freeze to death." To herself, though, Olivia admitted she wouldn't mind if Del saw her in costume. Maybe he'd be distracted enough to forget about that unauthorized visit she and Maddie made to Chatterley Mansion.

While Maddie unpacked her bags in the kitchen, Olivia took Spunky for a quick trip outside. Normally, he could stay in the store while Olivia was out, but she was afraid the revelry in the park might upset him. After Spunky had finished his business, Olivia took him up to her apartment for a relatively quiet day. He could watch the festivities in the park from his favorite perch, a small Queen Anne desk under the living room window. As she filled his bowl with a generous portion of kibbles, Olivia said, "You stay up here and protect the house, Spunks. Mommy is about to transform herself into something she'd rather you didn't see."

Once they had wriggled into their costumes, Maddie removed the mirror from the little bathroom in The Gingerbread House kitchen, so they could both get a look at themselves.

Olivia grimaced at her reflection. "Are you

sure this isn't a Victorian streetwalker costume?"

"Tavern wench," Maddie said. "Trust me. I did a costume search on the Internet."

"Aside from the color, I fail to see the difference between my costume and yours." Olivia studied her appearance in the small mirror. Her white mop cap was sliding off her auburn waves, so she adjusted it. Around her bare neck, she wore a necklace Maddie had strung from small flower-shaped cookie cutters. That touch, Olivia admitted, was sheer creative genius. As for the rest: the push-up bra was doing its job, and the teal laces in her gray bodice were tight around her ribs. At least she was able to breathe without pain. And Maddie had been right about the effect on her eyes, which looked blue-gray. The blouse was alluring, not as low cut as she'd feared, but . . . "I don't know, this outfit looks more Renaissance than Victorian. Not that I'm questioning your research."

"Oh, Livie, just go with it, okay? Karen ordered me to be a Victorian serving girl, but they wore black dresses and white aprons. Really boring. So I changed my character to serving wench. Besides, none of the costumes Karen suggested really had much to do with Chatterley Heights his-

311

tory. I think she wanted me to be a Victorian serving girl so I'd look dowdy."

"That I can believe," Olivia said. "Only why is my costume the same as yours. Unless . . . is this a sneaky way to get me to dress as a serving wench? Did Del put you up to this?"

"Don't be silly. Your costume has one distinct difference from mine. Look at your skirt, behind your right hip."

Olivia pulled her skirt fabric forward to smooth out the gathering at her right hip. "What?"

"Right there." Maddie pointed to a long, dark stain that dribbled down to the hem of Olivia's skirt. "That is the mark of a tavern wench. I had to use red wine so it would show up. I put it behind your hip because, of course, I didn't want it to look like you clumsily spilled the wine yourself. Some drunk would have tossed it at you. Probably because you spurned his drunken advances." Maddie's freckled cheeks bunched as she grinned. "Isn't this fun?"

By the time Olivia and Maddie had carted their decorated gingerbread cookies and cookie-cutter displays to their assigned booth, the town square park was already filling with early visitors. Olivia was aware of, and rather pleased with, the male glances tossed in their direction while they wound through the gathering crowd. As they passed the Chatterley Café booth, Olivia recognized the two servers, who were dressed as Puritans. The young woman glanced over Olivia's costume and gave her a thumbs-up. Pointing to her own costume, the server rolled her eyes heavenward.

In the next booth, Pete, owner of Pete's Diner, hawked meatball sandwiches and hot coffee. He wore his usual outfit: jeans and a stained T-shirt. Pete was timeless. Ida, his longtime waitress, wore a red-checked dress with puffed sleeves and a little white apron, straight from a fifties diner. Ida, now in her seventies, might easily have worn such a uniform, given she'd been waitressing for sixty years. As Olivia passed near the booth, Ida beckoned to her. "Livie Greyson, does your mother know you're dressed like a tart?"

"Well . . ."

"I'm pulling your leg," Ida said. "Listen, that mayor of ours is looking for you. She's on the warpath, even more than usual. That woman's got a personality problem."

"Thanks for the heads-up." Olivia didn't add that Ida was well known for her own brand of crankiness. "I love your costume."

"Found it in my closet," Ida said. "It still fits."

Maddie had gone ahead to the Lady Chatterley's Boutique booth, where her friend Lola wore a slinky 1920s gown, bright red. Maddie beckoned to Olivia to join them. "Listen to this, Livie."

Lola glanced over their heads as if to make sure no one was listening. Satisfied, she leaned close to Maddie and Olivia. "There's a rumor going around," Lola said in a low, sultry voice, "that our very own mayor once had a fling with Paine Chatterley, right here in Chatterley Heights."

Olivia did some quick arithmetic. "Isn't there something of an age difference between Paine and Karen? Are you sure it didn't happen in Europe?"

Lola shook her head. With her shiny, dark hair and nearly violet eyes, she looked like an exotic cat with a mouse in her sights. "Paine was older than he looked, and Karen . . . well, you've got to hand it to her, she looks terrific for a woman who is about to turn forty-eight. Even so, the affair was scandalous, which is why Paine took off for Europe."

With a small gasp, Maddie said, "You mean Karen was . . ." A concentration line formed between her eyebrows. "I know

Paine left for Europe when he was about twenty-four or five. Wouldn't Karen have been a teenager?"

"She was barely sixteen," Lola said. "I don't know if she was pregnant, but just her age was enough to force Paine to make tracks for Europe."

"Are you sure about all this?" Olivia asked. If true, it meant that Karen had a good reason to hate Paine. If Karen Evanson and Karin Evensong were the same person, she might not have traveled to Europe for art school, but rather to track down Paine Chatterley.

"Livie, I work at Lady Chatterley's Clothing Boutique for Elegant Ladies. Elegant ladies talk. Believe me, my source is unimpeachable," Lola said. "Karen and my customer were classmates and friends. They aren't close anymore, but she doesn't have any reason to lie about Karen. In fact, when she told me the story, she was still angry with Paine Chatterley for his treatment of her old friend." Lola's lovely eyes flicked over Maddie's head. "Uh-oh. Here comes Karen now. She's been looking for you, Livie."

Olivia and Maddie grabbed their bags of supplies and headed toward the band shell near the center of the park. The Gingerbread

House booth stood empty, waiting for them to festoon it with cookie-cutter garlands and trays of brightly decorated gingerbread cookies. Karen could be difficult, but she'd been thoughtful enough to position the booth near the old-fashioned streetlamp, so the cutters might sparkle at dusk.

Maddie tacked one end of a ribbon, strung with gingerbread man cutters, to an upper corner of the booth. She had a full view of the park. "Warning," she said. "Karen sighting. She's bearing down on us fast. Act natural."

"Easy for you," Olivia said. "You're not the one Karen is gunning for. Wish I knew why." She glanced over her shoulder to watch Karen's determined approach. "Hey, is that my mom I see behind her?"

"I do believe it is," Maddie said. "Ellie to the rescue! Wow, she can really carry off that slinky flapper look. Wish I looked that elegant in a straight dress, but it takes a slender, small-boned figure. The fringe on her dress is bouncing; she must really be moving."

"She caught up with Karen," Olivia said. "Oops, now they're both coming this way. Is my own mother mad at me, too? What did I do?"

Ellie gave Olivia a reassuring smile as she

and Karen reached the Gingerbread House booth. "Cookie-cutter garlands," Ellie said. "What a clever idea. This is going to be one of the most appealing booths at the fete."

"One of?" Olivia opened a covered cake pan and began to transfer cookies to a large plate decorated with a purple and yellow gingerbread house.

"Your costumes are outrageous," Karen said. "No Victorian serving girl would be caught dead in such outfits."

"I'm fairly certain," Maddie said in a dangerous voice, "that Victorian serving girls are mostly all dead, anyway."

Karen ignored her and said to Olivia, "I've been racing all over the park looking for you. For a member of the celebration planning committee, you've certainly been casual about our timetable." Before Olivia could formulate a retort, Karen said, "But never mind that now. I wanted to make sure you knew that we, the members of the celebration committee, are holding a meeting after the fete ends."

"Another meeting?" Olivia tried to keep the disappointment out of her voice, she really did.

"We need to dissect the weekend as quickly as possible, while it's still fresh in our minds. We don't want to repeat mistakes next time."

Olivia lifted another pan of cookies from a bag and selected a tray shaped like a gingerbread man. "I don't know about you, Karen, but I don't intend to be around in another two hundred and fifty years."

"You know what I mean. We'll meet at the community center after the fireworks end. The committee members are to go on ahead to the center, while I give a short speech to mark the official end of the celebration. Rosemarie York has promised to have coffee brewed. I think we'll all have had enough to eat, so no snacks are necessary. Try not to drink too much alcohol this afternoon; I want everyone's mind to be sharp." With a firm nod to indicate she'd finished, Karen turned and strode toward a forlorn group of madrigal singers gathering in the band shell.

Ellie waited until Karen was out of earshot and said, "Poor Karen, she is quite stressed. I tried to lighten her mood, but she is determined not to relax until the fete is over."

Olivia leaned closer to Ellie and lowered her voice. "Mom, did you ever hear anything about Karen and Paine being, um, involved? It would have been right about when I was born, I think."

As she watched Karen's retreating figure, Ellie said, "I was rather busy at that time, but yes, I did hear of such a relationship. Frankly, I see no reason the incident should be brought up again. It would only dredge up hurtful old rumors, and Karen has enough on her hands at the moment." Ellie's stern tone took Olivia back to her childhood. "Karen was a naive farm girl, which might be hard for you to imagine, but people do change over — what has it been? At least thirty-plus years now. How time does —"

"Mom? Details? Before the sun sets?"

Ellie arched a disapproving eyebrow at her only daughter. "Really, Livie, I never thought of you as a scandal monger."

"I'm going to ignore that comment," Olivia said with a haughty toss of her head. Her mop cap flew off, destroying the effect. Chuckling, Maddie retrieved the cap and plopped it back on Olivia's head. "I wouldn't ask if it weren't important," Olivia said. "Is the affair the real reason Paine left the country? Was Karen pregnant?"

"You think Karen might have killed Paine Chatterley all these years later? Why? Karen has gone on with her life; she has laudable ambitions. And no, as far as I am aware, she did not become pregnant, in case you're thinking she would have killed Paine for revenge."

"Well, it is a consideration," Maddie said. "Karen does want to run for Congress, right? Something like an abortion in her past wouldn't sit well with some voters."

Ellie's long gray tresses swung outward as she shook her head. "I knew Karen's mother, Iris. We belonged to the same quilting group. Iris was proud that Karen stayed in high school, despite her emotional turmoil. She never missed a day right up to graduation. Karen has always been a very focused person. The Evanson family was not well to do, but Karen put herself through college and has worked hard to succeed."

Olivia finished arranging cookies on plates and stretched plastic wrap over them. "By 'not well to do,' do you mean the Evansons were poor?"

"They were a typical farm family," Ellie said. "They had good years and lean years, but they managed. Iris was a fine seamstress. She made Karen's clothes and sewed for a number of Chatterley Heights women as well. I'll admit I didn't know Karen very well at the time, but I was close to Iris."

Olivia wondered if her mother's fondness for Iris made her overlook Karen's tyrannical behavior, but she kept that thought to herself. Ellie was highly intuitive about people, but she was only human. It was time to change the subject. "Hey, Mom, is that Allan I see in the band shell, hanging out with the madrigal singers?"

Ellie's face lit up. "It's so wonderful having Allan home more. Though of course, being so gregarious by nature, he has been looking for ways to get involved. He has such a lovely baritone, and the madrigal singers are so . . ."

"Awful?" Maddie offered.

"I was going to say they are a bit thin in the baritone range," Ellie said.

"Also tenor and bass," Olivia added, "given they seem to have only one male singer, and that would be Allan."

"Jason will be back in town soon, and he sings in the tenor range," Ellie said. "It will be so good for him to spend time with his stepfather."

Poor Jason. However, Olivia had no intention of warning her brother about their mother's plans for his free time. What fun would that be?

Two hours into the fete, the supply of decorated gingerbread cookies had been halved. "Wow," Maddie said during a pause, "these things are selling like . . . like decorated cookies."

"I'd pick a decorated cookie over a hotcake any day," Olivia said. She reached into a supply bag to get another covered cake pan filled with cookies. She heard a series of clicks, which turned out to be coming from a camera operated by Binnie Sloan and aimed right at Olivia's chest.

"Thanks," Binnie said. "I'll pick the best shot. Check it out on my *Weekend Chatter* blog. It ought to be good for a few extra hits."

Olivia kept her scathing retorts to herself. Knowing Binnie, she'd record and post them on her blog, along with the photo.

"How about a free cookie for the press?" Without waiting for permission, Binnie snatched two cookies. She made a sandwich of them, icing sides together, and took a bite. "Not bad," she said with her mouth full.

With a sideways glance at Olivia, Maddie slid the cookie tray out of reach. "Gotten any other good shots, Binnie?"

"Check my blog and see for yourself."

"I'm really busy these days," Maddie said. "Give me a reason why I'd want to see what's on that blog of yours."

Binnie eyed the cookies, just out of reach.

"Give me a cookie, I'll give you a reason."

Olivia smiled as she watched Maddie use a small sheet of bakery tissue to pick up one cookie and hand it to Binnie. Maddie was no fool. If she handed over the tray, Binnie would snag as many as she could hold.

Binnie's smug grin faded, but she took the cookie. "Got a great shot of our mayor," she said. "She needs to learn a little self-control." With that tantalizing comment, Binnie bit off a gingerbread man's head, shoulders, and upper torso. She spun around and walked off, but not before Olivia and Maddie saw her cheeks bulge as she tried to chew more cookie than her mouth could hold.

"*Who* needs to learn self-control?" Olivia said this under her breath, since it usually wasn't a good idea to antagonize the local press. Binnie had a camera and a tape recorder, and she knew how to use them. Maddie heard Olivia's comment and giggled softly.

"I am curious, though," Olivia said once Binnie was out of earshot, "what Karen lost her self-control about. And with whom did she lose it?"

By midafternoon, the excitement began to

323

wane among fete goers. The madrigal singers had lost their voices, and several busloads of visitors had departed, having eaten their way through the Chatterley Heights town square park. Given it was Sunday and getting chilly, Olivia figured the audience for the evening fireworks would be mostly tired locals. Just as well the crowd had thinned, she thought, since The Gingerbread House booth was running seriously low on decorated cookies.

"Hey, there's Heather and Matthew," Maddie said, pointing toward the Pete's Diner booth. "Matthew looks less tortured than usual."

"Rosemarie is right behind them," Olivia said.

Maddie waved as Heather looked in their direction. Heather waved back and took Matthew by the arm.

Olivia checked over their dwindling supply of cookies. "I hope they aren't too hungry."

Matthew paid Maddie for two cookies, while Heather engaged her in bubbling conversation. Rosemarie settled near Olivia, watching the young couple fondly. "Your cookies look delicious, as always," Rosemarie said, "but I'm stuffed."

"How is Matthew holding up?" Olivia asked.

"Quite well, considering . . ."

As Rosemarie's smile faded, Olivia noticed the puffiness around her eyes. "And how are *you* holding up?"

"Oh, I'm fine. Matthew is still under some suspicion, of course, but he was released from jail when a test of some sort showed he hadn't fired a weapon. The sheriff told me he did a second search of the mansion and grounds this morning and found two spent bullets."

"So someone did fire a weapon," Olivia said, "and it wasn't Matthew."

"That's what it looks like." Rosemarie leaned an elbow on the booth's sales shelf.

"You don't seem relieved. Are you sure you don't need a cookie?" Olivia edged the tray an inch closer to Rosemarie's elbow.

"So tempting, Livie, but no. Over the past few weeks, I've eaten enough sugar to fill the community center. And I really am relieved about Matthew . . . for now, anyway. I'm just feeling a touch of tattletale's remorse. I wish I hadn't told you what I did about Quill and Paine in high school. Now I've made Quill a suspect."

"Rosemarie, he really is a suspect. Quill had a strong reason to hate Paine, assuming he did mastermind the switched names on those tests."

"Oh, he did indeed," Rosemarie said with quiet force. "But I have sympathy for Quill. He took the fall for Paine, and I think I know why."

Olivia hesitated, uncertain how to encourage Rosemarie to say more but not wanting to seem too eager for the information. "If Quill had a reason to accept blame," she said, "that might weaken his motive for murdering Paine."

"It might," Rosemarie said. "Yes, I think it might." She edged away from Matthew and Heather, who were still chatting with Maddie. Olivia gestured toward the back entrance to the booth. Rosemarie nodded, and they met behind the booth. With the fete winding down, they'd have adequate privacy.

"Quill was quite shy with girls," Rosemarie said. "And Paine was popular. He was good-looking and brash, so girls were drawn to him. I'd noticed that when the two became friends, Quill began to double-date with Paine. Once I realized Paine was cheating, copying Quill's work, I suspected he was 'paying' Quill by getting dates for him. I wondered if Quill even understood that he was being bought. He was rather naive for his age."

"After Quill took the blame for the cheating, did Paine continue to find dates for him?" Olivia asked.

"Yes, he did. You see, that's why I think this information might actually help Quill — because he benefited from the arrangement. I'm sure Quill wasn't happy about the situation, but . . ." Rosemarie shrugged.

"That might help," Olivia said, more to comfort Rosemarie than because she believed it. Quill struck her as bitter and prone to brooding. He'd suffered in the long run, unable to achieve the education and career prominence he'd desired. Even the dating experience Paine provided him didn't seem to have helped Quill, since he hadn't married. In fact, Olivia had always thought he despised women. But maybe she'd been wrong.

"Rosemarie, do you . . . I mean, it surprises me to hear that Quill was eager to date girls. I've never heard that he was involved with anyone."

"He never married." Rosemarie scanned the dwindling crowd in the park.

"Are you sure he liked girls?"

"Positive." Rosemarie lowered her head, hiding her expression, but not before Olivia saw her features tighten. "All right, Livie, I get what you're implying. If Quill didn't like girls, then Paine wasn't doing him any favors by getting dates for him." Rosemarie raised sad eyes to Olivia's face. "But Quill was desperate to be admired. He wasn't an attractive boy, and girls ignored him. Or worse, they teased him, embarrassed him. Except . . ." Rosemarie shivered and tightened her light jacket across her chest. "Well, I tried to protect him, you see. I went to a lot of trouble to show that Paine had done the cheating. So I guess it was understandable. . . ."

"Quill fell in love with you?" Olivia heard the surprise in her voice and added, "Not that it's so startling."

Rosemarie's smile softened her features and drew attention to her striking dark hazel eyes. "I wasn't always fifty-eight and short on sleep, you know. And I truly believed that Quill had been wronged. I felt sad for him. I really wasn't aware of his feelings for me until he suddenly blurted out a proposal. I had to tell him I was already dating someone. He took it hard. I told myself he was young, he'd get over it."

"Did Quill feel you'd led him on?" Olivia asked. "Is that why he turned away from women completely?"

With a heavy sigh, Rosemarie said, "No,

not at all. Quill never quite let go of me. Oh, he didn't follow me around or anything, but he has always been, I regret to say, kinder to me than to women in general. It makes me sad."

"Does Quill know you're the one who revealed that he took the blame for Paine's cheating?"

"As soon as the sheriff questioned him, he knew it had to be me. He stopped by the community center that evening. I tried to explain, but he stopped me. He understood that I had to protect Matthew. He didn't even sound angry." Rosemarie asked, with a hint of hope, "Quill's calmness, does that imply he doesn't have a guilty conscience?"

"I hope so," Olivia said.

"Nine cookies left," Maddie said. "I'm getting hungry." She plucked one cookie off the tray, one of her "jailbird series" of prison-striped running gingerbread men. "This guy is doomed for two reasons," Maddie said. "First, his stripes are fuchsia and lemon yellow, so he's bound to get caught. And second . . ." She bit off his legs up to the knees.

"I never knew you had such a cruel streak," Olivia said.

"Yes, you did." Maddie's enunciation suffered from an excess of cookie in her mouth, but she got her point across.

"You two kids having fun?" Del appeared around the corner of the booth. He spotted the striped upper torso and fuchsia-capped head in Maddie's hand. "I've been looking for that guy."

"Has Karen released you from duty?" Olivia asked.

"Not a chance." Del took a dollar bill from his wallet. "I heard there were serving wenches, so I decided to take a cookie break. You look fantastic, by the way." He skipped over the last running gingerbread convict and selected a tangerine pumpkin. "It's the biggest," he said.

"Any word on Hermione?" Olivia asked.

"Still in intensive care. She was moved to Johns Hopkins by ambulance. It'll be some time before I can talk to her, and even then I can guarantee that I won't be allowed to ask upsetting questions."

"So I guess I won't be able to help with her," Olivia said.

"You've helped quite enough, Livie."

"Are you still mad at us?"

Del took a bite of his cookie and chewed in appreciative silence.

"Admit it, Del," Maddie said. "We found some interesting stuff at the mansion."

"Nothing that cracks the case, though. On the other hand, I will say this: no one got hurt, and I can forgive a lot for a good cookie and the presence of serving wenches."

"I'll have you know that I'm a tavern wench," Olivia said, flicking a crumb at Del.

"Even better." Del's pager buzzed, and he checked the message. "Gotta go. Her highness requires my attendance. Livie, I actually came over to see if you'd like a late dinner after the fireworks."

"Wish I could, but I can't. Her highness has called yet another meeting of the celebration committee. We're going to critique or deconstruct or something. I'm counting the minutes."

"You'll need to decompress after that, and the store is closed tomorrow," Del said. "Where are you meeting, at the store? I could drop by to rescue you."

"In the community center, the room with the gingerbread display. And yes, do please rescue me from the irritating boredom of yet another committee meeting." Olivia leaned toward him, across the display shelf, and gave him a quick kiss.

Del's pager buzzed again. He backed away from the booth, smiling. "Later," he said. "And thanks for the view!"

As Del sprinted off through the park, Olivia heard a familiar, husky laugh, and turning to its owner, said, "Struts! Wow, you look great. I was hoping you'd stop by. You deserve a free cookie for promising to hire Jason back. I was afraid he'd mope around, driving Mom and Allan crazy."

Struts Marinsky, gifted mechanic and owner of Chatterley Heights's lone garage, did not look the part. She'd forsaken her usual oil-stained jeans and T-shirt for an elegant pair of chocolate brown tailored pants, fine wool, and a matching sweater. The outfit showcased her long, lean figure. Her dark blond hair, usually captured in a ponytail to keep it out of moving engine parts, hung loose to her shoulders. "Yeah, I hired Jason back to save Ellie from aggravation, not because he's the best mechanic in Maryland. You didn't hear that from me. And I'll take that cookie. I'm starving. In fact, I'll buy the whole tray. That's enough for dinner." She handed Olivia seven dollars. "Hey, either of you seen Karen Evanson around? I wanted to tell her I won't go running tomorrow morning. Gotta late date."

"I'll be seeing Karen later," Olivia said. "I could give her the message."

"Great, thanks."

"I didn't know you two were friends." Olivia brushed some crumbs off the empty cookie tray and slid it into a canvas bag. Maddie began to clean up the booth, staying within listening distance.

"Yeah, we go back a ways," Struts said. "We were best buds in kindergarten, in fact. We had a lot in common. We both grew up on farms and have jobs that usually go to men."

"So you're still close?"

"Close, hm . . . I'm not sure Karen lets anyone get close. I suspect she's comfortable with me because I don't pester her to talk about her feelings. Come to think of it, that's probably why I'm comfortable with her, too. Although even I think she ought to loosen up a bit. Everything is too important to her, you know?"

"Mom says the same thing about her," Olivia said. "Karen seems secretive about herself."

"No kidding," Struts said. "I mean it's great that she doesn't get all sappy about feelings, but I literally know nothing about her life except for the early years, when I used to hang out at her farmhouse. Her mom and dad were just the opposite of Karen, laid-back and content with their lives. They really loved her, even though she was kind of a surprise. Her dad used to talk a lot about when he served in the army. He was stationed in Germany in the 1960s. Karen's mom moved there for a while to be with her dad, and that's when Karen happened."

"Karen was born in Germany? I didn't know that."

"I wouldn't either if her mom hadn't told me. Her mom was thrilled." Struts peeked into her bag of cookies and took a deep breath. "Ah . . . I'm going to find a nice private spot and inhale these beauties. Thanks for passing along my message to Karen."

"One question, Struts. This is sheer curiosity on my part, so I'll understand if you don't want to answer."

"I'm good with curiosity. Shoot."

"It's about Karen, or actually something Binnie said. She said Karen needed to learn some self-control. Any idea what she meant by that?"

To Olivia's surprise, Struts laughed. "I know exactly what that was about," she said. "I was there. I told Karen, 'Don't let Binnie get the upper hand. She makes stuff up just to see if she can get a reaction.' But Karen couldn't stop herself; she lost it."

Olivia didn't want to sound too eager, so

she forced herself to stay quiet while Struts selected a cookie from her bag and bit into it. She was relieved when Struts stopped at one bite.

"It's odd, too," Struts said. "What Binnie said to Karen, it was really a wild card. Binnie took out that little notebook she carries around and made like she was reading some notes. Then she asked Karen to swear she'd never known Paine Chatterley before he arrived back in town last Tuesday. Binnie emphasized the word 'known' in that sly way she has. When Karen got angry, Binnie started writing in her notebook. Karen grabbed the notebook and tore out all the pages. She ripped them up and tossed the pieces into the air. I have to admit, even though Karen lost her cool, I was silently cheering her on. I think it'll come back to haunt her, though. Binnie Sloan is the kind to take revenge."

CHAPTER SEVENTEEN

Olivia's head felt like a preschool full of hyperactive children. She'd absorbed too much information way too fast, and she felt a strong need to sort it all out with Maddie. If only they were back in the store kitchen, whipping up a batch of decorated cookies. . . . Well, why not? If there wasn't time to make cookies, at least they'd have privacy. The fete was still winding down, but The Gingerbread House booth was down to crumbs. They would only disappoint customers if they kept the booth open.

"Maddie, have you seen Karen lately?"

"Haven't seen her since you were out back of the booth, talking to Rosemarie. She snagged poor Del. Tell me you don't actually want to talk to Karen."

"Nope, I just wanted to confirm she isn't around. I'd rather talk with you. Preferably in private and with food. We need to compare notes, and the park is too public."

"Oh goodie," Maddie said. "Do you have a suspect for Paine's murder?"

"I have a brain crammed with bits of information that don't fit together yet, and I want to sort them out. Let's close up fast and head back to the store. We can hide out in my apartment and keep Spunky company while we brainstorm."

"Excellent," Maddie said. "I'll take care of the food issue. Ida dropped by and said Pete overestimated the public's craving for meatball sandwiches. I'll zip over to the diner's booth and pick up a couple sandwiches plus extras for you, so you can freeze the leftovers. It'll be a nice change from pizza."

"I like pizza."

"Yes, we all get that, Livie. I'll be right back."

While Maddie procured dinner, Olivia packed up empty cake pans, plates, and cookie-cutter garlands. They'd taken in a tidy sum, mostly in cash, which Olivia counted quickly. By the time she had recorded the amount and stuffed it into a zipped cash pouch, Maddie returned with two grocery-size take-out bags with "Pete's Diner" stenciled across them. "We won't starve," Maddie said, grinning. "Let's blow this cookie stand before Karen makes another appearance."

Heavily laden with bags, Olivia and Maddie skirted through the thinning crowd toward The Gingerbread House. Olivia felt a familiar lightening of her spirits as they neared the bright yellow Queen Anne. The house had wrapped its sticky fingers around her heart, and she could no longer imagine living anywhere else.

Olivia unlocked the store, and they headed to the kitchen, where they left their bags on the worktable. "We can clean up tomorrow morning, while the store is closed," Olivia said. "I want to take Spunky for a quick outing, then we can eat. We won't go far; too many strangers wandering around."

"Do you really have to go to that meeting at the community center this evening?"

"Yeah, I'll go," Olivia said, "but never again." She opened her apartment door and caught Spunky as he burst through. Holding the squirming dog in a firm grip, she said, "You're getting good at that, kiddo. Ouch." A red stripe appeared on Olivia's bare shoulder where Spunky's flailing claw had scratched it. "I desperately want to change out of this getup. Costume, I mean."

"Not allowed," Maddie said. "I'll show you why when you get back. I'll be in the kitchen, working down the mess."

After a short walk around the yard, Spunky was ready to go indoors. He wasn't happy with the noise level in the park. Olivia held on to him as they joined Maddie in the store kitchen.

"Now there's a sight for Binnie's blog," Olivia said when she caught sight of Maddie. "Serving wench loads dishwasher in The Gingerbread House kitchen. Inquiring minds want to know: does she do windows?"

"She does not," Maddie said. "She does, however, bring gifts from Aunt Sadie." Maddie reached into one of the bags she'd used to transport their costumes. She pulled out a folded white cloth, which she glanced at before tossing it back in the bag, shaking her head with impatience.

Olivia finished loading the dishwasher and added soap. As she pushed the start button, Maddie said, "And now, for your wearing pleasure . . ." She held an armful of fine white wool.

"What's that?"

"This is why we can't change out of our costumes yet," Maddie said. "Aunt Sadie sent along a couple of embroidered shawls for us. She used to embroider shawls before she turned to aprons. These have been packed away for decades, but she hand washed them to get out the mothball smell.

She wants us to keep them. I took the liberty of choosing mine first." Maddie wrapped one shawl around Olivia's shoulders and the other around her own.

"Nice and soft." Handing Spunky over to Maddie, Olivia slipped off the shawl to get a look at the embroidered decoration on the back. "It looks like a bouquet of passion flowers in pinks and purples. It's gorgeous. What's yours?"

"Aunt Sadie picked out romantic themes for us." Maddie turned her back to reveal two cardinals, a male and a female, touching beaks. "It's called courtship feeding. The male hops over to his chosen female and places a seed in her beak. When I was about eleven, Aunt Sadie called me to the kitchen window so I could see the real thing. It looked just like a people kiss, which melted my little prepubescent heart. Aunt Sadie embroidered this for me and put it away until I got engaged. I guess she figures that promising to think about being engaged is close enough."

Wearing their new shawls, they climbed the stairs to Olivia's apartment. While Maddie warmed the meatball sandwiches and set the little kitchen table, Olivia fixed Spunky's dinner. She was planning to head off her skittish Yorkie's reaction to a second round of fireworks, coming up after the fete. She'd made a quick call to Chatterley Paws, the animal shelter and vet clinic run by Gwen and Herbie Tucker. Gwen was skipping the celebration to stay home with their baby boy, but Herbie had stopped by the store early that morning to drop off a small dose of doggie sedative for Spunky. Olivia mixed the liquid into Spunky's favorite canned food, hoping he wouldn't notice. He licked the bowl clean, as usual.

Having feasted on meatball sandwiches and one glass of merlot each, Maddie and Olivia settled on the living room sofa to continue their discussion of murder suspects. Olivia said, "Okay, our suspects for Paine's murder are Karen Evanson —"

"My personal favorite," Maddie said.

"Duly noted." Olivia consulted her handwritten list. "Along with Matthew Fabrizio, Rosemarie York, Quill Latimer, and Hermione Chatterley, even though Johns Hopkins insisted she couldn't have moved Paine's body into the bathtub."

"Given Hermione's serious heart attack," Maddie said, "I guess we have to take Johns Hopkins seriously."

"But Hermione might have had help." Olivia ran her finger down the list. "Any of the other suspects could have dragged Paine and managed to maneuver him into the tub, even Rosemarie or Karen."

"Especially Karen," Maddie said, "since she works out and runs with your mom. I'm just saying."

"Each of the suspects had a key to the mansion — or access to one, in Rosemarie's case — and the murder happened overnight. Only Quill has an alibi for Thursday night. His friends confirmed he was inebriated at midnight, but he could have been faking."

"So we'll assume no alibis," Maddie said. "They all have motives. Matthew's motive is obvious. Paine tricked him into finishing the Victorian trim on the mansion in exchange for helping him prove he was a tried-and-true Chatterley descendant. Matthew finished the work — and you have to admit, Matthew's work is extraordinary — but Paine broke his promise."

"Matthew is a hothead and drinks too much," Olivia said. "Even Rosemarie and Heather admitted Matthew was enraged."

Maddie took a sip of coffee and added more cream. "According to Hermione," she said, "Matthew threatened her with a gun, which caused her to have a heart attack."

"Allegedly," Olivia said. "No one witnessed the encounter. Two spent bullets were found, but no gun. Although Matthew admits to getting drunk and going to the mansion to talk to Hermione. Which makes me wonder . . . this is pure speculation, but it strikes me that if Hermione has a partner in crime, it might be someone she doesn't quite trust. Hermione might think it wise to throw suspicion onto someone else, someone like Matthew. He makes such a good suspect. No one would believe him if he tried to implicate Hermione."

Maddie perked up. "But someone like Karen might be more dangerous if she decided to turn on Hermione."

Olivia massaged Spunky's ears as he snuggled next to her. "I keep wondering why Hermione drew attention to Karen's behavior as a young woman in London."

"Maybe Hermione and Karen actually became friends in London and hatched this scheme together?" Maddie twirled one of her many red curls as she considered the possibilities. "Except the story isn't true. Her so-called affair was with a fictional character in a crappy play."

"Right, and I find that interesting," Olivia said. "Why bring it up at all?"

Maddie stretched out her legs and perched her bare heels on the edge of the coffee table. "Well, according to your mom, the affair happened here in Chatterley Heights and seems to have ended badly. Then Paine returned to Chatterley Heights and refused to let Karen use the mansion for the celebration weekend. Karen already had reason to hate Paine, and she does not like to be crossed. So maybe Hermione approached her about doing away with the old reprobate."

"Maybe . . ." As Olivia jotted down a few notes, Spunky crawled onto her lap and curled up. The doggy sedative must have kicked in because he was acting like a very relaxed pup. Possibly too relaxed, Olivia thought as she scratched his ears. Spunky didn't open his eyes. "Karen and Hermione would be unlikely partners, but it's not out of the question. Even if they didn't like each other, they might have cooperated out of hatred for Paine. We do know that Karen did not become pregnant at sixteen, which lessens her motive."

"That's what your mom said, and I guess we should believe her," Maddie said.

"Mom is a superbly reliable source. I don't know how she learns so much."

"People just open up to Ellie," Maddie said. "I know I do. She has that empathetic and trustworthy thing going for her."

"What, and I don't?"

Maddie grabbed a small sofa pillow and held it across her midriff like a shield. "Livie, you have to admit there's only one Ellie, but you're no slouch. People tell you private stuff all the time. Why do you think you keep learning secrets that Del can't drag out of suspects? They trust you. Although, given your track record solving mysteries, they probably shouldn't trust you too much. . . . I'm digging myself in deeper, aren't I?"

"Yep, but nice try." Olivia yawned. "I'd slug you, but I don't have the energy, and it might disturb Spunky."

"Now see, that verged on empathetic. Could we go back to discussing Karen?"

Olivia pushed her hair back from her forehead. It felt sticky from the hair spray Maddie had used to puff it out to a more wenchlike volume. The thought of another meeting led by Mayor Karen Evanson made Olivia long for a shower and bed. However . . . "We do need to consider the possibility that Hermione was not involved in her husband's death. After all, did anyone know about her heart condition before the murder? Any of our other suspects might have assumed Hermione would become the obvious suspect in Paine's death."

"Like Karen, for instance," Maddie said.

"Yes, okay, like Karen. Or Quill or Rose-marie or Matthew. Let's move on to Quill Latimer. Rosemarie said he shouldered the blame for Paine's cheating in high school. She thinks it was because Paine was getting him dates."

"Flimsy," Maddie said, "and very sad. Maybe Quill had some shameful secret that Paine used to blackmail him."

"Good idea." Olivia turned a page in her notebook. "I'm going to start a list of unanswered questions." While Maddie carried the empty coffeepot and cups to the kitchen, Olivia brainstormed her list. "Here it is," Olivia said when Maddie plopped back onto the sofa. "Can you think of anything else?"

Maddie scanned the list and said, "Hermione was stealing from other stores in town, so let's assume for the moment that she stole baking supplies from the community center kitchen and used them to make decorated cookies. Why would she do so? I mean, if she wanted cookies, she could have bought them — excuse me, pilfered them — from The Gingerbread House. We put out a tray of free cookies every day. She wouldn't even have to steal them."

"Good point," Olivia said. "I suppose a neighbor might have brought over some cookies to welcome the Chatterleys to the neighborhood, though I've yet to hear of anyone in town who isn't furious with them for interfering with the celebration. From the picture Del sent us, with the remains of a decorated cookie on a plate in Paine's bedroom, it seems whoever made them isn't skilled at cutting and decorating cookies. Why bother? Why not just bring something simpler?" She added Maddie's question and reread the entire list.

UNANSWERED QUESTIONS

- Why was Quill willing to take the blame for Paine's cheating?
- Had Paine seen Rosemarie since his return and recognized her as the student teacher who accused him of cheating?
- Does Rosemarie believe in and hope to find the Chatterley cookie-cutter collection?
- Who has been vandalizing Chatterley Mansion and why? Why doesn't Hermione seem to care? (Were Paine and/or Hermione looking for the Chatterley cookie-cutter collection? Was anyone else involved in the search — or perhaps searching on his

or her own?)

- Why did Paine fake his own death? And why did the Chatterleys live in London under assumed names?
- Why did Hermione lie about Karen's connection to Paine and her? Did Karen have an affair with Paine in England, too?
- Why did Hermione steal items from several Chatterley Heights businesses? Were she and Paine broke, or was there another reason?
- Did Hermione steal ingredients to make decorated cookies and, if so, why?

Olivia checked her watch. "We should leave soon. Let's make a quick list of suspects and their motives for killing Paine, at least as far as we can determine. First, his wife, Hermione Chatterley. Wives always have to be considered, even when they have certifiable heart conditions." She turned the page in her notebook and started a new list.

"I don't suppose being a crappy husband is motive enough," Maddie said.

"Not usually. But I did sense undercurrents in the Chatterley marriage. Maybe losing a baby drove a wedge between them, and it widened over the years. Add to that the strain of being broke, as they seemed to be, and his possible affair. His drinking couldn't have helped much, either."

"I wonder," Maddie said, "whose decision it was to move back to Chatterley Heights. If Paine pushed the move, that might have added to Hermione's anger."

"And there's the cookie-cutter angle," Olivia said. "The simplest reason for the growing mess in the mansion is that someone has been searching for the Chatterley collection, hoping it would bring them wealth."

With some difficulty, Maddie maneuvered her serving wench skirt so she could sit cross-legged on the couch. "If Hermione thought Paine was wrong, that there was no collection, she might have lost it. Maybe she used lots of sleeping pills and whiskey to make it look like he died from a self-administered overdose. Then she could at least inherit the mansion and sell it. She did try to put it on the market right away."

"Then she took it off the market," Olivia said. "And that theory doesn't explain how Paine ended up in the bathtub. However, let's guess at hatred as Hermione's motive and leave the rest for now. Next, Quill Latimer. Paine copied his work in high school. When caught, Paine blackmailed the teacher to switch the tests so Quill looked guilty. Del thinks thirty-seven years is too long to hold a grudge, but during those years Quill never achieved what he had hoped for. Maybe he made his peace with his fate; maybe he didn't."

"It's a motive," Maddie said. "Can I do Karen Evanson? I will accept your groan as a yes. Paine seduced sixteen-year-old Karen and then left the country. A few years later, Karen was in London, acting in a forgettable play, and Hermione, then Paine's wife, knew about it. It's possible Karen and Paine became involved again."

Olivia gently massaged the paw Spunky had hurt during his escape from the puppy mill. "It's possible," Olivia said, "that Hermione intended to blackmail Karen and wanted to throw us off the track with her story about the fictional Sir Laurence and Ariana. If Karen's experience at sixteen and the hypothetical later affair became public during her campaign for Congress, it would surely hurt her chances. It's also possible that Paine tried to blackmail Karen, and after his death, Hermione decided to carry on."

Maddie reached over and lifted Spunky from Olivia's lap. He whimpered in his sleep but nestled in the folds of Maddie's skirt.

"Convoluted," she said, "but possible."

"Rosemarie York," Olivia said, "disliked Paine because he got away with cheating, shifted the blame to Quill, and embarrassed him in the process. More important is that Rosemarie disliked Paine for what he did to Matthew." Olivia tore the two completed lists out of her notebook and folded them. "I want to keep these with me." She frowned at her tavern wench costume. "If only I had a pocket."

Maddie grinned. "There's always your tight bodice. Nothing has fallen out of that yet."

CHAPTER EIGHTEEN

Olivia attached a leash to Spunky's collar and wrapped him in his favorite blanket. He didn't notice; he was sound asleep. "I've changed my mind about leaving Spunky home," Olivia said as she and Maddie headed downstairs from her apartment. "I was planning to snuggle him in my bed, but he's never had this sedative before, and he's sleeping far more deeply than usual. I want to keep an eye on him. We can settle him in a back room at the community center, farther away from all the noise. After that, how about giving me a quick guided tour of the gingerbread houses before my cursed meeting? I haven't had a chance to enjoy them. Heck, I haven't been able to get close to them."

"Excellent," Maddie said. "I'd like to see them again without hordes in the way."

They avoided the park, where the fete was finishing up, and walked up Park Street toward the community center. The sun dipped toward the earth, chilling the air. Olivia held Spunky securely with one arm while she pulled her shawl tighter around her shoulders. They were alone on the sidewalk as the fete goers in the park chose good spots from which to view the final fireworks.

The community center was brightly lit when Maddie opened the unlocked door. "Rosemarie will be relieved when she can keep the front door locked at night," Maddie said. "She's been fretting about security for weeks."

"Wow," said Olivia as she took in the full effect of the gingerbread house display, without crowds surrounding it. The scene was designed to look like a village, with curving rows of houses separated by paths representing streets, complete with street signs. In the middle, rising above the other buildings, was Chatterley Mansion.

"Stunned admiration is always accepted," Maddie said, "but I have to admit this was a team effort." She took Spunky from Olivia's arms. "I'll settle him down in the little room next to Rosemarie's office. No one uses it."

While she waited, Olivia wandered through the gingerbread village. She found

353

herself mesmerized by a gingerbread bakery and candy store with a crushed peppermint roof and a red licorice door. Gingerbread cookie shelves, visible through the open windows, displayed thin cookie plates covered with button-sized decorated cookies and iced cakes. Little cookie bowls held red hots, chocolate jimmies, pink sugar sprinkles, and pastel dragées.

Maddie returned in a few minutes. "Not a peep out of the pup," she said.

"I could devour this entire store," Olivia said.

"That's because we skipped dessert. Those little plates of candies and cookies are mouthwatering, if I do say so myself, given the fact that I created them.

"What's that?" Olivia pointed to a gingerbread church with two steeples. Half of the church was plain gingerbread with peppermint trim. Its windows glowed with yellow icing. The other half had gray iced walls, stained glass windows made of melted candy, and a marzipan gargoyle on the roof.

"Well, we were running out of time," Maddie said. "We wanted to play fair, so one side of the church is St. Francis, and the other is St. Alban's."

"The Catholics and the Episcopalians under one roof? There's a schism waiting to happen."

"Maybe no one will notice," Maddie said.

"What will happen to the gingerbread village after the crowds depart?" Olivia asked. "Can we pack it away? Should we invite Chatterley Heights citizens to feast upon it?"

Maddie strolled to the small yellow Victorian labeled "The Gingerbread House." Pointing to a gap in the green and purple railing, she said, "Looks like someone already took a bite out of your porch. You can see the pretzel I painted with green royal icing to make the top of the railing." She stood back to get the full view. "I made sure this one would be completely edible because, you never know, we might be hungry after your meeting. And all day tomorrow."

"And we'd be sick all night," Olivia said. "Are you saying that some of these gingerbread houses aren't edible?"

"The goal is to make a gingerbread house entirely of edible materials, but sometimes you need to cheat a little. These buildings are all at least mostly edible, but to be honest, we had to make concessions." Maddie led the way to the Chatterley Mansion gingerbread house. "For instance, the mansion was incredibly complex and quite large.

We had to use some wood here and there to shore up the structure. We could try to keep the mansion, but we'd have to spray it with shellac. And find a place to store it. Anyway, Lucas helped me shoot a complete video of all the houses, both during construction and once they were finished. I was thinking we could use it to advertise for the store."

"Good idea." Olivia pointed toward the mansion's upper floor, where the cookie of Paine Chatterley as a boy stared sadly out the window. "It didn't occur to me until now, but we probably should have canceled our contest," she said. "I'm guessing it didn't come across as sensitive after Paine's death."

"You'd think so, but in fact no one mentioned anything," Maddie said. "When I first put up the contest poster, I figured it would take about five minutes for someone to guess the boy was Paine. I put out a box for folks to leave their answers, and the thing filled to the brim by noon the first day. It's strange, though. . . . No one got the boy's identity right. Most of Chatterley Heights has been obsessed with the idea that they might be related to Frederick P. Chatterley, so they mostly guessed the names of their own obscure ancestors."

"They must have been fooled by the boy's

style of clothing," Olivia said.

"Also by wishful thinking." Maddie laughed and shook her head. "Everyone wanted to be a Chatterley. What really surprised me was that even Hermione Chatterley didn't get it. She came to visit the center when we'd just put the Chatterley Mansion gingerbread house out on display, and I'd posted the contest in several places nearby. I walked in and found Hermione starring at the mansion. She jumped when I greeted her. But she didn't say a word about the contest."

"Are you sure she didn't recognize Paine?" Olivia asked. "Maybe that's why she was staring so hard."

Maddie shrugged. "Maybe. But I asked her if she wanted to guess the identity of the little boy. Everybody else had gotten it wrong, so I figured what the heck. What's the point of a contest if no one can win it?"

"And?" Olivia prompted.

"And Hermione gave me this look, like I must be dense. She said, 'How would I know?' It was almost as if she didn't recognize the mansion, either. It was weird. Maybe she was having a little introductory heart attack that affected her brain. Then she came back to the kitchen and sat for a while, watching us work. She had plenty of opportunities to swipe the gel food coloring and whatever else she might need to make the cookies in the photo Del sent us. If so, she's quite an accomplished pilferer. The kitchen was swarming with bakers and decorators."

"Did Hermione say anything while she was in the kitchen?" Olivia asked.

"She never shut up, but she never really *said* anything. It was more like she was filling the silence."

Olivia heard popping sounds outside, which meant the fireworks had begun. She checked the community center's large wall clock. Twenty minutes had passed since their arrival. The fireworks could last up to forty minutes. Olivia hoped a few committee members would skip the fireworks and arrive early for the meeting, so she could probe for answers to her list of questions.

Olivia got her wish as the community center's front door opened, and Rosemarie York entered. After a slight hesitation, Rosemarie said, "Maddie, Olivia, hi." She glanced briefly back over her shoulder and added, "Olivia, you're a bit early for the meeting. I just thought I'd clean the place up a bit, get some coffee going." She stepped aside and added, "Matthew came along to help."

Matthew Fabrizio entered, wearing a flannel shirt and faded jeans. With his dark hair, he looked like a short, wiry version of Lucas Ashford. Matthew carried a bucket and a new professional-sized mop. His dark eyes flitted around the room before coming to rest at last on Olivia. "Ms. Greyson," he said, "I've been wanting to thank you. Mom said you tried to help me, and I appreciate that."

Matthew didn't sound like the raging maniac Hermione had described before succumbing to a heart attack, nor did he act like a tortured artist prone to drunken self-pity. However, Olivia knew that Matthew was capable of both roles. "I did what I could," Olivia said.

"We'll be cleaning up the kitchen while the committee meets," Rosemarie said.

With a sheepish grin that made him look younger than his twenty-five years, Matthew added, "The sheriff doesn't totally trust me, but Mom told him she'd watch me like a hawk. So I'm here to make sure I keep busy and don't cause any more trouble for her."

Okay, that verged on impressive. Olivia gave him a friendly smile. And she reminded herself that he had not always behaved like a mature adult, or even an entirely sane one.

Rosemarie patted Matthew on the arm

and said, "Honey, you go ahead and start working on the kitchen floor. I need to set up in here for the meeting." After Matthew left the room, Rosemarie opened a storage closet and began to remove folding chairs.

"Let me help with those," Olivia said. Without waiting for an answer, she reached into the closet and lifted out two more chairs. "I've been wanting to ask you something, Rosemarie." As she handed over the chairs, Olivia glanced at Rosemarie's face and saw her expression tighten. Olivia warmed her voice, hoping Rosemarie would relax. "When you spoke to me about Paine the other day, you didn't mention whether he'd seen you yet and recognized you from all those years ago when you were his student teacher."

Rosemarie picked up a chair and carried it past the gingerbread village, where she snapped it open and began a circle for the meeting. She paused to lean on the chair back. Olivia kept quiet. Clearly, she'd hit a nerve. All she could do was wait. Maddie, who'd witnessed the scene, exchanged a glance with Olivia before strolling to the far end of the gingerbread house village, out of sight.

Rosemarie turned to face Olivia. Her chest rose and fell as she took a deep breath.

With a slight nod, she returned to the storage closet, where Olivia awaited with two more chairs. "I know what you're wondering about," Rosemarie said. Her voice was quiet, tinged with anger. "I'm surprised the sheriff hasn't asked me that same question, but he's been so focused on Matthew. The answer is yes, Paine recognized me. Not at first, mind you. Paine only glanced at me when we passed each other on the street shortly after he and his wife arrived in town."

Three loud booms outside startled Olivia, and Rosemarie's body twitched. It took her several moments to calm herself enough to continue.

"Quill would never have said anything to Paine about me, I'm sure of that. And since I'm no longer a young woman, I probably didn't look familiar to Paine at first glance. Then I ran into him again outside the mansion, while Matthew was working on some trim. I'd brought him a sack lunch; he never remembers to eat. Paine was standing on the lawn with his back to me, inspecting Matthew's progress on the window trim. Matthew saw me and smiled, so Paine turned around and saw me. I couldn't just walk away. I gave Matthew his lunch, said I didn't want to interrupt his work, anything to get away fast, but . . . Paine kept staring at my face, and I could tell he'd recognized me. You see, when I was doing my student teaching, Paine . . . to be blunt, he tried to seduce me. He told me then that I had unforgettable eyes." Rosemarie reached for the chairs. "He didn't succeed, by the way, in seducing me."

"Paine knew you were the one who tried to prove he'd been cheating?"

"Yes." Rosemarie rubbed her thumb across the metal edge of a chair back, as if it comforted her. "He wanted revenge, I could see it in his eyes. That afternoon, Matthew came home with a bottle of whiskey. I could tell he'd already been drinking. He'd been sober for some time, so I knew something bad had happened. I grabbed the bottle away from him, and he started to cry. Finally, he told me."

The frequent popping sounds outside suggested the fireworks were building toward a dramatic finish. The committee would begin to arrive soon after that, and then Karen, following her wrap-up speech.

This time, Rosemarie showed no reaction to the noise as she said, "Matthew had nearly finished all the Victorian gingerbread trim on the mansion, and he was really proud of it. Some of the window trim still needed paint, but he figured he could do that the next day. Paine had promised they would talk more about his Chatterley lineage and how he would help him prove that he really was descended from the same family. Matthew was too impatient to wait, so he cleaned his brushes and went to talk to Paine about his connection to the family. Hermione was there, too. Matthew said Paine turned cold. He said he had no idea what Matthew was talking about. He sneered at Matthew and thanked him for all of his free work." Rosemarie's hand tightened into a fist. "After all he's been through, Matthew was so hoping he could prove he was a Chatterley descendant. He thought Paine was sincere and wanted to help. I could have killed him myself," she said in a harsh undertone. "I wish I had." Her hand relaxed as her shoulders drooped. "But I didn't. And neither did Matthew." Rosemarie met Olivia's eyes. "Are you going to tell the sheriff?"

"He's bound to figure it out," Olivia said. "But it would be better if you told him yourself, as soon as possible. And there's always the chance that Del won't believe you. If Paine didn't actually acknowledge that he recognized you, Del might write off your story as an attempt to blame the victim." Olivia didn't add that Paine had treated Lucas the same way, refusing to allow Lucas to benefit from his donated materials and labor. She was afraid Rosemarie was desperate enough to throw suspicion toward Lucas. She knew Maddie could vouch for Lucas's whereabouts the night of the murder, but there was no point in further complicating an already complex investigation.

A long burst of fireworks signaled the official end of the Chatterley Heights Celebration Weekend. Within moments, the community center door burst open. Binnie Sloan lumbered in, camera at the ready. Binnie let go of the door and didn't look back as it slammed against Professor Quill Latimer's foot. Quill scowled at Binnie as if he wanted to throttle her. Instead, he held the door open for Mr. Willard, who smiled his thanks. Lucas entered last, looking tired. He brightened as he caught sight of Maddie, peeking out from between the gingerbread versions of Lady Chatterley's Boutique and Frederick's of Chatterley, the men's clothing store. She blew him a kiss.

To Olivia's surprise, the front door opened again, and her diminutive mother appeared. A thigh-length, slim-fitting sweater covered much of her sleeveless, be-tasseled flapper sheath. Not for the first time, Olivia regretted inheriting her father's bone structure. Ellie saw her and waved. Maddie left Lucas's side to greet Ellie, and Olivia joined them.

"What's up, Mom?"

"Karen said the planning committee was meeting here," Ellie said. "Such a delightful weekend, it's hard to see it end, but then I am a bit of an extrovert."

"A bit?"

"Oh, Livie, you sound so much like your father when you're being sarcastic."

Maddie snickered.

"Now I won't interrupt your meeting," Ellie said, "but I'm at loose ends with Allan busy driving the madrigal singers home, which could take hours since they all missed their buses, and they live in several different towns. I thought I'd enjoy a last look at the gingerbread houses and help Rosemarie clean up."

"While you're at it, Mom, maybe you could convince Karen to go easy on us. I'm afraid we're in for an all-night critique session."

"And keep Karen out of the kitchen," Maddie added.

Ellie's normally sunny expression clouded

over. "I must have a chat with Karen, the sooner the better. Although I fear the damage has been done. Transparency is always best in these situations."

"Mom? Are you having a private conversation, or could Maddie and I join in?"

Ellie didn't respond.

Maddie touched Ellie's shoulder. "Are you okay?"

"Hm? Oh, sorry, I was thinking. . . ." Ellie pulled a hank of her long, wavy hair over her shoulder and began to braid it. Olivia recognized the gesture as her mother's reaction to worry. She followed the direction of Ellie's gaze. It led to the gingerbread village, where Binnie Sloan was trying to lift a cookie shingle off the Chatterley Mansion. Was her mother's worry focused on Binnie or on the mansion? Or, Ellie being Ellie, was she thinking about something else entirely?

Ellie snapped back as Rosemarie approached. "I'll go ask how I can be helpful," Ellie said, tossing her half braid over her shoulder.

"I'll go with you," Maddie said.

Olivia shrugged off the interlude. Karen would arrive as soon as she had delivered her closing speech. Knowing Karen, the speech would go on for too long, but it might not be enough time for Olivia to learn what she hoped to learn. She scanned the room until she saw the wispy hair on top of Mr. Willard's head behind the St. Francis/ St. Alban's gingerbread church. She hoped he was alone.

When Olivia sidled up next to Mr. Willard, he gave her a delighted smile. "Livie, I've barely caught sight of you since our last committee meeting. I hope your Gingerbread House booth was a lucrative undertaking."

"Too lucrative," Olivia said. "We ran out of cookies two hours early. Mr. Willard, I wonder if I could ask you a few questions about —" She heard murmuring voices nearby and realized she and Mr. Willard might be overheard if they stayed inside the gingerbread village. "I need to check on Spunky," she said. "He's afraid of fireworks, so I sedated him and brought him along. Would you come with me? I won't take much of your time."

"Take as much as you need," Mr. Willard said, his thin lips stretched in a sly grin. "Between you and me, I'd prefer to miss this final meeting. It promises to be uncomfortable."

"No kidding." To avoid walking back into the meeting area, Olivia led Mr. Willard to the end of the gingerbread village, where a door opened into the community center's staff section. The corridor was empty, the lights on dim. Near the back entrance to the building, beyond Rosemarie's isolated office, was a small storage room. As they passed Rosemarie's office, Olivia glanced at the bottom of the closed door. No light showed through. She hoped Rosemarie would be too busy to take refuge in her office for at least fifteen minutes.

Maddie had left the storage room door unlocked so Olivia could check on Spunky whenever she wished. Olivia inched the door open in case Spunky was awake and eager to escape. When no furry little snout tried to force the opening, she reached inside and flipped on the light. Even the sudden glare did not awaken Spunky. Olivia's heart began to thump against her chest. She slipped inside the room, followed by Mr. Willard, who closed the door behind them.

"Is the little lad all right?" Mr. Willard asked.

Spunky lay still on his blanket in a corner of the room. Olivia kneeled next to him and reached out to touch him. He felt warm, and he stirred beneath her hand. "He's okay," Olivia whispered, "but I'm worried about how deeply he is sleeping. I'll ask Maddie to check on him." Olivia settled cross-legged on the floor. Sliding her hands underneath Spunky's blanket, she lifted him and his makeshift bed onto her lap. "Sorry, this isn't very comfortable, but I'll keep it short."

Mr. Willard found a short step stool and placed it across from Olivia. When he sat on the top step, Olivia suppressed a giggle as his bony knees lifted almost to his shoulders. "You're a good sport," she said, "as well as a first-rate attorney."

"That is kind of you, but I'm not so sure about the latter. I made a dreadful error in declaring Paine Chatterley deceased. However, spilt milk and so on. You have questions for me? As you know, I cannot divulge certain information about any of my clients, but I have a feeling your interest does not extend to my current clients. I have not represented the Chatterley family since the death of Paine's parents."

Olivia gently rubbed Spunky's ears, hoping it would comfort him even in deep sleep. "My questions are more historical than legal," she said. "I know the Chatterley family was wealthy at one time. Do you know if any of their fortune remained when Paine was born?"

"Ah. I'm afraid I was regrettably uninformed about their financial situation. They relied on an accountant who is now deceased. I did have the impression that Harold Chatterley was inclined toward unreliable investments, as a result of which their financial state fluctuated a great deal. Clarisse could have told you more; she and Sally were great friends."

Olivia still missed her friend, Clarisse Chamberlain, and their almost daily talks about everything from family to business to cookie cutters. She felt a renewed sense of loss at the thought that Clarisse could have sat with her over coffee and answered so many of her questions.

"Did Paine ever communicate with his parents after leaving for Europe?"

"I know he did at least once. Sally was so excited to hear from him that she showed me the letter." Mr. Willard added, in a self-deprecating tone, "I can vouch for the fact that the letter was written with Paine's hand. His mother would have noticed if it weren't, and even I recognized the handwriting that time."

"Do you remember what the letter said?"

"Let me think. I used to have a photographic memory, which is quite useful in the legal profession, but it fades with age.

The letter arrived about a year after Paine left the United States, I believe. I do recall that the content was upbeat. Paine seemed happy. He reported that he'd recently married and that he and his bride were hoping to have a family. He mentioned nothing about his own income, but he said his wife came from a well-to-do family and had brought a dowry with her. Sally never mentioned receiving another letter, and Paine's death certificate was dated only one year later."

"One last question," Olivia said, "and then we'd better make an appearance. I've been puzzled by the continuing vandalism inside Chatterley Mansion since Paine and Hermione moved in. When I've visited Hermione, she ignores the destruction, as if it's of no concern to her. Her attitude makes me think she is involved, but with her heart condition I don't see how she could have been the main perpetrator."

"Ah yes," said Mr. Willard, nodding his skull-like head. "I have a theory about that, based on a visit Paine made to my office shortly before his death. By which I mean his actual death. He was quite irate. Paine insisted his parents had valuable treasures — that was the word he used, 'treasures' — which they had secreted throughout the mansion.

"When I mentioned the fine antiques throughout the mansion, Paine contended that they were merely of sentimental value, virtually worthless compared to his parents' hidden treasures. To be honest, I had the impression Paine was not entirely rational."

"I've wondered that myself," Olivia said. She relayed Aunt Sadie's memory of Paine's boyish excitement when he showed her two of the cookie cutters his mother had found. "They might have been part of the Chatterley collection," Olivia said.

"Ah," said Mr. Willard, stroking his gaunt chin. "Boys can be impressionable. Perhaps he formed the belief these cookie cutters were far more valuable than the mere antiques that filled his home. He was bitterly disappointed that he hadn't found any remaining cookie cutters in the mansion. When he consulted with me, he seemed unable to believe Harold and Sally might have sold all these treasures for their living expenses. Rather, he accused the town of Chatterley Heights — the entire town, mind you — of stealing them. Since I had been his parents' attorney, he wanted me to confirm or deny the town's involvement in the alleged crime. He planned to demand reimbursement. I knew that Harold and

Sally had sold many family possessions, and I told him so. He accused me of lying and stalked out of my office. It was quite disturbing. I needed two café lattes to calm myself."

CHAPTER NINETEEN

Karen's high heels clicked a staccato beat on the tile floor as she strode across the meeting room toward Rosemarie and Olivia. "Rosemarie," Karen said, "I'm glad you're here. The committee has a great deal to discuss, so we'll be working here for some time. I'm sure you would like to go home, but I'm afraid we'll need lots of coffee."

Quill appeared at Rosemarie's shoulder.

"Please have Matthew stay as well," Karen said.

Rosemarie paled. "I don't see why Matthew can't go —"

"I passed him outside, cleaning up the lawn," Karen said. "Honestly, people think nothing of tossing trash on public property. When he's finished, perhaps he could sweep the floor in here. I find a messy room distracting." Karen left without waiting for a response.

"I'd better see about the coffee," Rosemarie murmured.

Quill shifted his weight from one foot to the other. Staring at the floor, he said, "I'll give you a hand with the refreshments, if you like."

Rosemarie gave him a brief smile. "Oh no, Quill, it's sweet of you, but I can manage. Maddie already offered to help out, and you must be tired."

Quill raised his eyes to Rosemarie's face. "I'm sorry you've been put in such a difficult position," he said. "I mean, because of what happened to Paine."

Rosemarie touched his arm lightly. "That is kind of you, Quill."

So Quill does still care for Rosemarie. Olivia hoped he wasn't naive enough to believe Rosemarie might turn to him in her time of trouble. "Go ahead and start the coffee, Rosemarie," Olivia said, "I'll finish putting out the chairs." She picked up two folded chairs, which Mr. Willard rushed to take from her. Before joining her fellow celebration committee members, she looked around the room for Maddie. Unless she was hiding behind a gingerbread house, Maddie had left the room.

Ten minutes later, clattering cups and a squeaky wheel announced Rosemarie's arrival with a coffee cart. Olivia used the distraction to slip into the hallway and head for the kitchen, where she found Maddie emptying the community center's large dishwasher in preparation for a final load of soiled items from the gingerbread house baking extravaganza.

"Hey there," Maddie said. "You must be desperate to avoid one last committee meeting, if you're so eager for cleanup duty."

"Kitchen duty sounds heavenly compared to what awaits me, but I wanted to ask a favor. Spunky's little calming medicine should have worn off by now, but he's still sound asleep. I'm a bit worried. Would you keep checking on him? If he's awake, maybe you could take him for a walk?"

"Sure . . ." Maddie studied Olivia's face. "Anything else?"

"I worry about the little guy, that's all."

"Uh-huh."

"What's with the intense stare? Spunky is sensitive; I'm his mom."

"You're planning something, aren't you? You have that look. I'll bet you want Spunky out of here because you're afraid somebody might get violent or something. I'm right, aren't I?" Maddie pushed aside a stack of dirty bowls and hoisted herself up onto the counter. "Come on, spill," she said. "Should I hide in the gingerbread village and take notes? Should I call Del and Cody?"

"Don't be silly," Olivia said. "I'm not planning to unmask a murderer. I just don't want Spunky to wake up in a strange room and panic. However, since you bring it up, I have been thinking more about that list of unanswered questions we brainstormed." Olivia patted her ribs. Her décolletage had prevented her from stuffing the folded lists down the front of her blouse, so she'd laced them inside her gray bodice. However, she knew the questions by heart. "Karen ordered Rosemarie and Matthew to hang around, which means all our suspects except Hermione are in the building. I'm hoping a detail or two might slip out. Maybe I can fill in a few blanks. Then I'll spill it all to Del, and he can take it from there."

"But you don't want me to be there, right? That is so not fair."

"You're blowing this all out of proportion."

"Of course I am." Maddie's eyes sparkled. "I'll check on Spunky, don't worry."

"You're going to eavesdrop on the meeting, aren't you? Because if you aren't, who are you, and what have you done with Maddie?"

Maddie clasped her hands like an excited child. "I'll bring out refreshments, make sure there's plenty of coffee, maybe clean up a bit. . . ." Maddie opened the pantry door and retrieved the shawl embroidered with passion flowers. She tossed it around Olivia's shoulders and said, "Better wear this, or no one will take you seriously."

"Listen, Maddie, if you insist on loitering in the meeting room, I have an assignment for you."

"Name it."

"If it looks like the meeting is breaking up, and you hear me say something about going home and getting some rest, leave the room and call my cell. You can hang up right away. I just want it to ring."

"No way am I hanging up," Maddie said. "Tell me your plan."

"Really, there's no plan. It's just in case —"

Rosemarie poked her head into the kitchen, and Ellie's head appeared beneath Rosemarie's chin.

"Livie," Rosemarie said, "Karen is getting impatient to start the meeting, and she's in a mood."

"I'm afraid Binnie has been taunting her," Ellie added.

"You'd better get in there fast, or you'll be Karen's first victim," Rosemarie said before disappearing.

Ellie bestowed a gentle, concerned smile. "I'll be wandering among the gingerbread houses, should you need me. And I'm rather afraid you will."

Mayor Karen Evanson cast a stern glance around the circle of beleaguered volunteers. Olivia prepared for an unpleasant experience by renewing her vow to avoid any future involvement with committees. Or any group led by Karen Evanson.

Karen reached into her ever-present, ever-expanding file and produced her voice-activated handheld recorder. "Overall," she began, "the Chatterley Heights two-hundred-fiftieth birthday celebration went fairly well. By that I mean none of our visitors appeared distressed by the myriad gaps and errors in the organization and administration of the event." Karen's piercing gaze focused on Olivia. In the artificial light, Karen's eyes reminded Olivia of a great horned owl. "Did you have something to add, Ms. Greyson? I distinctly heard you sigh."

Before Olivia could think of a response, rescue came from the seat next to hers. Binnie Sloan produced a small notebook, a pencil, and her own recorder. "Just so you know, Karen, I intend to record and take notes on everything that's said here tonight. It'll be in next week's article about the celebration. You might want to think about that."

"Put the recorder and notebook away," Karen said. "This discussion is privileged."

Mr. Willard cleared his throat. He still wore his British barrister's outfit, minus his white wig. Tapping his fingertips together, Mr. Willard said, "I would need to review the Maryland sunshine laws, but I believe our little gathering might qualify as a public meeting."

Olivia heard a faint click as Karen turned off her handheld recorder.

"In which case," Mr. Willard said, "we must allow public access to the content of our discussion. If we do not, it might appear as though we have something to hide. The press does have a right to provide an accurate, and I stress the word 'accurate,' report to the citizenry."

Karen clicked her recorder on again. "Very well then, Ms. Sloan, we will begin our discussion with a summary of your behavior last Friday, the day of Paine Chatterley's murder. As I recall, you were arrested by Sheriff Jenkins for entering the Chatterley Mansion without permission and taking unauthorized photographs. If that tidbit isn't in your so-called article, I will see that it does appear in public records."

Binnie shrugged her plump shoulders. "Why would that scare me? Reporters horn in on police investigations all the time. I was just doing my job."

"Let me explain," Karen said. "The sheriff did not consider you to be a murder suspect because he assumed you had no personal involvement with the victim. But what if the sheriff was wrong? As mayor, I would feel it necessary to order an investigation into your movements, your past, every detail of your life, in case you did, in fact, have a relationship with the victim and/or his wife. During such a thorough investigation, I suspect we'd uncover a number of libelous comments and doctored photographs you and your niece have published about our citizens. So far, we've tolerated your unprofessional behavior, but that can change. Lawsuits might result. It could get very messy for both of you."

Olivia couldn't say she'd ever seen Binnie hesitate in the face of a threat, but hesitate she did. She cared about her niece Nedra's future. With another shrug, Binnie stuffed her notebook and pen back in their assigned pockets. "Have it your way." Her secretive half smile said that her capitulation was temporary.

Karen skipped over Lucas Ashford, whose strong, sculpted features couldn't hide his intense discomfort. Olivia cringed as Karen focused on Mr. Willard. Mild-mannered, gentlemanly Mr. Willard had crossed Karen by bringing up the sunshine laws. He was about to be disciplined.

"Now we have the matter of Paine Chatterley's false death certificate," Karen said. "Mr. Willard, would you care to explain to us how such a mistake was made?"

Olivia had underestimated Mr. Willard. Unfazed, he cleared his throat and said, "I do apologize for the error. At the time, the town was hoping to open Chatterley Mansion to the public and could do so only if all 'legitimate' descendants were deceased. I contacted the appropriate officials about Paine Chatterley's whereabouts and was sent a death certificate and other supporting documents. The examining physician's description of the deceased was a good match to Paine Chatterley. Since this was nearly thirty years ago, DNA was not analyzed. Death occurred as a result of a skiing accident in Switzerland, and Paine's identification papers were found on the body."

"And yet, it wasn't Paine," Karen said.

"It was not," Mr. Willard said. "A mountain climber came upon the body and reported it to the authorities. I was sent a copy of his account, which he was required to sign before being allowed to return to his native England. Everything seemed in order. I did not recognize the name and therefore failed to examine the signature thoroughly. The name was Howard Carswell, but the handwriting bears distinct similarities to examples of Paine's writing I have in my files. Again, I do apologize."

There wasn't much Karen could say to such a straightforward explanation. But she couldn't help herself. "Well, it created quite a mess. Try to be more careful in the future."

Olivia tightened her shawl around her bare shoulders as the mayor's gaze shifted to her. Perhaps no juicy criticism sprang to mind because, after several tense moments, Karen moved on to Quill Latimer. Quill appeared comfortable in his cloak and PhD hood. His mortarboard lay on his crossed knee, the tassel hanging down the side of his shin. He answered Karen's stare with the faintest of smirks, as if he found her personal critiques entertaining.

"Quill, we saw very little of you during the festivities. I thought I made it clear that, since you were not conducting tours of the mansion, you were to circulate among the visitors and talk about the history of Chatterley Heights. We deserve more prominence in Maryland state history, and the celebration was our chance." Karen's attempt at scathing criticism was a stretch, but she didn't flinch under Quill's disdainful stare.

"Isn't it a shame," Quill said, "that Paine Chatterley's murder spotlighted your town, and you as its mayor, for all the wrong reasons." Karen's recorder clicked off as Quill leaned back in his folding chair and stretched out his long, thin legs. "Paine did seem pleased to see you last week when he and his wife first arrived in town. He sounded almost . . . lascivious."

Olivia's peripheral vision caught a movement from across the room, near the gingerbread town. She didn't dare turn her head. She hoped Maddie had slipped into the room to eavesdrop on the meeting.

Karen wasn't about to back down. Her eyes never wavered from Quill's face as she restarted her recorder and said, "I have no idea what you are talking about. Paine obviously mistook me for someone in his past, someone who happened to have the same first name. Years of heavy drinking addled the man's brain; that was clear from his erratic behavior. You, on the other hand, did have a prior relationship with Paine, didn't you, Quill?" A hard smile sharpened the perfect lines of Karen's face. "It goes back, doesn't it? All the way to high school?"

Quill's body stiffened. "Everyone knows Paine and I went to high school together, and some people know the truth about what happened during that time. If I were you, I wouldn't toss out vague insinuations. I could sue you successfully for slander, and if I decide to do so, good luck winning a congressional seat."

Karen drew in a breath, as if to retort. Instead, she consulted her notes and said, "We need to move on. Local shops did a brisk business during the fete, and the town more than covered its expenses for decorations and so on. The opening parade could have gone more smoothly. Certainly the high school band needs improvement, but the spectators seemed appreciative."

Lucas Ashford had neither contributed to the discussion nor found himself an object of criticism. Nevertheless, he looked like a lumberjack facing a hungry grizzly bear. Gazing around the circle, Olivia saw Mr. Willard's eyelids drooping. He was, after all, well into his seventies, and it had been a demanding weekend. Quill Latimer scowled in the direction of his extended feet, and Binnie Sloan reminded Olivia of Spunky after he'd captured the steak from the Chatterley Mansion garbage can — triumphant and stubborn. Binnie wasn't finished with Karen. Olivia herself felt both drained and intrigued.

Maddie appeared, as if on cue, carrying a plate laden with gingerbread cookies she'd whipped up in the community center during the last days of gingerbread house preparation. She had left her shawl in the kitchen and looked every inch the serving wench as she presented the cookie tray to each committee member in turn. Olivia grinned inwardly when she saw Mr. Willard's eyes stray to Maddie's impressive cleavage, then flick away. Quill took a cookie and ignored Maddie's charms. As she served Lucas, his face lit up with relief. Rosemarie abandoned her dust cloth to join the group, and Matthew followed, bringing along his mop.

Olivia nibbled on a running gingerbread man, iced with magenta and pink prison stripes, while she reviewed the tense meeting. She needed more information. Decorated cookies had such a relaxing effect on most people, maybe they would lower their guard. Unfortunately, the meeting was winding down, and no one felt like chatting. Then she thought of Binnie.

As Maddie repeated her cookie rounds, Olivia joined her. In a conversational tone, she said, "I heard a rumor the police are investigating Paine and Hermione's years in England, now that they know about the assumed names. I guess the police are interested in any contacts they had with Chatterley Heights citizens."

Olivia's comment triggered a moment of suspended animation. Binnie broke the silence by saying, "Is that all you could get out of your boyfriend?"

"It sounds like normal background investigation to me," Quill said. "If there were anything to find, we'd have heard about it by now."

Olivia hesitated, pretending to search her memory. "I think the names were something like Sir Laurence and Lady Ariana."

Karen's cup clattered on its saucer. "That's absurd. No one would fall for that."

"You would know, wouldn't you?" Binnie said. "Karin."

Bingo. Olivia had guessed correctly. If anyone would think of hunting down personal information about suspects on the Internet, it would be Binnie Sloan. Binnie might be obnoxious, but she was no fool. She'd come to the same conclusion Olivia and Maddie had. The actress named Karin

Evensong — who'd played Doris, the betrayed wife, in the London play, *Malice and Teacakes* — was a twenty-ish Karen Evanson.

"This meeting is over," Karen said. She plunked her half-drunk coffee on the metal table and reached for her expandable file.

"Now it's getting interesting," Quill said.

Mr. Willard gave the impression he was confused, but Olivia noticed his watchful eyes shift between Binnie and Karen. Smiling to herself, Binnie strolled toward the gingerbread houses. She stopped at the conjoined St. Francis/St. Alban's Church and pretended to listen at the candy stained glass window on the Episcopalian side. "I think I hear music," Binnie said. I wonder what . . . yes, of course. The congregation is singing. . . ." Binnie looked directly at Karen. "It's the right time of day for *Evensong,* isn't it, *Karin?*"

The only color remaining in Karen's face came from artificial sources. Niggling discomfort made Olivia wish she hadn't started what was turning into an all-out attack on Karen to the exclusion of other perfectly good suspects.

Ellie's petite form appeared from behind the gingerbread bakery and candy store. She strolled over to join the group. "Karen dear, your mother and I had lovely talks about your exciting year studying art in Europe. I wish all young people could have an opportunity to live in another culture. It makes one so much more appreciative of differences, don't you think?"

"Studying art," Binnie sneered. "Yeah, right."

"I studied art at the Sorbonne," Karen said. "When the year ended, I went to London and tried out for a play. To my surprise, I got the part. I decided to use a stage name. It was all simply a lark."

"I'll bet it was." Binnie rummaged in several pockets and produced her recorder, notebook, and pen. Switching on the recorder, she said, "Did your lark include continuing your torrid affair with Paine Chatterley?"

"Binnie Sloan, stop it this instant!" Ellie's curt tone took Olivia back to one day in seventh grade, when she'd come home from school in a cranky mood and flung her backpack on a table. It smashed a porcelain indigo bunting, her ornithologist father's first gift to her mother.

A stunned Binnie gaped at Ellie, which gave Olivia enough time to snatch the recorder and notebook from her slack grip. Since her tavern wench costume had no pockets, Olivia handed Binnie's weapons of torture to Karen, who slipped them into the pockets of her blazer. Karen gave Ellie a startled yet grateful smile, then turned to Olivia. "Livie, I . . ." Karen's eyes moistened, and she blinked rapidly to clear them. For a moment, Olivia noticed flecks of copper in her light eyes.

"Hey, that was illegal!" Binnie's pudgy face reddened. "You saw that, Mr. Willard. They stole my equipment. This is a blatant attempt to muzzle the press."

Mr. Willard's long, bony fingers stroked his chin for a thoughtful moment. "I'm afraid," he said, "that my eyes are not as reliable as they used to be."

Quill snickered and said, "Deeply satisfying as this scene has been, Binnie does have a point. Don't the citizens of Chatterley Heights have a right to know if our mayor has had an ongoing relationship with a murder victim?"

"I did no such thing," Karen said. "As everyone in Chatterley Heights seems to know, Paine took advantage of me when I was underage. I recovered and went on with my life. I never saw him again until he and Hermione arrived here last Tuesday. I didn't even recognize him."

With a sly smile, Binnie studied the

gingerbread bakery and candy store, which had several cookie rosebushes in front. Olivia cringed as Binnie yanked up a pink and red rosebush by its royal icing roots and took a substantial bite.

Karen checked her watch. "I hereby declare the celebration committee disbanded," she said. "I'm going home."

"Not so fast." Binnie pointed the remains of her cookie at Karen. "Last Wednesday evening, you spent nearly two hours inside Chatterley Mansion. You were renewing your affair with Paine, weren't you? Poor old Hermione was probably sound asleep. She's six or seven years older than Paine was, isn't she? He married her because she had family money." Binnie had done her homework.

Karen glanced toward the community center's front door and hesitated. She reached inside her blazer pockets for the confiscated recorder and notebook. Handing them back to Binnie, she said, "I have nothing whatsoever to hide. Good night." She strode toward the door.

"What happened, Ms. Mayor?" Binnie was beginning to sound desperate. As Karen reached for the doorknob, Binnie said, "Tell us what happened during that visit to the mansion, Karen, or we'll have to assume the worst. Did Hermione walk in on you and Paine having a —"

"Nothing happened." Karen spun around to glare at Binnie. "Paine never appeared. Hermione said he was asleep, which I assume meant passed out. I talked to Hermione about opening the mansion for the celebration. Period. And if you print anything else, I will sue you. *The Weekly Chatter* will cease publication. Do I make myself clear?"

"You're lying," Binnie said.

"I don't think she is." As all eyes turned to Olivia, she added, "At least not about the meeting being amicable. I think there might be a compelling reason for Karen to have spent two hours with Hermione Chatterley." Olivia knew she might be wrong, in which case she'd have started a lurid rumor, but it made sense as several pieces clicked into place. "Karen, you were adopted, weren't you?"

Karen stiffened. "That's ridiculous. My parents were living in Germany when I was born."

Ellie said softly, "Livie, are you sure this is —"

"Yes, Mom. Karen, I know the story your parents told you, and you always believed it. Until last Wednesday evening. That's when Hermione Chatterley told you she is your mother, wasn't it?" Before Karen could respond, Olivia said, "Hermione carried a photo of an infant. I wondered if she and Paine had lost a baby, but . . . I think that baby was you, Karen. I wondered because of your eyes. They are such an unusual color. I'd never noticed before. They are amber, aren't they? A rare color. Amber can look coppery or golden or light brown, depending on the light, so I didn't put it together until now. Hermione's eyes are the same color. And Hermione knew all about the play you were in, as if she'd kept track of you. I wondered why Hermione took the mansion off the market so quickly. I think she was worried you would be implicated in her husband's death, and she wanted to stay to protect you."

Karen's shoulders drooped. Ellie walked over to her and guided her back to the group, clustered near the gingerbread village. "Why don't you tell us the story, dear," Ellie said. "You'll feel better. And Binnie will be very quiet, won't you, Binnie." Ellie's voice had a steel edge, and Binnie gave her a slight nod.

Maddie pushed the coffee and cookie cart closer. Karen accepted a fresh cup and began her story. "I had no idea I was adopted. I don't think Hermione intended to tell me, but when I came to talk to her, she couldn't help herself. She gave birth to me before she married Paine when she was just sixteen, the same age that Paine . . . anyway, her parents forced her to give me up. There was no formal adoption. Hermione's parents simply gave me to a childless American couple, through an intermediary. As soon as she left home, Hermione hired a private detective to find me. That's how she knew I lived on a farm near Chatterley Heights. She said she couldn't believe her luck when she found out years later that Paine Chatterley was living in London."

"Are you saying . . . ?" Olivia remembered Hermione's insistence that she always loved Paine. "Did Hermione seek out and marry Paine because she thought he could lead her to you because you lived in the town he was from? That sounds extreme."

To Olivia's surprise, Karen smiled. "It was a bit extreme," she said in a gentler voice than Olivia had ever heard her use. "Though Hermione insisted she actually did fall in love with Paine. She said he was charming and attractive when he was young. She hated what he had become."

Olivia thought of Hermione's odd reaction to Aunt Sadie's embroidered little boy in the mansion window, which Maddie had copied for the gingerbread mansion. Hermione must have known the little boy was Paine, though she'd pretended not to recognize him. But that little boy no longer resembled the bitter, manipulative man Paine had become.

"Hermione showed me the photo of me, taken right after my birth," Karen said. "Her parents weren't in the hospital room at the time, and Hermione never told them about it. She never gave up hope that she would find me someday. She spent years trying to convince Paine to move back here, so she could find me again. He hated the idea until about six months ago, when all of a sudden he announced they should take back Chatterley Mansion, that they could live in it for free. They were destitute, you see. Paine was alcoholic, no longer able to work his scams, and several nasty people were after him."

"Most intriguing." Quill Latimer sipped his coffee, his eyes fixed on Karen's face. "The two of you spoke for two hours. Can we assume that you told Hermione that her husband seduced you when you were sixteen?"

Quill's question hung in the air like an airplane with a sputtering engine. Olivia's thoughts tumbled chaotically as she tried to connect the dots. She suspected Hermione had told the convoluted story about Karen and the fictional Sir Laurence to distract Olivia from the close connection between herself and Karen.

"Karen," Olivia said, "if Hermione knew where you lived, why didn't she try to contact you earlier?"

"Oh, she explained all that." Karen sounded more relaxed now that she'd told her story. She picked a red hot candy from the roof of the bakery and candy store. "Paine absolutely forbade Hermione from contacting me. He said he'd leave her if she brought me into their lives. He was trying to protect himself. He didn't want her to find out what he'd done to me, her daughter. Hermione complied because she wanted him to bring her to Chatterley Heights. She didn't know about Paine and me until I told her, but I didn't do that until after he was dead." Karen popped the red hot into her mouth.

"Couldn't she have come to Chatterley Heights on her own?" Olivia asked.

Karen shook her head. "Hermione brought a tidy sum of money to the marriage, but Paine went through it almost immediately. She said Paine got involved with some shady characters to restore their finances. He couldn't stand to be poor."

Maddie refilled Karen's coffee cup and asked, "Is that why they were using assumed names in London?"

Karen frowned. "Paine never talked to Hermione about his criminal activities. He said she was better off not knowing."

The mood in the meeting room had lightened considerably. Even Quill joined in with the others as they tore shingles off gingerbread houses and cookie vegetation from iced lawns. Binnie ripped a hole in the bakery and candy store roof. She reached her entire arm inside and lifted out the little cookie plate piled with tiny cookies. A greedy sweet tooth had overtaken Binnie's hunger for embarrassing information about her fellow citizens. At least for the moment.

Olivia poured herself another cup of coffee, adding generous portions of cream and sugar. Maddie sidled up to her and said, "Your brain is still crunching data, isn't it?"

With a quick glance at the gingerbread village, Olivia whispered, "I've got lots of new information, but the pieces aren't telling me who murdered Paine or why. It might be time to shake things up. Call my cell, like we talked about, and I'll take it from there."

"I can do that," Maddie said. "Give me a

few minutes, though. I want Lucas in on it, in case we have need of impressive muscles."

As Olivia watched Maddie lead Lucas toward the kitchen, she tried to sort out the information she needed. She lightly touched the bodice of her costume. Most of the questions on the list she and Maddie had brainstormed were now answered. As yet, two questions puzzled Olivia. Who was vandalizing the mansion, and for what reason? And did the Chatterley cookie-cutter collection play a role? She realized at once that the questions could be linked, and they came close to answering each other. Perhaps someone believed in the Chatterley collection and wanted it badly. Speed was important. The search might involve one person or more than one. If Hermione was involved, she wasn't alone.

Matthew Fabrizio was least likely to care about cookie cutters, but the level of destruction in the mansion implied anger. Matthew was definitely angry. Rosemarie loved both antique cutters and Matthew. Quill was passionate about history. Karen . . . well, Karen had a newly revealed motive for murdering Paine: revenge. Olivia glanced at Karen, who was chatting with Ellie and nibbling on a chunk of periwinkle-iced gingerbread siding from the Chatterley

Mansion. She looked more relaxed than she'd been for as long as Olivia had known her, but maybe she felt safe now. If Karen killed Paine, her devoted mother might try to take responsibility. But Hermione couldn't have done it alone.

Olivia felt her phone vibrate. That would be Maddie, faking a call from Del. Olivia would pretend to hear that Hermione was out of danger and ready to talk to the police. Time to boogie. Without bothering to look at her caller ID, Olivia flipped open her phone and said, "Hi, Del."

"Hi, Livie, glad I caught you."

"Del." Olivia couldn't come up with more words, given she'd expected it *not* to be Del.

"I believe we established my identity," Del said. "Livie, are you okay? Is something wrong at your end? Just say 'yes,' and I'll get an officer over there right away."

"Everything's fine. Really. So what's up?"

"I called to give you an update on Hermione," Del said. After another pause, he asked, "Are you absolutely positive you're all right? This isn't your normal sparkling dialogue."

"I'm sorry, Del, I guess I'm tired. Yes, tell me, how is she doing?"

"Worse," Del said. "The docs decided to risk surgery. They said she won't make it otherwise. All we can do is wait. Nothing I can do here, so I'm heading back to Chatterley Heights. We could still have that dinner. How about if I stop by the community center and pick you up? It shouldn't be long."

Six months ago . . .

When Olivia didn't respond, Del said, "Livie, what is going on?"

"Del, I'm sorry, it's sort of chaotic here. Yes, dinner would be great. See you soon."

Olivia looked around for Maddie but didn't see her. She called Maddie's cell.

"Hey," Maddie said, "I've been trying to call your cell, like you asked me to, but the call kept going to voice mail. So I figured I'd check on Spunky. He's fine, just waking up."

"Can you come back to the meeting room right away? And bring Lucas." Olivia flipped her phone shut without waiting for an answer. Her mind was on overdrive.

Karen had said Paine suddenly changed his mind and decided to claim Chatterley Mansion about six months ago, which implied he knew about the renovation. The Chatterleys' arrival in town was perfectly timed. Someone had told him when to show up.

Hermione wouldn't have known about the

400

renovation. Karen? The celebration was dear to her heart; she would never have risked losing access to the mansion. Matthew hadn't moved back to town yet. Rosemarie had every reason to avoid contact with Paine. It was hard to believe Quill would ever want to see Paine again. There'd been some coverage of the birthday event on the Internet, but the mansion renovation hadn't rated a mention.

Nothing makes sense.

Maddie waved at Olivia from across the room. She took Lucas by the hand and pulled him along as she headed toward the gingerbread village. Rosemarie stopped Maddie halfway across the room and spoke to her. Olivia instinctively turned to the Chatterley Mansion gingerbread house, which proudly displayed the lovely renovation work Lucas's team had accomplished in a mere six months. She stared at the little boy in the window . . . the little boy who had bubbled with excitement when he showed Aunt Sadie the treasures his mother had secreted in the coal bin.

The Chatterley cookie-cutter collection. Olivia stood in front of the mansion gingerbread house, oblivious to anything else. That little boy . . . aside from Aunt Sadie, there was only one person Olivia could think of who might have known about the antique cookie cutters Paine had found. Someone Paine might have confided in, if for no other reason than to make him jealous.

Maddie was poking Olivia in the side to get her attention. Except she could hear Maddie's voice, and it sounded far away. Whatever pressed against her ribs was much harder than a finger.

"Were you aware you've been muttering to yourself?" Quill's voice was soft but far from gentle. "When you stared at the mansion, you whispered something about 'Chatterley cookie cutters.' I suspected you'd figured it out. I was afraid you might, so I came prepared."

Olivia looked down at her side and saw something tubelike and metal. "So there *is* a gun," she said.

"Paine asked me to get it for him. For protection," Quill said with a derisive snort.

"How did you get Hermione to fire it when Matthew came to the mansion?"

"That was almost too easy. I told her she killed Paine with those sleeping pills, that I was just trying to help her by making it look like he'd drowned. She believed me. Paine had mentioned how Hermione desperately wanted to reconnect with her daughter, so I told her she'd go to prison and never see

her daughter again if she didn't help implicate Matthew in the murder. I even hinted I
could convince the police that Karen put
Paine in the bathtub to protect her long-lost
mother. Hermione is a very stupid woman."
Quill spoke quietly, but his voice snarled
with anger and arrogance.

Hoping to keep Quill talking, Olivia asked,
"Did you know about Paine's early relationship with Karen?"

"Oh yes, Paine couldn't resist bragging
that he'd seduced Karen when she was
sixteen. He enjoyed torturing me with his
sexual conquests and his superior breeding.
Even after I told him about the mansion
renovation and when it would be finished,
he showed me nothing but disdain. Sure, he
let me look for the Chatterley cookie-cutter
collection with him. Only, if I admired an
antique for its historical significance, Paine
would smash it before my eyes."

Olivia could hear the rage and the hurt in
Quill's voice. She almost felt sorry for him.
Except he had all but admitted he'd murdered Paine. If she could only get him to
tell her how . . . She felt the gun poke her
hard, as if Quill were taking out a lifetime
of rage and frustration on her.

"But if you could prove that Hermione
—"

"No more questions."

Olivia took a deep breath and made one more attempt. She tried to sound admiring as she asked "How did you even find Paine?"

"That was an accident," Quill said. "I traveled to London several times to research Chatterley family history." For a moment, he sounded like his old pedantic self. "I followed him back to his flat. He was using a different name, so I deduced he was in hiding. I devised the plan that enabled him to return here, and in exchange, he let me search the mansion for the Chatterley cookie-cutter collection. It had always been my dream to find that collection. The historical significance . . . I doubt there is a collection any longer, but it was worth the risk. If I'd found those cookie cutters, I'd finally have gotten the respect I deserved, that was stolen from me."

Out of the corner of her eye, Olivia saw Maddie watching them, looking puzzled. Olivia didn't dare try to signal.

"But I didn't find the collection," Quill said, "and now it's too late. I must, as they say, get out of town fast. You are going to walk me out of here, very casually, and then you're coming along for the ride. For a while, anyway. I think you know what I'll do if you scream. I have nothing left to lose."

Shifting the gun so it was hidden by Olivia's shawl, Quill guided her down the gingerbread village street. Maddie was talking with Lucas and Matthew, now paying no attention to Olivia. Rosemarie, Karen, and Ellie were having an animated conversation near the coffee urn. Of all times to be ignored. She could try screaming, but she'd heard the despair in Quill's voice. He might shoot others as well.

As Quill forced Olivia toward the end of the gingerbread village, Maddie called across the room, "Olivia Greyson, what makes you think you can get out of cleanup duty?" Lucas and Matthew had disappeared.

Olivia Greyson. Maddie had used her full name. Since becoming best friends at age ten, Maddie and Olivia had reserved the use of their full names to communicate distress, danger, a warning . . . or a question: *Is anything wrong?*

Olivia said nothing. If Maddie approached, Quill might panic. Ellie was watching them, too, her face puckered with concern. She started toward them.

Quill squeezed Olivia's arm hard, pulling her in front of him, like a shield. She felt the gun in the small of her back. "Stay away,

Mom" Olivia said. "He has a gun."

Every head in the room swiveled in their direction. Olivia's heart quivered as she saw her mother's face blanch.

"There's something I don't understand, Quill," Olivia said, desperate to distract him. "You had an alibi for the night of Paine's murder. Your friends said you were too drunk to do anything when you left them."

With a mirthless laugh, Quill said, "You'd be surprised how easy it is to fake inebriation, especially when everyone around you is imbibing with abandon."

"So you knew you didn't have a solid alibi," Olivia said. "Is that why you made Hermione wave the gun at Matthew, to throw suspicion on both of them?"

"The opportunity presented itself, and how could I foresee the happy accident that my antics would frighten Hermione into a heart attack?" Quill said. "Now stop trying to slow me down." Quill prodded Olivia past the gingerbread mansion. She could feel him twist around behind her as he checked that no one was following. The pressure from the gun barrel lightened, but she couldn't break away. Quill's grip on her upper arm was tight enough to bruise. He was moving faster now, as they prepared to leave the relative shelter of the gingerbread village. The door to the staff area was a few steps beyond. Quill could lock it behind them and take one of several ways out of the building.

In the gingerbread village, each house stood on a separate platform, leaving open space between the buildings. As Quill and Olivia reached the joint gingerbread church of St. Francis and St. Alban's, the business end of a wet mop sloshed across the floor in front of them. A moment later, Matthew appeared, having followed his mop through the open space between the church and the gingerbread cottage at the end of the village. Matthew and his mop stood between Quill and escape through the door to the staff area.

"Move aside or I shoot Olivia," Quill ordered. "I'm deadly serious. Move away or —"

From behind the staff door, a ferocious yapping drowned out the rest of Quill's threat. Spunky. Olivia's heart rate took off at a gallop. If Quill aimed his gun at Spunky . . . Olivia heard a thud as Spunky hurled himself against the closed door.

Startled by Spunky, Quill shifted sideways. In that split second, Matthew shoved his wet mop between Quill's and Olivia's feet, separating them. Olivia yanked her arm away from him and succeeded in breaking Quill's hold on her. As Quill let go, another strong arm grabbed her wrist and spun her out of Quill's reach. It was Lucas, who'd stepped from between the gingerbread mansion and the church. Lucas hurried her to a safer distance and ran back to the gingerbread village.

Olivia turned back to see Matthew flip the heavy mop straight up in the air, knocking the gun out of Quill's hand. Instead of letting the mop drop to the floor, Matthew whipped it over Quill's head and down behind him. Before the soaking fibers reached the floor, Matthew whacked them against the backs of Quill's knees. With a yelp, Quill lost his balance and crashed into the combined church of St. Francis and St. Alban's. Lucas kicked the gun aside, grabbed Quill under his arms, and dragged him away from the gingerbread village. Quill didn't resist.

Once Quill had been subdued, Maddie opened the staff door, and Spunky shot through. As he skidded on the linoleum floor, Olivia ran to help him. When Spunky spotted Olivia, he yapped his joyful yap and leaped into her arms. As she held her panting pup close, Olivia had a thought that made her giggle. In a sense, Chatterley

Heights Catholics and Episcopalians had joined forces to defeat evil. Quill Latimer had been defeated by one grand ecumenical event.

The community center's front door flew open, and Del rushed inside, his gun drawn. He took in the scene and slid his weapon into his holster. Behind Del, a tall, skinny, boyish figure wandered through the open door. His dark eyebrows lifted high as he took in the smashed gingerbread church. "Wow," he said. "You guys sure know how to party."

"Jason! You're home!" Ellie ran to greet her son, Olivia's younger brother. "I thought you'd be arriving earlier."

"Me, too," Jason said, "but the bus had a leaking fuel line. The driver wanted to call for help, but I patched up the leak with duct tape. Otherwise, we'd still be out there by the side of the road. You okay, Olive Oyl?" Assured that his sister was fine, Jason inspected the remains of St. Francis and St. Alban's. "I'm starving," he said. "Would it be sacrilegious of me to eat this?"

CHAPTER TWENTY

Olivia awakened at dawn on Monday morning. She had fully intended to sleep in, but Spunky had other ideas. He trotted back and forth across her stomach like a pooch who needed to go out. Now. Olivia hoisted herself up on one elbow. "Young man," she said, "I distinctly recall that we went on a late walk last night to calm our nerves. Go back to sleep."

Spunky jumped off the bed, ran to the open doorway, and looked back at Olivia. "You had too much sleep yesterday," she said. "That's your problem." Spunky whimpered.

Olivia curled in a ball underneath her covers and took a deep, relaxing breath. Spunky jumped on top of her. Olivia whipped the covers off and said, "What the . . . Oh." She heard the faint whir of a mixer. A moment later she smelled the sharp sweetness of orange oil. Maddie was baking cookies.

"For cookies, I'll get up." Olivia rolled out of bed and into her favorite slippers, a pair of worn tennis shoes without laces. She was looking forward to wearing jeans and a sweatshirt while the store remained closed for the day. Maybe she'd dress up for dinner, which she had promised to cook for Del. After the previous evening's adventure, their dinner plans had fallen through.

Olivia took Spunky on a brief, chilly run around The Gingerbread House yard before she let both of them into the store. Locking the front door behind her, she said, "You guard the place, Spunks, while I confer with Maddie." Spunky knew the drill. He set out to sniff every corner of the store, while Olivia entered the kitchen.

It always amazed Olivia that Maddie could dance and roll out cookie dough at the same time. Maddie was listening to music, so it took a few seconds for her to notice Olivia. "Well, hello, sleepyhead," Maddie said, taking out her earbuds. "I realized we had no cookies left for the store's cookie tray. I put orange zest in the dough."

"I know. I could smell it upstairs." Olivia began to fill the dishwasher.

"Is it too much of a good thing? The orange zest?" Maddie smoothed her rolling pin over a high corner of dough to even it

411

out. "Too bad. It's going into the icing, too. I'm in an orange mood."

"Maddie, what's this?" Olivia was emptying the canvas bags Maddie had left in the kitchen. Their wench costumes and fete decorations filled several of the bags, but one bag held only a single fold of cloth.

Glancing over at the cloth in Olivia's hand, Maddie said, "I think it's a rag that accidentally slipped into the bag when Aunt Sadie was packing our embroidered shawls."

"It looks too good to be a rag." Olivia unfolded the cloth and held it up. "There's embroidery on it, all in one color. Maddie, are these what I think they are?"

"Bring it here," Maddie said. "Hold it under the light." She washed the dough off her hands before taking the fabric. "Wow," she said, "Aunt Sadie is good. Those are cookie cutters. She put in all sorts of detail using only shades of gray."

"That's what I thought they were," Olivia said. While Maddie selected cutters to work with, Olivia spread the cloth on the kitchen counter, under a new full-spectrum light. Aunt Sadie had managed to show dents, scratches, soldering marks. . . . Olivia traced a shape with her finger. "Maddie, tell me again about the two antique cookie cutters Paine brought to show Aunt Sadie when he was a boy. Wasn't one a horse?"

Maddie paused, her cookie cutter poised above the rolled dough. "Yeah, a rearing horse with a rider, and there was something on the rider's back. The other was a cat with its tail in the air. Pretty common, but Aunt Sadie was sure it was antique, maybe Moravian or something like that. Why?"

"Because Aunt Sadie embroidered those two shapes, along with six others. Do you know if Paine brought more cutters to show her?"

Maddie pressed her cutter into the dough and left it there to join Olivia. "I remember her saying that Paine kept bringing cutters until she ordered him to stop. She was afraid he'd get in trouble with his parents." Leaning closer to the embroidered shapes, Maddie said, "Unfortunately, she didn't mention any of the others, but these all look like they were antiques. Aunt Sadie has a stellar visual memory. Maybe she embroidered these shortly after seeing the cutters, while the imperfections were clear in her mind."

As Maddie returned to her cutting, Olivia said, "This might be the only memento we'll ever have of the Chatterley cookie-cutter collection. I should have it framed and hung in the town hall." She had trouble taking

her eyes off the embroidered piece, but . . .
"Time's a-wasting," she said. "I need to
start cooking."

"You? Cook? Whatever for?"

Olivia traced another shape with her
finger, a bird of some sort. "I promised Del
I could cook something besides frozen
pizza."

"But you can't," Maddie said. "Listen, I
was hoping you and Del could have dinner
with Lucas and me this evening. How about
I do the cooking? Then I could give you
cooking lessons for, say, six months before
you make another rash promise to Del."

Olivia didn't answer. She had traced two
more shapes. They'd begun to trigger a
memory.

"Earth to Livie."

"Hm?"

"Dinner this evening? I'll make a big pot
roast with carrots and potatoes and onions,
the works. Plus a salad. Cookies for dessert.
You provide the wine."

"Sounds great," Olivia said. "We can eat
here. In fact, could you call my family and
ask them to come? And Rosemarie? I guess
we should invite Karen, too. Oh, and if you
bring Aunt Sadie, that would be terrific. We
can eat downstairs in the cookbook nook,
so she won't have to negotiate stairs. That

414

used to be a dining room, anyway." Olivia grabbed her phone and car keys. "Gotta run an errand. I might be a while."

"Uh . . ." Maddie's eyes had widened in confusion.

"Thanks, Maddie. You're the best. I'll take Spunky with me. This is going to be so fun."

As the kitchen door swung shut behind her, Olivia heard Maddie say, "You're channeling me, you know that, right?"

Olivia did not return home until four p.m. She opened The Gingerbread House door to find the cookbook nook filled with folding tables already set with tablecloths and dinnerware. Instead of orange zest, she smelled garlic and onions. Spunky raced around the store at top speed, excited by the possibility of meat in his immediate future.

A note taped to the kitchen door read

Gone home to shower and pick up Aunt Sadie. Lucas, too. Everyone coming except Matthew, who is working late for Constance the Tyrant, and Karen, who's staying in the hospital with Hermione. Arriving 5:30. Baste the pot roast.

Maddie

p.s. Del said Hermione is doing well after surgery.

p.p.s. If you don't know what "baste" means, look it up on the Internet.

Olivia entered the kitchen, holding Spunky under one arm so he wouldn't lunge for the roast when she opened the oven door. She did know what "baste" meant, and she did it quickly. "Now for your real food," she said to Spunky. "Upstairs we go."

By the time Olivia fed Spunky, showered, and dressed in new burgundy wool pants and a matching sweater, it was five twenty. She found two unopened bottles of merlot and headed for her apartment door. Spunky whined and whimpered until Olivia changed her mind about leaving him upstairs. "Okay, Spunks, you deserve to come, too. But if you beg food from the table and end up sick, you'll have no one to blame but yourself." Spunky yapped his agreement.

As Olivia unlocked the inner door leading to the store, she heard a key in the outer door. Maddie held the door open while Lucas escorted Aunt Sadie and her walker into the foyer. Maddie wore her serving wench costume without the mop cap, and Lucas looked uncomfortable, yet handsome, in a suit. Aunt Sadie, Olivia noted with approval, wore a periwinkle blue sweater over navy pants. Del followed behind, bearing a case of wine.

Within ten minutes, all of Olivia's guests had arrived. Olivia felt her cheeks flush with excitement, but she intended to wait until dessert to share her news. The atmosphere felt perfect. The tables were arranged in a large, loose circle, so everyone could see everyone else. As Maddie settled Aunt Sadie near Olivia and Del, her promise-to-think-about-it engagement ring flashed in the light.

"Maddie," Olivia said, "show me your ring. It's suspiciously sparkly this evening."

Maddie held up her ring finger for everyone to see. The emerald was no longer alone. It had been joined by two rows of tiny diamonds, one row along each side of the emerald. "I decided I'd thought about it long enough," Maddie said. "After all, Lucas saved my best friend's life. So I let him buy me some diamonds to go with the emerald."

"And?" Olivia prompted.

"And we're getting married in the spring. Now let me sit down and eat."

With Maddie soaking up the attention, Olivia asked Del, "So is Hermione going to be all right?"

"It looks good so far. I suspect that finding her daughter has given her a strong will to live."

417

"But wasn't she involved in Paine's death? If she recovers, will she be prosecuted?"

"Hermione might luck out," Del said, twirling his wineglass. "Quill claimed she masterminded the whole thing, but that's doubtful. Hermione did keep tabs on Chatterley Heights over the years, hoping to find a way to return and look for her daughter. According to Quill, Hermione contacted him and promised he could search for the Chatterley cookie-cutter collection if he would tell her when the mansion was ready to be lived in again."

"That doesn't make sense to me," Olivia said. "Quill lived here; he could have searched the mansion any time he wanted."

"Exactly. Quill needed Paine to identify secret hiding places in the mansion. Thanks to you, we know that Quill made numerous trips to England over the past ten years to research the Chatterley family, and during one trip he saw Paine and followed him."

"But the cookie-cutter collection was long gone," Olivia said.

"Apparently." Del refilled their wineglasses.

"And I was so sure Quill had found something important in the front parlor while Maddie and I were in the root cellar. All that for nothing." The room was growing warm, so Olivia pushed up the sleeves of her sweater.

"You should have worn your tavern wench costume, Livie. You'd be nice and cool right now."

"Dream on," Olivia said. "Hermione and Paine were in hiding, weren't they? They were using assumed names to stay under the radar."

"We still aren't sure why, but yes. Paine probably killed the man who was identified as him. It might have been a crime of convenience: Paine was in Switzerland, met a man who looked like him, invited him skiing, and pushed him off the mountain."

"It's all very sad," Olivia said. "I mean, I adore cookie cutters, but Quill went off the deep end."

"That collection was his life's passion," Del said. "You should hear him talk about it, even in jail. A Chatterley ruined his life, and the Chatterley cookie-cutter collection was going to restore it. It probably didn't help Hermione's heart condition to watch those two lunatics go at each other. When she got out of surgery, she told us that while Quill searched the house for cookie cutters, Paine would drink and taunt him. Paine followed Quill from room to room, breaking anything he seemed to admire. Hermione tried to clean up the shards, but it was a hopeless job."

Olivia remembered the small cuts she'd noticed on Hermione's fingers after Paine's death. Poor woman.

Del said, "Hermione said she even tried to sedate Paine, so he'd go to bed and shut up. She tried to bake his crumbled sleeping pills into cookies, even a steak, but she couldn't figure out how to do it right." Del smiled toward Spunky, who had worn himself out and fallen asleep on one of the stuffed armchairs in a corner of the cookbook nook. "By the way, Hermione begged me to assure you that the meat she fed Spunky had no sleeping pills in it."

"Thank goodness," Olivia said. "What will happen to Hermione? She did steal from a number of businesses."

"All the owners said they didn't want to prosecute a Chatterley, though they do want their merchandise back. Hermione apologized. She said she'd grown up in a well-to-do family, and Paine had squandered everything. She was stressed beyond endurance by Paine's behavior. It isn't an excuse, but she's returning what she stole, and we're inclined to release her to her daughter's custody. Karen is dropping all plans to run for office so she can care for her mother.

And as Karen pointed out, she was born of British parents, so her citizenship is questionable." Del drained his wineglass and said, "On the night Paine died, he'd drunk enough whiskey that Hermione was able to fool him into thinking he hadn't taken his pills. In fact, she managed to get him to take at least three doses."

"The sleeping pills didn't kill him?"

"No, but they gave Quill the opportunity to do so." Del glanced around the table; the guests had clustered nearer Maddie to admire her ring and discuss her upcoming wedding. "Quill did confess to the murder," Del said quietly. "He told us that Hermione was afraid she had given Paine too many sleeping pills and killed him, rather than simply sedating him. She began to feel faint. Quill told her to stay downstairs while he checked on Paine. He wasn't aware of Hermione's heart problems."

"I can believe that. Maddie and I noticed how hard she worked to hide her condition." Questions whirled around in Olivia's head, but she kept them to herself. She was aware Del was sharing information that he would normally keep under wraps. He trusted her. Olivia wanted more than anything to keep that trust. Rather than ask another question, Olivia said, "While Quill was using me as a human shield, he told me he'd pressured Hermione into throwing suspicion on Matthew by claiming she really had killed Paine with her pathetic attempt to sedate him. He said she'd go to prison and never see her daughter again."

"I remember that from your statement," Del said, nodding. "No wonder the poor woman had a heart attack. In fact, Quill had determined that Paine was alive, though the sleeping pills plus alcohol had induced such a deep sleep that he couldn't be shaken awake. Quill believed Paine had already found the Chatterley collection and hidden it just to torture him. So while Paine was out cold, Quill searched his room for antique cookie cutters. When he found nothing, all those years of rage overcame him. He suffocated Paine with a pillow, then filled the tub and slid him underwater. Quill isn't a mystery fan, so it never occurred to him that the body should have been faceup or that forensics could tell a drowning from suffocation."

"So in the end," Olivia said, "Paine outsmarted him again."

Olivia's mother and stepfather had brought cognac to round out the evening. While they served the drinks and Maddie passed the cookie tray, Olivia made a quick trip to the small safe in the store kitchen. She extracted a box and brought it back to the gathering.

"Before everyone heads for home," Olivia said, "I want to share something with you." As a murmur went through the group, Olivia said, "Let me quickly add that Maddie is the only one currently engaged to be married. What I have to share really comes from someone we all knew and loved: Clarisse Chamberlain. As you know, Clarisse was my dear friend. I wish she were with us tonight. Something of her spirit is here, though." Olivia opened the box she'd set on the table. "Clarisse left me her wonderful cookie-cutter collection, in honor of our shared passion for cutters. I still haven't gone through the entire collection, it's so extensive. She left me a list, which highlighted the most valuable pieces, and I've put those in locked storage. The shapes in this box were on the list, labeled as 'possibly valuable, no information.' I hadn't gotten around to examining the contents until today, after I realized Paine had shown some of them to Aunt Sadie." Olivia smiled at Aunt Sadie.

"When I opened the box," Olivia said, "I found a note from Clarisse on top of the cutters." She unfolded the note. Her breath caught in her throat. "Maddie, I can't quite . . . would you read it?"

Maddie took the note and skimmed it. With a wide-eyed glance at Olivia, Maddie read:

Dearest Livie,

You might not receive these cutters for many years, by which time I might be too dithery to have told you their history. These are the last of the Chatterley collection, secreted for decades throughout Chatterley Mansion. My friend, Sally Chatterley, sold them to me. She needed the money, so I did not drive a hard bargain. I intended to keep them for her or for her young son, but both of them have died.

Sally told me she'd left one cutter, a teapot shape, in Paine's childhood bedroom. She'd put the cutter inside an old Spode teapot and left it in a hiding place in Paine's closet where he used to keep his little treasures. It was a gesture of love for the little boy who'd loved tea. I left it where it was.

Olivia heard a quiet gasp and scanned the guests. Aunt Sadie was dabbing her eyes with an embroidered handkerchief.

Maddie continued:

424

After you and I became friends, Livie, I determined you should have my cookie-cutter collection. Until then, I wished to keep the existence of the Chatterley cutters a secret. I am including this note to alert you to the value of these rather worn specimens. They are yours to do with as you wish. I know you will be kind to them.

Love, Clarisse

"I think Clarisse would be pleased to know I am donating the Chatterley cookie cutters to the town of Chatterley Heights. But first I wanted to share a few of them with all of you, my friends and family."

"Ooh, I did the cooking, so I get to help." Maddie jumped up and stood next to Olivia.

"I'll need an expert to authenticate the cutters," Olivia said, "but I think these are probably the oldest." Olivia held up two cutters. "One is a rearing horse and its rider, who carries a quiver for arrows on his back. The second is a cow. They are made of hot-dipped tin, so they are heavier than most later cutters."

Maddie held one cutter in each hand, like an offering. "I'll bet Amelia Chatterley brought these with her when she and Frederick P. came to the colonies." She passed them on only when Olivia picked out three more.

"And these," Olivia said "are simple shapes — a heart, a star, and a bird. They are typical of early American cutters made from tin scraps."

"Okay, so probably from the 1800s, right?" Maddie examined the cutters one by one before relinquishing them. "A later Chatterley wife might have bought these from an itinerant tinsmith who appeared at her door. Very cool. Next?"

"Next," Olivia said, noticing a few drooping heads, "it's time for bed. Most of us have to work in the morning."

"Olivia Greyson, you are such a —"

"Poop head, I know," Olivia said. "You can help me catalog all the antique cutters."

"Okay, I forgive you." Maddie grabbed Lucas's hand and pulled him toward the front door. "But you can do the dishes."

The other guests said their good-byes and filed out, leaving only Del. "I just got a text message that Quill is ready to make a full confession, so I'd better take off soon. Tell Maddie that she needs to turn in that old cookbook she took from the mansion. I believe that belongs to Chatterley Heights, too."

Olivia took Del's hand. "So are you upset

with me for butting in again? I should have been more careful around Quill."

"Agreed," Del said. "Don't do it again. Or at least think twice before you do." He intertwined his fingers with hers. "My heart nearly stopped when I realized how close I came to losing you. However, I will forgive you on one condition." Del pulled Olivia to her feet and toward the front door.

"Which is?"

"Take me to Bon Vivant on Friday, seven p.m." Del kissed the tip of her nose and stepped onto the porch.

"Done," Olivia said, following him down the front steps.

Del checked his cell and sprinted toward his squad car. Olivia watched as he slid inside and slammed the door. Before starting the engine, Del rolled down his window. "And one more thing," he said.

"Yes?"

"I'll expect to see you dressed as a tavern wench."

The employees of Thorndike Press hope you have enjoyed this Large Print book. All our Thorndike, Wheeler, and Kennebec Large Print titles are designed for easy reading, and all our books are made to last. Other Thorndike Press Large Print books are available at your library, through selected bookstores, or directly from us.

For information about titles, please call:
  (800) 223-1244

or visit our Web site at:
  http://gale.cengage.com/thorndike

To share your comments, please write:
  Publisher
  Thorndike Press
  10 Water St., Suite 310
  Waterville, ME 04901